BURIED LEADS

A NICHELLE CLARKE CRIME THRILLER

LYNDEE WALKER

SEVERN RIVER

PUBLISHING

Severn River Publishing
www.SevernRiverBooks.com

ISBN: 978-1-64875-512-5 (Paperback)

ALSO BY LYNDEE WALKER

The Nichelle Clarke Series

Front Page Fatality

Buried Leads

Small Town Spin

Devil in the Deadline

Cover Shot

Lethal Lifestyles

Deadly Politics

Hidden Victims

Dangerous Intent

The Faith McClellan Series

Fear No Truth

Leave No Stone

No Sin Unpunished

Nowhere to Hide

No Love Lost

Tell No Lies

To find out more about LynDee Walker and her books, visit

severnriverbooks.com/authors/lyndee-walker

For Justin, who has always been my hero. Thank you for believing in me when I didn't, and for sharing this crazy ride with me. I love you.

1

Dead people can have the worst timing.

After a ridiculously long day of deadlines, criminals, and cops who did not want to talk to me, I wanted a hot bath and my warm bed. Is that too much for a girl to ask? Apparently so, because there I was, traipsing around the woods looking for a half-eaten dead guy who got himself discovered at eleven o'clock. At night. The glamorous life of a journalist.

Since the body recovery came over my police scanner while the TV stations were all seconds from their last broadcast of the day, though, I knew going out there would likely get me an exclusive for morning. Which meant the bath and bed could wait.

Ducking under another branch, I grimaced as I jerked the heel of one aubergine Manolo out of the composted leaves and pillowy moss that blanketed the ground. Someday, I was going to remember to put rain boots in the back of my little SUV. I didn't often have to slog through the middle of nowhere chasing stories, but I wrecked a pair of shoes almost every time I did.

I picked my way closer to the investigators' voices, reaching to the waistband of my khaki capris and turning down the volume on my police scanner.

Finally finding the scene, I tucked my pink flashlight into my pocket and scanned the faces inside the bright yellow tape. I didn't see any cops or coroners I knew, so I flashed a smile at the uniformed Richmond police officer who stepped toward me, then handed him my press credentials.

"Nichelle Clarke, *Richmond Telegraph*. I spoke with Detective White on my way here," I said, hoping the public information officer's name would lend an air of authority. I left out the part where I hadn't told the detective I was headed to the recovery site.

"Nothing I can tell you until the official report is complete." He handed my press badge back without looking at it, the lines in his face evidence of a perpetual scowl.

I smiled at him again and leaned forward a little. "I'm sure there's something you can tell me. Who discovered the body? Is there a reason to suspect foul play?"

His expression didn't change. "Report will be available in the morning." The radio handset clipped to his shoulder crackled to life. He stepped backward and turned away.

Thank you, Officer Charming.

I peered through the hundred-foot trees, wishing this part of the woods smelled more like woods and less like decay. I wasn't entirely used to the forest scent after more than half a decade in Virginia, but I still loved it. It smelled green—dank and loamy, with a hint of pine. Texas had nothing like it. At least, not the part of Texas where I grew up. Fresh-cut St. Augustine grass, hay fields, and skunks: that's what the great outdoors was supposed to smell like.

Skunk is preferable to rotting human, though. Mercifully, the remains had already been zipped into a rubber bag and loaded into the back of the coroner's van, but the lingering stench of decomposing flesh snatched the woodsy fragrance right out of the air. It wasn't the first time I'd smelled a dead body, but the faintly sweet, acrid smell didn't get less putrid with repeated exposure.

The scene was quiet for a body recovery, just as I'd hoped. Not another reporter in sight.

But maybe witnesses? Off to my left, I spotted a pair of teenagers. A boy, in purposely-worn jeans and a navy shirt, sat on the trunk of a police cruiser, his arms around a petite girl in short-shorts and a lavender silk tank top.

They looked like they'd seen a ghost. Or a half-eaten corpse.

I hurried toward them, sure Officer Charming had called their parents. If I wanted to talk to them, it was now or never. I stood by the back end of the squad car for a long moment, but the kids could've been rehearsing for a living art show, they were so indifferent.

I tried clearing my throat in an obvious manner, and when that didn't work, I offered a greeting followed with an apology. Still nothing.

I touched the boy's shoulder, and he flinched away like it had shocked him.

"I'm sorry." I pulled my fingers back. "I'm Nichelle. What's your name?"

His eyes were brown, and looked clouded when he focused them on me.

"Jack," he said. "I'm Jack. And this is Tina. We were just looking for a place where we could sit under the trees and look at the stars."

Sure you were. The leaves eclipse the view of the stars out here, Romeo. Aloud, I said, "I'm sorry. Definitely a different kind of night."

"That was a person," Jack said, his muddy eyes fixed on something behind my right shoulder, his fidgeting fingers strumming imaginary chords across Tina's shoulders. "Wasn't it? It didn't look like there was a whole person there, but there was enough. I know I saw a hand. And a shoe. But part of it was buried. And ..." He pulled in a hitching breath and closed his eyes. "It looked like something ate the face."

The hairs on my forearm pricked up. People don't turn up half-buried in the woods when they die of natural causes. And scavenging animals help dump sites get discovered. An exclusive on a murder victim was definitely worth postponing my bedtime.

"Do you feel like telling me what happened?"

"We were just walking along through the trees," he said. The girl whimpered, and Jack stroked her hair absently as he talked, his eyes still far away. "There's not a path out here, and I was looking at the ground, trying to make sure we didn't trip over anything. First, there was the smell. I thought there was a dead animal around somewhere. I told Tina to cover her nose and tried to walk faster, but then I saw a shoe."

His Adam's apple bobbed with a hard swallow.

"What kind of shoe?" I asked.

"Armani. It was on the sole. There was a hand, and part of someone's face." The choked voice was high and came from Tina, muffled by Jack's t-shirt. "I saw a face. A person's face. But it wasn't all there—" a sob cut off her words and her fingers curled into fists around the cotton tee.

Armani. So the dead guy probably wasn't destitute.

"And you didn't move anything before the police got here?" I asked. I was pretty sure I knew the answer, but I'd been wrong before.

"Move anything?" Jack looked confused for a split second, then his expression twisted into one of horror. "Like, touch it? God, no."

I thanked them and turned back toward the crime scene tape, shoving my right hand into my pocket in search of the pink flashlight my closest girlfriend, Jenna, had given me as part of an "investigative reporter essentials" kit she'd made for my birthday. It had latex gloves, big sunglasses, and a little magnifying glass, too. This was the first night I'd had occasion to use any of it, and I made a mental note to tell her.

The little white flags poking out of the dirt told me the police had already swept the area for evidence and footprints. I wanted a firsthand look at the depth of the makeshift grave, so I ducked under the tape, glancing over one shoulder. Officer Charming was talking to the coroner, his back to me. Not that it mattered—there's no law preventing reporters (or anyone else) from entering a crime scene. It's not a great idea if the forensics crews are still working, though. I'd had fingerprints taken, DNA typed—I'd even lost a gorgeous pair of silver Louboutins because I'd once accidentally stepped in blood at a murder scene. Plus, doing it too much can get a reporter on the PD's "no calls" list, the professional equivalent of a time-out.

Though I could tell forensics had likely come and gone, I walked softly, watching for objects on the ground. I wasn't trying to cause trouble. I just wanted to get the story right.

The grave was about three feet wide. I guessed my leg would fit to about mid-shin, though I didn't actually put my foot down to see, because—well, ew. So about a foot and a half deep. Not a very careful hole. Which meant the person who dug it didn't give a damn about the deceased or was in a hurry. Or both.

I turned at the sound of tires on the leaves, wishing I'd known I could drive back here so I wasn't facing a hike back to my car in the dark. A late-model Jaguar stopped near the teenagers and a petite blonde flew out of the driver's seat and swooped both of them into her arms.

I ran the flashlight over the hole one last time, to see if I could guess the height of the deceased, and the beam glinted off something white, nearly buried about halfway up. A missed bone fragment? I turned toward Officer Charming, but he was deep in conversation with Ms. Jaguar. I knelt carefully next to the hole and poked at the soil with my pen, unearthing a small piece of odd paper.

Not regular office paper, and not cardboard, either. It was shiny, which was why the light had hit off it. I used the pen to brush the loosened soil away. The dirt had been sifted, but it looked like the paper had been turned just right to slip through and escape notice. I had no idea whether or not it had anything to do with the dead guy, but my curiosity was piqued.

It wasn't even an inch square, torn on two edges with a pair of tiny holes punched in the top, like a staple had been removed. Using the pen, I flipped it over and found ink along the torn edge on the backside. I fished my cell phone out of my pocket and took pictures, laying the pen next to it for size reference. Standing, I brushed my knees off and waved to Officer Charming.

"What the hell are you doing nosing around in my crime scene?" His face flushed, eyebrows drawing down.

I explained what I found, and he glared at me as he used tweezers to slide the scrap into a baggie. "If your prints are on this, I can charge you with interfering with an open investigation. Damned reporters."

"This 'damned reporter' is not stupid, officer." I handed over my pen. "Here. I dug it out of the soil with this. You're welcome."

I shoved my cell phone into my pocket and ducked under the tape, leaving him muttering as I strode away.

I passed the Jag on my way to my own car and the woman turned from tucking the still-silent kids into the backseat and waved at me.

"My son said you asked him questions for the newspaper," she said, her voice neutral, but guarded.

I introduced myself.

"Is there any reason you must use his name in the press?" She fiddled with a heavy gold charm bracelet, then dropped both hands back to her side. "I can't imagine him having to relive this for reporters until a better story comes along. I'm not looking forward to the therapy bills, just from what he told me."

"Not at all." My beat didn't often involve minors, but when it did, I didn't use their names without consent unless they were being tried as adults. Moreover, this was protecting a child's privacy—the poor kids huddled on the calfskin seats in the back of that Jag were victims of being in the wrong place at the wrong time.

She thanked me and slid behind the leather steering wheel, nodding in my direction before the engine purred to life.

I pulled in a few lungfuls of blissfully uncontaminated air when I got closer to my car, thankful for the relief. On the drive home, I ran through what I wanted to lead with, not even noticing the sleeping city that blurred past the windows.

By the time I turned into my driveway, I was torn between wanting to take a shower—my default response to eau de dead guy—and wanting to write my story.

Shower first, I decided. I could work when the olfactory evidence of a decidedly odd late night was swirling toward the water treatment plant. Grabbing my bag out of the backseat, I completely overlooked the sleek black Lincoln sitting in front of my neighbor's house.

I'd made it almost to the kitchen steps before the smooth, familiar voice stopped me.

"Nice night to be outside. I thought I might interest you in a walk. But that was a couple of hours ago."

Joey. I turned and stepped toward the front porch, ignoring the tiny flip my stomach did. My sexy Mafia friend enjoyed his air of mystery, stopping by whenever the whim struck him. Or whenever something important stirred in Richmond's criminal world.

He strolled into the light spilling from the kitchen porch lamp, and my insides positively cartwheeled. It had been several weeks since I'd seen him, and his olive skin, strong jaw, and straight nose looked even better than I remembered. The shoulders under his Armani suit coat were broad; his lean, strong frame obvious through his tailored clothes.

"I might have gone for that. But if you come much closer, you'll get a whiff of why I can't. I've been poking around a body dump in the woods out toward Goochland."

"Anyone interesting?" He didn't look surprised, a sardonic smile tipping up the corners of his full lips. That was an upshot to having a Mafia boss as a friend. I could talk to him about the more disgusting aspects of my job and not freak him out.

"No ID yet," I said. "But I was the only reporter out there, so I'm going to write it up anyway. We can get it on the web first thing in the morning. The coroner will probably know who it is by tomorrow."

"Bodies don't get dumped in the woods by good guys."

"Could be interesting." I nodded.

"You all right?" he asked. "How much did you see?"

It took a minute for me to figure out that he was asking if my mental state had been impaired by the sight of the half-eaten dead guy.

"Yeah. I'm jaded enough that I don't go catatonic or throw up anymore. I think I might understand a little bit of how doctors get to be clinical about telling people they have some horrible disease. After a while, it's just a bad day at work. Not that I don't love my job. I just love the dead guys less than the rest of it."

"I can appreciate that." He nodded, starting to step forward and appearing to think better of it. "I suppose I should let you get to work."

"I need a shower before I do anything. I feel like there should be a little Pigpen-esque cloud of funk around me." I grinned, stepping toward the kitchen door when my toy Pomeranian started yipping and scratching the other side of it. "But thanks for coming by. I'm sorry I wasn't here. It might work better if you called first, you know. My cell number is eight-oh—"

He held up a hand. "I know your phone number. I like surprises. Maybe we'll get to take that walk next time. I need to talk to you."

"Anything pressing?" I asked.

"It'll wait. Watch yourself on this one, okay?"

"Why?" My stomach flopped again, for a different reason. What if Joey knew something about the dead guy? That idea wasn't nearly as appealing as a moonlit walk.

"We'll talk," he said with a low smile before he offered a tiny nod, then turned and strode back to the car.

The taillights disappeared around the corner before I shook off the uneasy feeling and hurried inside.

* * *

Two teenagers looking for a peaceful view of the stars found a body in the woods near the Richmond City limits late Tuesday, sending police on a search for the identity of the man, estimated by coroners at the scene to be in his early thirties.

"There's not a path out here, and I was looking at the ground, trying to make sure we didn't trip over anything," one of the youths, whose name was withheld at parental request, said at the scene. "First, there was the smell. I thought there was a dead animal around somewhere, and I told [my companion] to cover her nose and tried to walk faster, but then it was right there, and I saw a shoe."

My editor was thrilled with the early story, especially since the mystery dead guy led the morning TV news. He was also ecstatic to have exclusive comments from the scene.

"Good move, getting all that on the record." Bob sat back in his big leather chair after he finished reading it before the morning staff meeting. "Very nice, kiddo."

I returned his smile and stifled a yawn. I'd gotten up a half-hour early to run in lieu of my usual body combat class. "Anything for the team," I said.

I clicked my pen in and out. "I found something out at the scene last night," I began, but Eunice Blakely interrupted. Our features editor came bearing a foil-covered pan of deliciousness, as she did at least once a week —in spite of Bob's restricted diet. He may have had a heart attack last summer, but he still longed for Eunice's southern culinary creations.

"What'd you bring me?" I grinned, my growling stomach taking precedence over the paper scrap.

"Armadillo eggs in honor of Texas clinching their division last night." She grinned and set the dish on the corner of Bob's desk closest to me. "I know how much you love them."

I lifted the foil and snatched up an oval lump of yummy wrapped in amazing before she could lower herself into the other orange armchair. They were still warm.

"Not as much as I love you," I told her, the words muffled by the food.

"Cheese-stuffed jalepenos coated in sausage and Bisquick? What's not to love?" Bob stared sadly at the tray, and I stopped mid-chew.

"I brought you something, too." Eunice pulled a Ziploc of brownies from her oversized pink tote. "Carob, black bean, and cocoa. Taste one before you turn your nose up. They're pretty damned good."

Bob took a tiny bite and grinned. "Eunice, you could put topsoil in that stand mixer and it would taste like heaven." He popped the rest of the square into his mouth.

Brownies that wouldn't widen my ass?

"Can you do that with white chocolate?" I asked, watching the rest of the armadillo eggs vanish as the other section editors filed in.

"I don't know, sugar, but I'll give it a shot." Eunice winked over the sports editor's head as he wolfed down an armadillo egg and asked her to marry him, which he did every time she brought food. Spence swore his wife wouldn't care, either, if Eunice would cook.

Bob started the rundown with sports.

"It's September." Spence tapped a pen on his notepad. "I got baseball winding down and college football gearing up, a Redskins injury report that ought to make the fantasy diehards cry into their Coors, and a great column from Parker on that foundation the Generals set up in Nate DeLuca's memory."

The meeting flew by. My feature on an inner-city family and part one of the baseball season wrap-up led as the big stories for the coming weekend. When the international desk chief started arguing ideology with our political reporter, Trudy Montgomery—who had more big D.C. names in her phone's favorites list than I could count on both of her perfectly-manicured hands—I pulled out my cell phone and checked my email.

"Politics is perception," Trudy's words faded into background noise as I clicked an email from Aaron White, the police department's public information officer. "This election isn't going to come down to the economy or the schools or the roads or any of the things people should give a damn about. It's going to come down to the guy who looks best on camera or the one who doesn't say something stupid in the next seven weeks."

She went on about the senate race, hotly-contested for the first time in almost two decades, and I tore my eyes from the "loading" icon on Aaron's email. Covering politics was my dream job, and Trudy was one of the best on the east coast.

"Trudy, polling shows voters are more concerned about the environment and foreign relations than ever," Edwin Caruthers, who'd been covering foreign affairs in Richmond since The Bay of Pigs, objected.

"People don't always tell pollsters what they really think," I said. "Sometimes they say what makes them sound smart."

Trudy winked at me. "Thank you, Nichelle. My point exactly. The polls are close because they both look good on TV and they're both suave. Add that to the uproar in DC, and of course it's tight. But Ted Grayson's smart. He's also got a well-oiled campaign and a gift of charisma I haven't seen since Clinton. He'll pull it out."

I nodded, and Bob thumped a paperweight onto his desk to recall order. He quizzed the business editor, and I returned to Aaron's email.

Hot damn. The coroner hit on the dental. My dead guy was Daniel Amesworth, twenty-nine, of Henrico. By the time Bob dismissed us, my fingers itched to hit the keyboard.

I detoured through the break room to refill my coffee mug, frowning at the light weight of my white mocha syrup bottle. My coffee habit was going to get expensive if I started pigging up a seven-dollar bottle of syrup a week.

Back at my desk, I searched Amesworth's name in Google. He was a lawyer. Private firm in Henrico, single, no police record. Not even an unpaid traffic ticket. I found a picture of his whole, smiling face on his Facebook profile. Poor guy.

"How did you end up bobcat chow, counselor?" I mused, sipping my coffee and staring at his blue eyes. He was good-looking, in his tan jacket and azure silk tie. And he had a mother somewhere who would miss him.

People are the reason I do my job—finding the truth, bringing them closure. It makes the grisly parts bearable.

Grabbing the phone, I called Aaron for an update.

"I heard you poked around our scene last night," he said in lieu of hello. "I wish I'd known you were going out there."

"Did I forget to mention that?" I asked.

Aaron and I got along well after nearly seven years of working together, so I could tell he wasn't really upset. I could also tell he wasn't going to say much about the victim. Which meant there was something worth hearing.

"You did. But I forgive you. You get my email on the dead guy?"

"I did, thanks. It's kind of thin. Google tells me he's a lawyer. You know anything else about him?"

"Not really."

"Liar."

"Sorry, Nichelle. No one gets anything but the basics."

"Has his family been notified?" I clicked back to Amesworth's Facebook account. Nothing helpful in his public information, which wasn't terribly fleshed-out.

"They have," Aaron said.

"Then why so cryptic?"

"I'm sorry, Nichelle."

That was Aaron-ese for "no comment."

I thanked him for being no help at all and hung up, turning back to my computer. There was something about this guy, because Aaron wasn't that tight-lipped about anything unless he'd been ordered to be.

I went back to the search results, staring at the name of the law firm for a long minute.

"Where have I heard that?" I tapped a pen on my desk and waited for their corporate page to load.

Holy Manolos. The pen fell to the desk when the firm's logo came onto the screen. Trudy. I'd heard Trudy talk about this firm because they did corporate and tax law—and political lobbying.

The latter wasn't advertised on their website, of course, but a quick search of the firm name plus "lobbying" landed me a list of the most influential lobbies in Washington and how much cash they funnel to campaigns.

The victim's firm was number five. And their biggest client? The largest tobacco company in the world, headquartered less than twenty miles from where I sat.

A dead lawyer is one thing. A dead tobacco lobbyist is entirely another. Washington. Politics. Murder. Everything I'd ever dreamed of.

I sighed, slumping back in the chair. It could be a hell of a sexy story. It also might not be my sexy story.

I opened an email and typed Trudy's name in the address line, tapping out the victim's name and where he worked, because anything inside the beltway was her domain in the pared-down twenty-first century world of newspapers with too little space and too few reporters. Twenty years ago, it had taken a bureau of four people paid by the *Telegraph* and living in D.C. to do Trudy's job, and it had taken three to do mine.

Arrow hovering over the send key, I scanned the message again.

There was no evidence, really, that the guy's death had anything to do with politics. Except I knew Aaron White. What he didn't say this morning told me way more than what he did: Something was up.

I trashed the draft I'd started, telling myself I just wanted to poke around, see what was going on. Between the upcoming election and budget deadlock, Trudy was swamped. She didn't need me bothering her with a murder.

Maybe I shouldn't have bothered me, either.

2

Twelve hours since Jack and Tina found Amesworth's body, and the coroner's office still hadn't released a cause of death. Someone had to know how he died. Fortunately, an agent at the Richmond FBI office owed me a favor. Maybe he'd talk.

"What can I do for you, Miss Clarke?" Craig Evans asked when he picked up the phone.

"To tell you the truth, I'm not a hundred percent sure," I said. "I have a hunch, and I was hoping you could answer a few questions."

"Yes. Yes, I can," he said with a chuckle.

Hooray for guilt trips. I tossed out a few roundabout inquiries concerning lobbying and impropriety, hoping maybe he knew something. He just said the FBI commonly did months of planning and undercover work when they suspected such things.

"Why?" Evans asked as I scribbled the last of his comments. "You uncovering more corruption?"

"Corruption seems to have fitted me with a LoJack," I said. "But I don't have anything definite on this yet. Can I call you back if I get something?"

"Please," he said. "We can't have you people stealing all our fun. You want to share what you've got so far? If I can come up with anything on this end, I'll tell you what I find."

Come again? The FBI was notoriously tight-lipped with the press, and the public information officer in Richmond was a nice enough woman, but she'd rather have a root canal than willingly give up details on anything they were doing.

"I thought media contact with agents working on an investigation was against policy," I said, regurgitating the line Agent Starnes had burned into my brain.

"It is. But I'm not working on an investigation, now, am I?" There was a hint of mischief in his tone. I laughed.

"I guess you're not." I paused and decided to be candid. "There was a lawyer found in the woods near the city limits last night. I don't think he was an ordinary lawyer."

Evans fell silent for a minute.

"You think right," he said. Something in his tone twisted my stomach into a knot. "You sure you haven't ever thought about being a cop, Miss Clarke?"

"Couldn't handle the shoes." I tried to keep my tone light. "Can you tell me anything about cause of death on that case?"

I heard papers rustling. "Let me find it," Evans said.

"They said an animal got to him. They weren't sure if it was before or after–" my words came slowly. I clenched the phone in my suddenly-sweaty palm.

"It was after," Evans interrupted. "The prelims I got this morning say the guy was hit over the head with something and shot. Not sure which came first, but someone really wanted him dead."

Indeed. I scribbled that down and thanked Evans for his time. Then I clicked back to the Google results. There was nothing that would mark him as a target, except the lobbying job. I clicked over to the Channel Four website. Charlotte Lewis at Channel Four was my biggest competition in Richmond, usually just a step ahead of or behind me on any given story.

If Charlie knew this guy was a lobbyist, she hadn't run it yet. Her story was a basic report that identified Amesworth as a lawyer. She might be onto it, but I had time to figure out what happened to the guy, at least. And if I could beat Charlie to the answer, it'd be worth big brownie points with the suits upstairs.

I pulled a file folder out of my desk and flipped it inside-out, writing Amesworth's name on the tab and printing off copies of his Facebook page, the firm's homepage, and the list from the *Post*. I added my notes from Evans and tucked it into the back of my drawer before I turned to the day's police reports. Amesworth's murder wasn't the only crime in Richmond that day, and as the lone cops reporter, I had other cases to check on.

Only one needed my attention: another drive-by on Southside. That part of town had a whole city's share of troubles, currently serving as Richmond's own drug war demilitarized zone. Every small-time dealer and wannabe badass fought by the hour to win control of the cash that changed hands on every other street corner.

I also needed an update on a rash of break-ins in the Fan—the part of Richmond named for its geography, the way it splayed out from downtown like the hand-held works of art favored by ladies in the days before air-conditioning. It was also the part of town where I lived, not that I had anything worth stealing except footwear. The police attributed the outbreak to a talented cat burglar, but Aaron got less forthcoming with information every time the guy got away.

I called Aaron back.

"You're not tired of being blown off yet?" he asked when he picked up.

"I've moved on. I'm good at that," I said. "I need to talk to you about this shooting on Southside."

"Another day, another shooting. I'm surprised it wasn't a reporter who got shot, with every TV camera within fifty miles hanging out down there all day." He sighed. "One of these folks is going to get themselves killed trying to get better footage or asking the wrong person for a comment. You people and your scoops."

"Hey, you haven't seen me out there dodging bullets." I twisted the phone cord around my index finger. "I've had enough of that for one lifetime. Let Charlie at it. She might win an Emmy for some of what she's done lately. More power to her. I'll stay here, far away from the crack-high teenagers with automatic weapons."

Banter with Aaron aside, I did hope Charlie was watching herself. Covering cops is not the safest gig in journalism.

"You do that," Aaron said. "I'll give you all the details you want. The victim is young, again, with a record, again. I'll fax you everything."

"Thanks, Aaron. I need an update on the cat burglar, too. Any leads?"

"Not a one." He was annoyed, though he tried to keep his voice neutral. In a month, someone had managed to get in and out of some of the biggest homes in town (with some of the most influential residents) without leaving a fingerprint. The detectives were stumped, and cranky. "The good news? It's been nine days since the last report of anything stolen."

"So he found what he was looking for?"

"Or he's on his way to the islands with the money from fencing that stuff."

"Any indication this is a team effort?"

"Who knows? This whole thing is bizarre. How the guy knows which houses have the fancy security and which don't, and how he can find and crack any type of safe without making a sound is beyond me. Guys like this usually work alone if they can. The more people involved, the better chance we have of catching someone."

I scribbled that down and thanked him before I hung up, glancing at the clock. Lunchtime. I didn't have anything on my calendar until the interview for my feature story at five, so I called my friend Jenna and asked if she wanted to grab a bite at the cafe across the street from the rare bookstore where she worked. I hadn't seen her in nearly a week, and her birthday was coming up.

Ten minutes later I settled into a little metal chair, struggling to keep my mind off the dead lobbyist and on Jenna's crisis of the month, which involved her husband and a certain medical procedure.

"He's right. We always said thirty-five was the cut-off for kids for us," she said, plucking the wedge of French bread that had come with her soup into a pile of snowflakes. "But staring down the barrel of it when Carson's getting so big, so fast, is a lot different than talking about it ten years ago. What if I want another baby in a year?"

I knew she wanted me to say something, but I wasn't sure what "something" she wanted to hear. I shoveled salad into my mouth and studied her as I chewed. The bread was gone and she moved on to her napkin.

"I'm sorry, Jen," I said finally. "But, do you really think you might?"

She sighed as she dropped the last piece of the shredded napkin. "No. I'm nearly thirty-five. I have a girl, I have a boy. I'm done with three a.m. feedings and my boobs are my own again."

"So why are you so upset?"

"I don't know. Honestly? Maybe I have PMS. But he didn't even tell me first. He just comes home and says 'I'm doing away with our ability to procreate as of nine o'clock Friday morning.' No warning. No, 'Honey, what do you think about this?' Happy freaking birthday to me."

"You're pissed because he didn't talk to you about it before he made the appointment," I said. "That's when your tone went from 'I married such a great guy' to 'My husband is the world's biggest asshat and I may end up on that Oxygen show about the women who go batshit and bludgeon their men to death with a garlic press.' "

She peeked up at me and smiled. "A garlic press? Nah. I'm definitely a *Wives With Knives* sort of girl."

"Hey, that was a joke. A small one, but still. See? It's not all doom and gloom."

"No, but it still sucks. Isn't it fun to be my friend?"

I laughed. "That it is. I certainly learn a lot about the mechanics of marriage, at any rate. Not that I'll ever need to understand them. But knowledge is good, on the whole."

She grinned. "Nothing from your sexy Italian friend?"

"I don't know that he's actually Italian. But in fact, he did stop by last night. I really wish I could stop wondering if he's a murderer, though. There was a dead guy in the woods just before I saw him." I clung to the hope that forensics would determine Mr. Animal Food had been there for a while, but I didn't know yet whether it had been days or hours.

"More dead people?" She raised her eyebrows. "We're going to have a population shortage around here before long."

"This was a gross one, too." I paused and looked at her half-eaten lunch. I didn't want to ruin the rest of her meal, but I had the borders of a new puzzle in my head, and Jenna was a good sounding board.

"You don't need details." I smiled. "Suffice to say that the FBI said this morning that the guy was shot and hit over the head with something. The exact quote was 'someone really wanted him dead.' " I paused, thinking about Jenna's joke about Chad. Was the killer someone Amesworth knew?

"What the hell are you getting yourself into now?" Jenna's eyes widened and she shook her head. "You can't go getting killed chasing a story, Nicey. Who else will listen to me bitch about my fantastic life with such convincing sympathy?"

"Gee, thanks," I said wryly. "I have no intention of getting myself killed. I just want to beat Charlie to this story, and I have a hunch I'd like to run down before my interview tonight. Thanks for listening to me."

"Back at you."

I stood up and leaned in to hug her. "It really will be all right, Jen," I whispered into her reddish-brown curls. "These things work out the way they're supposed to. Talk to him."

She nodded. "I know. I will."

I cranked the stereo on my way back to the office and let the Red Hot Chili Peppers lead my mind back to college political science class. Lobbyists in democracy gave me a place to start. My first order of business after filing my copy for the day would be to see if I could find where the money was going.

Back at my desk, I pulled up my story on the body and rewrote the lead to include the victim's name (Daniel Amesworth) and profession (attorney, as far as anyone else needed to know).

I found Aaron's fax and wrote up the shooting, too. The nineteen-year-old female victim had three prior arrests, and had been patched up at St. Vincent's and sent home overnight. The cat burglar story was easy, essentially rehashing what I already had, plus Aaron's comment about the nine-day lapse in the robberies, the longest since they started.

Once I'd sent those to Bob, I was free to hunt for background information on Amesworth. Clubbed, shot, and left as dinner for the local wildlife. If he'd pissed someone off that badly, there had to be a record of it in cyberspace. I just had to find it. Preferably first.

I typed a few words into the Google box, drumming my fingers on the desk as I scrolled through the results. He was a lobbyist for the tobacco industry, and that was big business in Virginia, from farming, to manufacturing, to sale. And yet, Google had nothing for me in ten pages of results. If there was one thing I'd learned from better than six years at the crime desk, it was that the answer to almost anything could be found on the Internet. The trick was knowing where to look.

I clicked over to the image results and scrolled through a surprising number of photos. Amesworth appeared to be a fixture in Richmond society. I ran my cursor over the thumbnails, finding loads of charity event shots from the *Telegraph's* site. I jotted a list of places he'd been, wondering who else had been there, too. Lucky for me, I had the means to find out.

I got up and hurried back to the photo cave. A darkroom in its former life, it now held high-resolution monitors for photo editing. The smell of stop bath and fixer still hung in the air ten years into the digital age. Larry Murphy, our senior photographer, was the only one not out on assignment that afternoon.

"Hey Larry, how long do you keep images from big charity events and society stuff?" I leaned on the table next to the monitor he was studying.

He pushed his wire-rimmed glasses up the bridge of his nose and peered up at me, his gray hair sticking out from under his faded Richmond Generals baseball cap in a dozen different directions.

"Forever," he said. "It's a nice little side income for the paper, because those people order reprints all the time, so Les won't let us trash them." Les Simpson was our managing editor. He was also a pain in my ass, since the copy editor he was sleeping with wanted my job. I felt my nose wrinkle reflexively at the mention of his name. I'd had a pretty successful run of flying under his radar lately, and I hoped to keep it that way.

"I'm not used to Les being helpful." I handed Larry the list of events where I'd found Amesworth. "Do you have time to find and copy the shots from these events for me?"

"Sure. And don't worry, Les didn't mean to be helpful. I heard him bitching last week because you've been writing about too many murders on Southside. His focus groups don't like it."

I shook my head. "I'll be sure to let the trigger-happy dealers know they're boring our subscribers."

Larry plugged a little USB drive into his computer, clicked his mouse, and handed me the drive. "Have fun. There are about twenty-three-hundred photos there. What are you looking for?"

"Needle. Sounds like I have myself a haystack. I see another late night in my future. Thanks, Larry."

I tucked the drive in my pocket, went back to my desk, and unplugged my computer. Amesworth's social life would have to wait. Eunice was counting on my feature for Sunday, and I had an interview appointment.

3

Graffiti-covered storefronts hawking liquor, cigarettes, and soul food lined one side of the street. On the other, narrow front porches cluttered with junk sagged from years of neglect. My little red SUV slowed to a crawl as I looked for address markers. Some houses had them, some didn't.

The row house where Joyce Wright raised both a drug dealer and an honor student had three out of five numbers over the front door.

I made the block and parallel parked the car on my first try. Not bad for a girl who'd learned to drive amid the sprawl of Dallas' plentiful parking lots.

Joyce's was the neatest of the block's porches, occupied only by a battered ten-speed and a couple of metal yard chairs that looked like their best days had come and gone back when Lucy was trying to finagle a way into Ricky's acts on Monday night TV.

I smoothed my beige linen slacks, eyes on my sapphire Louboutins, and pushed the doorbell.

It opened quickly, and I looked up to meet Troy Wright's deep brown eyes.

"Miss Clarke!" His face lit with an infectious smile.

"It's nice to see you again, Troy." I returned his grin. "How's school?"

"Good." He stared at me for a long minute. "School is good. Life is getting better." Troy dropped his eyes to his shoes and shuffled backward, holding the door. "I should thank you for that. I didn't expect you to listen to me when I told you what I thought about my brother and why he died. So thanks."

"You're welcome." I laid a hand on his arm and stepped into a cluttered living room. The furnishings matched the era and wear of the porch chairs. No air conditioning, but the warmth in the homey little room was more than temperature. Love oozed from every chip in the once-white paint on the walls.

"Thank you, too. For trusting me." I squeezed his outstretched hand and laughed when he pulled me into a hug.

He shoved his hands into pockets of faded jeans that were at least two sizes too big. "So, what brings you to my neighborhood? Mama said you wanted to talk to us. Are you doing another story about Darryl?"

"No. I want to write a story about you. What it was like to grow up in the city with a single mom. I'd also like to talk about your academic achievements. Have you started applying to colleges yet?" I looked around. "Is your mom here?"

"She's...sleeping." He dropped his gaze to the worn red carpet. "She does a lot of that when she's not at work since Darryl ... well. She said to get her when you got here. I'll be right back."

He disappeared through a narrow door into a dim hallway. I studied the photos that covered the wall. Troy at different ages. And another boy, a happier one than the Darryl Wright I'd seen in mugshots. They posed next to a Christmas tree with vastly different-sized, new-to-them bikes. In another picture they sprayed each other with super soakers on the tiny lawn I'd crossed on my way to front door.

I could tell Joyce Wright loved her sons. Both of them. My throat tightened at the thought of her holed up in her bedroom when she wasn't at work. No parent should have to bury a child. A voice breached my reverie with a soft "hello," and I spun around, arranging my features into a bright smile.

"It's so nice to meet you, ma'am," I said, extending my hand to the robust woman who shuffled into the room. She was two heads shorter than me, with a full figure and close-cropped hair. Her handshake was firm, but the smile on her face didn't reach her eyes. The same extraordinary espresso color as Troy's, Joyce's eyes betrayed anguish.

"Likewise, Miss Clarke," she said. "I want to thank you for what you did for my Darryl. Not many people would care much about a black boy with a record who got shot with a house full of dope."

"They should," I said. "And thanks to Troy, they do now. Thank you for taking time to see me today."

She gestured to the small sofa that ran the length of one wall, and I settled myself on the floral fabric and dug a pen and a notebook out of my bag. Joyce took the La-Z-Boy in the room's opposite corner, and Troy dropped his long frame to the floor in front of her, pulling his knees to his chest.

"You want to talk to us about Troy's schooling?" Joyce asked.

"Among other things." I smiled. "But why don't we start there? Troy, have you made any decisions about what you're going to study in college?"

"I want to be a sportscaster." His eyes lit up, excitement creeping into his voice. "You know, like on ESPN. Sometimes when there's a game on TV, I turn the sound off and call the plays myself."

"He's good." Joyce rested a hand on top of his head. Her voice brightened the tiniest bit. "I tell him all the time, I don't much care for watching sports on TV, but I love to watch the games with him when he does the commenting. He knows everything there is to know about it, it seems like. And he's funny, too."

"That's great." I smiled. "Just know it's not quite as glamorous as it looks on TV. But this business is never boring."

"My baby boy here's done so much to make his mama proud." Joyce's fingers closed around her younger son's shoulder. "This is just one more thing. My boy in the *Telegraph* for being a smart kid. This one's not going to spend his life cleaning up other people's messes. He's going to do better. My Troy is going to be the first person in this family to go to college."

I nodded and smiled. "Do you know which college will be lucky enough to have you, Troy?"

He plucked at a dingy shoelace, his eyes trained on something on the floor. "That depends on whether or not I get my scholarship, and I won't know that until after Christmas," he said. "I'm going to apply to UVA and Tech, and we're going to try for financial aid."

"And we'll get it," Joyce said, determined. "And we'll get loans. And I'll mortgage this damn house if I have to. It's paid for. You're going to college, baby."

I stared at her ragged nails, betraying the work she did with her hands every day to keep food on the table and buy a home for her children, as her fingers sank into Troy's shoulder. I had no trouble believing she'd mortgage her soul to see her son get his bachelor's. She reminded me so much of my own mother a lump formed in my throat.

"If it's my choice, I go," he said. "There were a few kids in my school last year who got picked to go to Blacksburg to the Tech campus overnight, and I was one of them."

"He won an essay contest," Joyce interrupted. "First place."

Troy rolled his eyes. "Thanks, mama. Anyway, I've never seen anything like that. All the buildings are so big and the campus is huge. We went in the spring and there were people just sitting under trees reading and guys playing catch in the middle of the grass, and the library...I didn't think there were that many books anywhere."

I smiled at his enthusiasm as I scribbled, remembering the first time I'd ever stepped foot into the library at Syracuse. I'd had that same thought, staring at the shelves that soared toward the heavens on every floor of the four-level building.

"Troy, your mom is right to be proud of you. You should be proud of yourself. And put that essay contest on your applications. College applications are no place for modesty. You have to toot your own horn loud enough to get noticed among the other kids who are blowing theirs."

"Yes, ma'am," he said, nodding. "My counselor at school is helping me, and I'm taking the first SAT in October so if I have to re-take it I can."

"You ain't gonna have to re-take no test," Joyce said. "You might get an award for the last one."

"The National Merit program is a big deal, Troy," I said. Our schools reporter had forwarded me the Richmond finalist list when Troy's name popped up on it, and Eunice had jumped at my pitch of a feature on a drug dealer's brother up for such an award.

"Damn right," Joyce said. The first real smile I'd seen on her face radiated pride at her son. "I didn't spend my whole life cleaning other people's toilets for nothing. I made sure my boys had plenty to read and took them places when I could, too. I think Troy's read every book in that library up the street, and he could be a tour guide for most of the historical stuff 'round these parts."

"Can you tell me a little about your work, ma'am?"

"I don't see how that's going to make interesting reading. I wasn't much older than Troy is now, when I found out I was expecting Darryl. I'd have starved right to death waiting for their lazy-ass daddy to get a job. I thought he was Richmond's own Billy Dee Williams, he was so charming." She kept her eyes on her hands. "I learned charming wasn't everything, but not 'til I had my boys to take care of. I'd do anything for my boys. Scrubbing toilets may not be the proudest work there is, but it kept food on our table."

"You don't need to defend anything to me," I said, something in my tone bringing Joyce's eyes back to mine. "My mother was seventeen when I was born. And she's been a single mom all my life. When I was little, she worked as a secretary all day and went to school at night until she got a business degree. She owns a flower shop now, but it took a lot of work to get there.

"Things happen," I told Joyce. "I believe it's what you do when things happen that defines your character. And I'm looking at a young man who scored better than ninety-five percent of high school kids in the United States on a test that's not exactly easy, as I remember. I don't see where you have much to defend to anyone."

She sat a little taller in the chair and her chin lifted slightly.

"I saw an ad in the newspaper," she said. "It said they needed people to clean houses. I figured I could mop a floor or scrub a toilet if it would buy diapers and formula for my baby. When Troy came along, I figured out I'd have more money if I wasn't supporting their daddy's lazy behind. So I threw him out, got a second job and paid a lady down the street to watch my boys for me in the evening. When Troy was two, they give me my own crew at the cleaning company, and I could afford to quit moonlighting.

"In almost fifteen years, I've only had one employee leave my crew. They say I'm fair. I got the best crew in the city. We work mostly over to the

Fan. Clean houses for big executives. Even got a few doctors and a senator on my list."

I nodded, my hand moving like lightning to catch every word exactly as she spoke it. She told me about the weekend days she'd spent showing her boys around the Civil War battlegrounds scattered across the Mid-Atlantic, and taking them to experience the living colonial history that defined the Williamsburg corridor.

Troy beamed at his mother. "My mama was like the Energizer bunny. She'd come home after being on her feet for ten hours and clean our house, cook us supper, and help us with our homework. I definitely learned the value of hard work. I don't care if I have to start out bringing someone coffee or making copies. I'll make the best coffee and the cleanest copies they've ever seen, and I'll have my own mic in the press box one day, you wait and see. When I was just a kid in middle school, I wanted my own column in the newspaper like Grant Parker. But then I started watching SportsCenter, and they get to report on all the games that happen everywhere, not just the ones that are in their town. I like that."

I kept writing, but I had an idea. "Troy, I know you want to work in TV, but how would you like to spend a day hanging out with Parker?" I looked up from my notes and felt a smile tug at the corners of my lips as his mouth dropped open.

"Seriously? Do you really think he might let me tag around after him? I won't be a pest, I swear it! Do you know him? Can you ask him if that would be all right?" He sounded like a little boy who'd just been told he might go to Disney World.

Parker owed me a favor. He had been walking around in a megawatt-grin daze for weeks, since I'd decided to play cupid with him and Melanie from the city desk. "We're friends. I think I can go ahead and tell you it'll be fine." I matched Troy's grin with one of my own. "Do you think you could miss a day of school next week? Parker's not much for coming in on the weekends."

"I'm ahead in all my classes, anyway," he said. "I have a part-time job at the grocery store two blocks up, but I'm off on Mondays and Tuesdays."

"Parker's column runs Tuesday, Thursday..."

"And Saturday," Troy interrupted. "I read it every time it's in. This is the baddest thing ever, Miss Clarke."

I laughed. "I'm guessing you'll see more of what he does on Monday, but I'll double check that with him and call you later."

"Thank you," Joyce mouthed over her son's head. I nodded.

I asked a few more questions about Troy's classes, and thanked them both as I shoved my notebook back into my bag and capped my pen.

Troy stood up to get the front door, and Joyce rose when I did. She crossed the shoebox-sized room in three steps and took both my hands in hers. I felt calluses under my fingertips.

"I'm obliged to you for coming, Nichelle," she said, holding her back straight. Tears swam in her eyes again, but she didn't blink them back. "My boys are the world to me." A tear fell, followed closely by another. "This is something. I'm obliged."

"Thank you for sharing your story with me," I said, returning the pressure she was putting on my fingers. "I hope I can tell it right."

* * *

Larry's USB drive full of photos burning a hole in my pocket, I pulled back into the garage at the office at ten after seven, detouring past the break room's vintage soda machine on the way to my desk.

Sipping a Diet Coke and thinking about Troy's game-show-host grin, I checked the clock and went past Parker's office, hoping he'd stayed late. Dark and empty. Damn. There wasn't a game that night, so he was probably out with Mel. I'd have to catch up with him tomorrow.

I plugged the drive into the side of my computer and waited for the photos to load, opening a slideshow so I wouldn't miss anything important.

Three hours and over a thousand images later, my head was starting to hurt. I rifled through my desk drawer for a bottle of Advil and washed two down with the last of my soda before I clicked to the next photo.

And found something.

I checked the information in the sidebar. It was from a charity casino night in April. There was Amesworth, laughing and leaning one hand on the shoulder of a tall, dark-haired man in a sharp tux. They looked chummy, which was interesting, since the dark-haired man was Senator Ted Grayson.

A tobacco lobbyist and a U.S. Senator in the middle of a bone-crushingly tight reelection campaign laughing over drinks and cards might mean nothing, except that Grayson could deliver a good punchline. But it was a hell of a coincidence. I'd covered crime for long enough to know true coincidences are few and far between. Playing the odds here, I might have an exclusive. The photo hadn't been published, so no one else had access to it.

I copied the photo to the Amesworth folder on my hard drive and clicked over to Google.

A search for the good senator's name brought up all the usual suspects: his official Senate page, his campaign site, a long list of minutes for both the Senate and the Virginia House of Delegates, where he'd served for six years before winning his first federal campaign, and a slew of articles. Some of them were written by Trudy, some were from the *Washington Post*, and some were from various other websites and publications that covered national politics. I clicked on news articles covering political campaign speeches and appearances, scanning the stories and photo cutlines for mention of Amesworth or the tobacco industry. Four pages and seventy minutes of Ted Grayson 101 later, I had bupkis.

Grayson had a background that consisted almost exclusively of public relations and politics. He did a short stint at his father's PR firm and then ran for Richmond City Council, leapfrogging through just two terms in the House of Delegates into the national spotlight. Then he went on to the U.S. Senate, where he was running for a second term. Ted Grayson was a political wunderkind.

I stared at the photo of the dead lawyer and the senator for a long while before I packed my computer up for the night. The pose was too familiar for strangers at a party.

But with no other link between the two of them, Bob wouldn't touch it, and I knew it.

I'd have to keep looking.

4

My toy Pomeranian was positively indignant when I walked into my house at nearly midnight for the second night in a row. I bent and scratched her head, then opened a can of Pro Plan and scraped it into her bowl, ignoring my own rumbling stomach for the moment. I kicked my sapphire Louboutins off and flipped the TV on, my mind still on Grayson.

I fiddled with the five-thousand-piece jigsaw on my coffee table, while mulling over the mental puzzle of the story. My cell phone erupted into "Second Star to the Right" and I jumped, dropping a piece under the table.

I glanced at the screen. Agent Evans.

It was midnight. What the hell was the FBI calling me for?

"Clarke." I braced the phone against my shoulder, bending forward at the waist to reach for the lost puzzle piece.

"I have a tip for you that won't go to anyone else for another twelve hours," Evans said in a warm tone I wasn't used to hearing from the FBI. "I think we're even after this."

I forgot the jigsaw piece. "I appreciate that, Agent Evans," I said, rifling through a nearby basket for pen and paper. "At the risk of sounding redundant, you don't owe me anything, but I'm not turning down an exclusive from the FBI."

"There was an arrest this evening in that murder case we discussed earlier."

I scribbled, holding my breath. "Who?"

"James Robert Billings, age fifty-six, of Henrico," Evans said, rustling papers in the background. "He's a senior vice president at Raymond Garfield."

The tobacco company. Hot damn.

"Did he confess?" I asked.

"This is an inter-agency operation with the ATF, and I wasn't there for the questioning, but I'll go with no. Bank records show he was paying the vic off the books, and the bullet was fired from a rifle that belongs to Billings."

"How do you know that?" I asked. "Private citizens don't have to register guns in Virginia." I listened to Aaron complain about that often, because it made it harder to build a case in a shooting.

"Good question." Evans rustled more papers. "I don't have an answer. This isn't my case, but the warrant lists the gun as the reason and a judge signed it."

"I see. Do they have the weapon, then?"

"I don't know. What I do know is this: a guy like Billings won't talk without a lawyer in the room, and the kind of lawyer he can afford isn't going to let him give up anything. I imagine his attorneys will call in as many favors as it takes to have him on the early docket."

"Who's the ACA handling this one?" In Virginia, prosecutors are known as Commonwealth's Attorneys instead of district attorneys, but after covering cops for six years, I'd finally gotten used to the quirk.

"This paperwork says Corry's going to take it himself," Evans said.

Wow. That in itself was newsworthy. At thirty-four, Richard Corry was the youngest head prosecutor in Virginia history. He rarely showed up in a courtroom or in front of a TV camera, preferring to stay out of the limelight. I'd heard he was a damned fine orator. That should make for great copy when the trial rolled around.

"Anyway, they're going to try to get him through without the press knowing what's going on," Evans said. "So I thought you'd appreciate a heads up. If you're at the courthouse by eight in the morning, you won't miss it."

I thanked him, adding a last bit of chicken scratch to my notes. An exclusive was always a good thing. Especially on something like this. The senator would have been a sexier angle, but this was good stuff.

I stared at my notes and then lifted Darcy onto the sofa when she bounced and scratched at my bare foot. Sifting my fingers through her silky russet fur, I couldn't help wondering again how well the dead lobbyist knew the senator.

I texted Bob to tell him I would miss the morning staff meeting and flicked the TV off. Grabbing a protein bar out of the pantry to stave off starvation, I took Darcy out for a quick round of fetch so I could get to bed. Maybe Billings's hearing would shed some light on what was fast becoming a tangled mess of a story.

* * *

Dressed in unobtrusive neutrals right down to my most practical square-toed cream heels, I stepped out the door at seven-oh-one for the eight-mile drive to the John Marshall Courts Building on the east side of downtown Richmond. Traffic here was nothing compared to trying to get the same distance on Dallas' clogged roads, but I wasn't taking chances.

I sipped coffee from a tumbler with a hot pink Texas emblazoned across the silver—a gift from my mom—as I watched a jogger cross in front of me at Monument and Malvern. I was excited about the prospect of Billings being the killer. A powerful executive engaging in corporate political hijinks now suspect in murder? It was a hell of a sexy news story. And all mine.

I pressed the gas pedal and the legendary statues of Arthur Ashe, Stonewall Jackson, and Robert E. Lee that sat in the middle of the road blurred past. I barely noticed them, a moral conundrum worrying around my head. The story would be even sexier if Grayson really was involved. And while the "sexier" factor was definitely there, I was having trouble convincing myself that my intentions were completely honorable. Did I want the story because it was rightfully mine, or because it might give me a taste of covering politics?

While getting ready that morning, I'd spent a good deal of time brainstorming a way to sell Bob on the idea that the murder should trump the senator's involvement, if he was involved.

It was a valid point, but one that made my skin tighten with self-directed anger because it reminded me too much of Shelby Taylor, the copy editor who was perpetually after my beat. Resolving to talk to Trudy if I needed to, I parked at a meter in front of the courts building, forty-five minutes early. I flipped the sun visor down to avoid the glare of the perfect September morning and texted Jenna, "Happy Birthday! Tell Chad feel better. You stocked with frozen peas?"

Finishing my coffee, I watched bailiffs and attorneys enter the thick glass doors. Getting into the courthouse was a bit of an ironman event, involving heavy lifting to open the door and quick reflexes to avoid losing the hide off an ankle.

I wished for an arrest report to read, but I wasn't even sure if the arrest had been made by the Richmond PD or the FBI or the ATF. For all I knew, Batman could be bringing Billings to the courthouse.

I reached for my cell phone and dialed Aaron's cell number.

"I thought you went to the gym in the mornings," he said when he answered. "Didn't you tell Anderson Cooper that's where you learned how to fight?"

"I usually do, but decided the courthouse would be more exciting than body combat today," I coughed off the throat closure that came when I thought too much about how close I'd come, in June, to dying. At least the nightmares had dialed back to weekly from nightly. "You have an arrest report to email me?"

"For something going on down there this early? Not that I know of," he said. "Whose arrest are you nosing around?"

"James Billings."

"Who?"

So not the PD. I hoped whoever picked Billings up had at least notified someone at the PD, or I was about to find myself smack in the middle of a jurisdictional pissing contest.

"He's a big fish over at Raymond Garfield. And about to go before a judge on a charge of murdering the lobbyist those kids found in the woods the other night."

"Oh, really?" Aaron tried for interested, but annoyance bled through in his tone. "And do I get to know where you heard that?"

"From the FBI," I said, scrunching my nose apologetically even though he couldn't see me. "But, you know, maybe they called someone else and you haven't gotten the memo yet."

"Not likely. Damned irritating, them waltzing in and arresting people without telling anyone what the hell they're doing. If *you're* down there, every other reporter in town will be looking for information on this before I finish my second cup of coffee. And you know who they're going to call? Not the goddamned FBI, that's who."

"Well, thank me for the heads up later then," I said. "You're welcome."

"I'm not counting that as a favor," he grumbled. "Have fun with your hearing. I'm gonna go find out what the hell's going on before my phone starts really ringing."

I clicked the end button and dropped my press credentials over my head, stepping out of the car as the parking lot across the street started to fill up. No TV trucks. Not yet, anyway. I wrestled the door open and scuttled into the lobby.

Laying my bag in a battered plastic bin on the conveyor belt, I waited my turn before shuffling through the metal detector, offering the bailiff a smile and a good morning as I grabbed my x-ray inspected tote.

"What're you looking for this early, Nichelle?" Hurley asked over his shoulder as he waved a pinstripe-suited gentleman with salt and pepper hair through the detectors. "I haven't seen Charlie this morning. And when she's late she always gives me a hard time about security. Is she fixin' to holler at me because she got stuck in traffic?"

"Not sure, Hurley," I said, already striding toward the courtrooms and realizing I had no idea whose docket Billings was on. "Sorry."

I was about to stick my head into the clerk's office and ask when an auburn head in the middle of a throng of suits outside number four caught my eye. I stared at the profile, fear of smudging my makeup the only thing keeping me from rubbing my eyes. Kyle Miller. My old flame had grown up to be some sort of Bureau of Alcohol, Tobacco, Firearms and Explosives supercop. But he was supposed to be in Texas. What the hell was he doing here? I didn't have time to find out, but I walked over to the edge of the huddle anyway.

I cleared my throat and touched Kyle's shoulder.

"Nicey!" He pulled me into an unexpected hug when he turned and I lost my balance, clinging to his broad shoulders such that we drew a couple of snickers from his entourage. He still wore Eternity. Same old Kyle. Except for the biceps. The arms I remembered were skinny. The ones crushing into my ribcage were not. I pushed away memories of some very nice evenings spent in those arms as I gathered my wits.

I kept one hand on his arm and straightened myself, then smoothed my flared navy skirt and smiled.

"Nice to see you, too," I said.

He turned to his colleagues, all of whom also sported gun-bulges under their jackets. "This is Nichelle Clarke. She's the cops and courts reporter at the *Telegraph*."

"We've heard." A barrel-chested man with cocoa skin and a voice that belonged on the radio offered his hand, his teeth flashing stark white when he grinned. "It's a pleasure, Miss Clarke."

I shook his hand firmly and turned back to Kyle, one eyebrow up. "Some reporter I am. I wasn't aware you were back in town."

He ducked his head. "Busted. I was going to call and ask you to dinner. I got a transfer to the Richmond office. Meet your newest local ATF special agent."

I stared in silence for a full minute, my brain in hyperdrive. Once I'd thought Kyle Miller was the love of my life. It had taken me a decade to stop thinking it, actually. And now he decides to move halfway across the country to my city? Fabulous.

"Well, welcome to Richmond," I said finally.

His eyes told me that wasn't the reaction he hoped for.

The other three men laughed and introduced themselves as members of Kyle's new team.

"What brings you to the courthouse this morning, Miss Clarke?" Agent Silky Voice asked.

"I'm covering a bond hearing. James Billings. I need to go find the courtroom before I miss it. It was good to see you, Kyle." I turned back to the clerk's door.

"The courtroom is right here," Kyle said. "Billings is my collar. How the hell did you find out about this hearing? His lawyer got him set for bond before the ink on the arrest report was dry."

Interesting. I glanced around at Kyle's team, and everyone had the same casually-curious expression. Something told me it was a face they practiced in front of the mirror. Possibly as a group.

"I'm just that good." I winked and brushed past them, opening the massive cherry-paneled door and nodding to the agents. "Gentlemen first."

Kyle brought up the rear, pausing on his way in. "No reporter is that good. Who tipped you off?" he asked in a low voice.

"If I wanted you to know that, I'd have told you." I returned the no-nonsense tone and flat stare syllable-for-syllable. "If you don't mind, this door isn't as lightweight as it looks."

He narrowed his ice-blue eyes and looked like he wanted to say something else, but turned on the heel of his Justin ostrich dress boot and took a seat in the front row instead.

I slipped into the back and pulled out a pen and notebook as the bailiff called the court to order and announced the Honorable Reginald S. Davidson's entrance. Sure enough, Corry was at the prosecution's table, dark blond head bent over a yellow legal pad. He wore a tan suit that fit his lanky frame well, his wire rimmed glasses pushed up on top of his head as he studied his notes.

A petite bailiff who didn't look strong enough to restrain a schoolyard bully led Billings to the defense table. In his wrinkled Hugo Boss, with a silver-flecked shadow beard playing across the angular planes of a face that had aged well, he looked like a rumpled movie star. A haggard, terrified movie star who had not enjoyed the jailhouse experience.

Kyle thought this guy was a murderer?

I had seen stranger, I guessed. I pulled a notebook and pen from my bag.

Billings didn't fidget or drop his head as the judge read the charges being levied against him. His attorney, wearing enough Aramis that I could smell the musky cologne from my seat, launched immediately into a plea for the court to allow Billings to be released on his own recognizance pending trial.

Kyle erupted into a coughing fit.

"Your honor, Mr. Billings is a model citizen, a pillar of this community, and a major contributor to many charities." The lawyer threw a glance over his shoulder at Kyle, who was still shaking, though whether it was with laughter or coughing was hard to tell from behind. "He has no prior record. These charges are false, insulting, and defamatory, and we will more than prove that at the trial. In the meantime, my client would like to return to his family, his job, and his community service."

The judge scooted his glasses down the bridge of his nose and looked over them at Billings and Overused Aramis, Esq.

"I appreciate everything Mr. Billings does for the community," Judge Davidson said. "However, in light of the severity of the charges, I'm not prepared to let him out without bond."

Billings nodded and leaned toward his lawyer, whispering.

Corry stood. "Your honor, Richard Corry for the Commonwealth. If I may, I'd like to request that Mr. Billings be held without bond until his trial."

Oh, my. Totally worth skipping the gym. I scribbled, not taking my eyes off the key figures in what had just become an even more interesting hearing. Kyle's head bobbed like a fishing lure with a prize trout on the business end, and Billings' lawyer gaped as though Corry had just branded him the antichrist.

"Ob-Objection!" he stuttered. "Your honor! Again, my client has no prior record. I've never heard of the Commonwealth holding a defendant with no priors over for trial."

"I'll hear him out," the judge said, his eyes on Corry. "Mr. Corry, that is a highly irregular request. Care to tell me why you're asking?"

"Your honor, Mr. Billings is a flight risk," Corry said. "Most of the murder defendants our courtrooms see don't have his resources, or his connections. The commonwealth wants to ensure that he stays in Virginia until the trial."

The Honorable Reginald Davidson nodded, his eyes flicking from Billings to Corry for a full minute.

"The court concedes the commonwealth's point," he said, raising one hand when Captain Cologne knocked his chair over jumping to his feet. "However, Mr. Kressley has a point, too. The defendant has no record, and the Commonwealth of Virginia believes very strongly in the notion of innocent until proven guilty. At least in my courtroom it does. The defendant may choose to post bond of two million dollars, but will wear an electronic tracking device at all times between now and the end of his trial."

My pen moved so furiously my hand cramped, but I ignored it until I had every word in my notes.

The judge waved his bailiff over for a quick conference before facing the attorneys again.

"I'll hear opening arguments on February sixteenth." He adjusted the specs for the look-down-the-nose thing again. "Mr. Billings, it would behoove you to keep every toe in line between now and then. Court is adjourned."

5

Kyle filled in Billings's attorney's full name, which sounded vaguely familiar, and the particulars of the arrest warrant, much of which I'd gotten from Evans the night before. But the story coming from the arresting officer sounded better. I thanked him and hightailed it back toward my office, grateful my scanner was silent throughout the ride. Speeding back down Grace, I slowed as I neared police headquarters, wondering if Aaron might be irritated enough with the feds to tell me whatever he'd been keeping quiet the day before.

I zipped into a tight spot in front of a meter and hurried inside, punching the elevator button for the ninth floor impatiently and hoping Aaron was there. The detectives' offices were bustling, as usual. Crime pilfers on.

I looked around the maze of map-and-photo-covered cubicles for a familiar face, my ears pricked for interesting bits of conversation.

"Can I help you?" A pretty brunette in a uniform cradled the phone in her hand and looked at me expectantly.

"They called from downstairs when I came in. Nichelle Clarke, from the *Telegraph*? I'm here to see Detective White."

"Is he expecting you?"

I shook my head. "I was driving by and had a question for him. I can call him later if he's busy."

She smiled and gestured to the chairs between the elevators. "I'll let him know you're here."

I turned toward the olive green vinyl seating, but before I'd made it half a step, a frustrated man's voice stopped me cold.

"But, ma'am, this break-in has to be investigated with all the others. We have a procedure." My head snapped around to find a middle-aged, shirt-and-tie detective who was running one hand through his graying hair while he held a phone to his ear with the other. Cat burglar strikes again? That story got more interesting every time the crook managed to get away. "Yes, I understand that. People tend to get upset when their home is violated. Yes, we know there have been robberies in the Fan lately. We're working on it."

I scooted closer to the chest-high wall of his cubicle, attempting to feign disinterest by skipping my eyes around the drab gray decor.

He dropped his hand from his head to the desk blotter and picked up a pen, flicking the button on the end of it. "I assure you, we're doing everything we can to catch this guy. We have every detective we can spare working on this case. But we do need your cooperation."

"Can I help you, miss?" A ringing baritone from behind me made me jump.

I turned, confused smile already in place. "Please. I'm waiting for Detective White, but I was looking for a restroom," I said, straining to hear the detective's phone conversation over my unwanted Samaritan.

"We generally like visitors to this floor to be escorted." He was shorter than me, stocky, with sandy brown hair, wearing pressed chinos and a cerulean Polo. His friendly smile didn't cover the questioning look in his hazel eyes.

"I've been here before," I said, offering a hand for him to shake. "I'm Nichelle Clarke, from the *Richmond Telegraph*. First time I've needed y'all's restroom."

He shook my hand, his grip firm. "The restrooms are right back there." He pointed toward a long hall that extended off the end of the row of cubicles where my frustrated detective was still clicking his pen. I took three steps, but just past the door to the cubicle where the interesting phone call was going on, I purposely failed to lift my foot high enough and stumbled over my stilettos, leaning far forward and dumping my bag all over the floor. My little flashlight, peppermint lifesavers, Godiva white chocolate pearls, pens, change, and tampons rolled and bounced into a scattered formation worthy of a broken piñata. I dropped to my knees and glanced up at the detective who'd given me directions, willing him to either go away or shut up.

He leaned on the edge of the empty cube across from me and watched me crawl around the floor picking up my belongings, his thick arms folded across his chest. Not one for touching tampons, then.

I focused on Detective Frustrated's voice behind me, taking my time and trying to keep from looking up.

"No, I don't have any idea how someone could have circumvented the security system." He sighed heavily. "Yes, I really do understand that. But I still need statements from everyone who was in the house. Are you sure we've spoken to everyone?"

I crawled forward a bit and snagged a runaway nickel, reaching behind me to make sure my skirt was still covering my lavender undies. I'd never be able to go to a crime scene again if half the detectives in Richmond had seen my Victoria's Secrets.

I stuffed the last pen back into my bag and stood up carefully just as Detective Frustrated finished his call.

His shoulders heaved with another sigh. "Of course. Thank you." All that eavesdropping effort for no information. Damn.

He hung up the phone, and I smiled at Cerulean Shirt. "Oops." I waved a hand toward my shoes. "I love them, but they're not always the best for balance."

"They're very nice," he said, not glancing down. "Right this way." He started toward the hallway and I followed, my thoughts still back in the tiny cube with the graying detective.

Another robbery. Now I just needed to know if it was connected to the others, but Aaron grew less fond of talking every day the cat burglar story stretched on.

My new friend watched me go into the bathroom, but wasn't there when I came out, three minutes of silent mulling bringing me no closer to a way to ask Detective Frustrated for the address of the most recent robbery. Which meant digging through every police report from the last few days to find it.

I made my way back to the vinyl chairs just in time for the pretty brunette to come back without Aaron.

"Detective White is very busy this morning, but he said he'll call you as soon as he has a chance," she said. "Is that all we can do for you today?"

"I think it is, thanks." Smiling, I flipped my notebook closed and tucked it back into my bag as I stood. I had some reports to read, and I still wanted to talk to Aaron, but maybe it wasn't an entirely wasted side trip.

* * *

As an exclusive, the hearing story took precedence over everything else when I returned to the office. Except for coffee.

Pulling my syrup bottle from the cabinet, I shook my head as I tipped it over my cup. It was definitely lighter than it had been the day before. Was someone else using it? I pushed it to the very back of the shelf and took a couple of sips before I started for my desk with an over-full mug.

I tried to stay focused on Billings and his arrest as I typed, but my brain raced ahead, ready to file this story and move on to the robbery.

Agents from the Richmond office of the Bureau of Alcohol, Tobacco, Firearms and Explosives made an arrest Thursday in the murder of Daniel Amesworth, 29, the Henrico man whose body was found in the woods near Goochland earlier this week.

James Billings, 56, also of Henrico, was held overnight and released early Friday despite the objection of Commonwealth's Attorney Richard Corry, who made a rare courtroom appearance to argue for keeping the Raymond Garfield executive in custody until after his trial.

"Mr. Billings is a flight risk," Corry told Judge Reginald Davis. "Most of the murder defendants our courtrooms see don't have his resources, or his connections. The Commonwealth wants to ensure that he stays in Virginia until the trial."

Corry didn't outline the particulars of the Commonwealth's case, but the Tele-

graph *has learned that the firm where Amesworth worked does political lobbying for Raymond Garfield.*

I debated that sentence for a full three minutes, but left it in because I wanted to have it first. Once Billings's arrest was live, all it would take for Charlie to find out Amesworth was a lobbyist was a Google search for the relationship between Raymond Garfield and the dead lawyer. I clicked over to my browser and typed the name of Billings's attorney into my Google bar to see where he worked. Holy shit: the guy's name sounded familiar because he was a principal in Amesworth's firm.

I clicked back over to my story, shaking my head. "Defending the guy accused of killing one of his own employees," I said. "How does Captain Cologne sleep at night?"

By the time I finished pounding out the story and sent it to Bob, it was nearly lunchtime. Which meant my three o'clock deadline for filing my feature with Eunice was fast approaching, and I hadn't even written the lead yet.

The morning's police reports sounded so much sexier after my eaves-dropping adventure, though. I stared at my notes for the feature, ignoring my noisy stomach and three emails from Eunice wanting to know where her story was. I clicked over to the PD reports database and scrolled, hunting for the one on the robbery. I found it just in time for my scanner to start squawking. I turned up the volume.

"Why the hell do they need a structural engineer for a car accident?" I wondered aloud, jotting down the address and typing it into Google maps. They were calling an awful lot of ambulances out there, too.

When the little red pin popped up, I scrambled to my feet and threw my bag over my shoulder.

"Where's the fire, sugar?" Eunice asked as I almost mowed her down on my way to the elevator.

"The west end," I called over my shoulder, not slowing down. "Someone ran a truck through a jewelry store. I promise I'll have your feature ready by the end of the day."

* * *

It took twenty minutes to get out there. I stopped and rolled down the window to flash my press pass at the RPD uniform guarding the parking lot entrance.

"Miss Clarke." It was the officer who'd been at the body dump. And I couldn't remember his name to save my shoe closet.

I squinted, but I couldn't see his nametag in the glare from the sun, so I stayed with the generic. "Hello again, officer."

"You here to trespass in another crime scene?"

"Nice to see you again, too, officer."

"You can park over there." He pointed to a stretch of concrete shaded by a line of Magnolia trees where the Channel Four van was already sitting. Damn. "A word of advice: don't try to go inside this time. They aren't sure they can even pull that thing out of there without the whole place falling down. I'd hate for you to get hurt." His smirk said that last part wasn't true, and I shook my head, having learned the hard way that some cops just despise reporters. Period.

I looked past him at the back end of the double-cab that was buried in the side of the building.

"That's why I love my job, officer. Never a dull day."

He grunted and stepped out of the way.

I parked next to Charlie's van, climbed out of the car, and crossed the parking lot, picking my way around the shattered glass that littered the pavement as I waited for Aaron to finish talking to Charlie's TV camera. He rolled his eyes when he turned to me, waving an arm at the truck.

"Can you believe this shit?"

"Hey, who needs stealthy?" I grinned. "Just plow through the wall in broad daylight and clean the joint out while people are still shaking from the adrenaline."

"That would at least be funny," he said. "This was just a stupid mistake, best I can tell. Fool's lucky he didn't kill anybody. We had to transport the driver and three other people to St. Vincent's by ambulance, but the medics said none of the injuries looked life-threatening."

I scribbled as he talked.

"How does one manage to run a truck into a jewelry store on accident?"

"From what he said while they were loading him into the ambulance, the guy came into town to buy a gift, and when he was leaving, he thought he had the truck in reverse. But it was in drive, and he plowed right through the side of the building. That thing has some horsepower. There was a sales clerk who got cut up pretty bad by the flying glass, and a couple looking at engagement rings who got hit. The guy tried to throw his girl out of the way, so he took the worst of it."

"The driver was alone in the truck?"

"Yeah. It's entertaining, but it doesn't look like there was anything sinister here. Just an accident. Glad it wasn't a tragic one."

"Non-tragic is always nice," I said.

"Hey, I got a message that you came in this morning," Aaron said. "What did you need?"

"I wanted to pick your brain about the hearing I covered this morning," I said. "The story's done, though, and I'm buried today." I did want to talk to Aaron about Billings, but he didn't have time for a sit-down in the middle of an accident scene, and I didn't want to ask him about the burglary until I had time to find out if it fit the cat burglar's profile.

"Don't have to tell me twice," he said. "I know the feeling, and if I can brush you off, I'm going to. No offense." His grin brought out the lines around his eyes, but his round face was eternally boyish. Aaron had two girls in college and didn't look a day over thirty-five, if you didn't notice the flecks of gray at his temples.

"None taken." I thanked him and let him go back to work while I looked around the parking lot. There was a young woman sitting alone on the curb, hands buried in her auburn curls. Her pale pink pantsuit was splattered with blood.

I cleared my throat when I stopped next to her. She squinted up at me.

"Can I help you?" she asked. The pale features under her smattering of freckles looked tired.

I introduced myself and asked if she felt like telling me what had happened. Over her shoulder I saw Charlie stop on her way back to the van, poking her cameraman and pointing at me. I waved discreetly before I turned back to the pretty redhead, determined to get something good.

"Sure." The redhead shrugged and gestured for me to have a seat beside her. "I'm Brittany."

When I'd settled on the sun-warmed concrete and taken down the correct spelling of her name, she launched into her story.

"I was helping this couple with the engagement rings," she said. "They were really nice, and she was so excited about picking out her ring. They had been here for a while—she didn't like anything we had in the case and wanted to look at settings and diamonds to see if we could do a semi-custom. I love the engagement rings. Everyone's always so excited when they come in to look at those."

I nodded. "I can imagine. This was the couple who were taken to the hospital?"

"Yeah. I would've been hit, too, but I had turned around to get a color grading guide for diamonds out of the file cabinet. I got sprayed with the glass from the case when he crashed into it. Anyway, there it was, out of nowhere. This guy had just left with some big expensive tennis bracelet for his wife. Or his girlfriend." She snorted. "He was a character. Big, loud dude in boots and a cowboy hat. Made a real fuss of wanting the biggest diamond bracelet we had in the place, and paid cash for it. Most of those are looking for make-up jewelry for the wife or suck-up diamonds for the girlfriend."

I jotted notes, trying not to laugh. I knew the type: Dallas has its fair share of big, loud cowboys. They can be colorful, for sure.

"I see. Was this one a regular customer?"

"No. He lives out in the sticks. I heard him say he owns one of those big farms out in Powhatan." Her green eyes rolled skyward. "Been in his family for generations, he said. And something about his regular jeweler not having anything big enough. He wouldn't talk to anyone but my manager."

"That explains the truck and the boots," I said.

"The truck, maybe. Those boots hadn't ever seen a field, though."

I nodded, jotting that down.

"Are those people going to be okay?" she asked. "They were so happy. Excited about getting married. And my friend Janie—she was in the way. The glass from the windows cut her up pretty bad."

I patted her hand. "The police spokesman said the paramedics expected everyone to be fine. Thanks for your help."

"No problem. I guess I can go home now. I think we're closed."

I turned back toward the building, intent on finding the structural engineer, and saw a blue SUV turn into the parking lot.

I shaded my eyes with my notebook and stared as Kyle stepped out of the driver's seat. He paused when he saw me, then raised one arm and waved.

"You're just underfoot today, aren't you? What's this got to do with the ATF, Mr. Special Agent?" I asked when I met him halfway across the lot.

"On the record? No comment." He grinned. His eyes said he was happy to see me, and I smiled back. I had missed Kyle. Not that he needed to know that.

"Really?" I arched an eyebrow at him. "All right, then. I'll figure it out for myself."

He pointed to a group of men who were surveying the damage. One had a tie and wire-rimmed glasses, and two of the others had hard hats and clipboards.

"Looks like someone really did a number on this place," Kyle said.

"Yeah. The cops said they're waiting for a structural engineer to tell them if they can even pull the truck out of there. I'd bet that's one or both of the hard hat crew over there. Store clerk said the guy who did it was a real piece of work. Flashing a lot of cash and buying big diamonds."

Kyle's eyebrows went up.

"Really? Who did you talk to?"

I turned back toward the sidewalk, but she was gone.

"Oh. She said she was going home," I told Kyle, scanning the parking lot for the auburn ringlets. "I guess she meant right now. I didn't get a phone number, but I do have a name."

"That's okay," he said. "I'm sure I can find someone else. And if not, I know where to find you."

"Sure," I said. "If you're going to keep secrets, I'm going to go see what I can find out from these guys and get back to the office before deadlines eat me alive. I now owe Bob three stories, and I still have a feature due today."

"No rest for the wicked." He shook his head. "Though that doesn't really suit the Nichelle I remember."

I smiled a goodbye and turned back to the building. The engineers spouted a lot of technical jargon about load-bearing walls and danger of spontaneous demolition, and I wrote it down carefully. Climbing back into my car, I waved to Kyle, who was taking notes while he talked to Aaron.

Driving back to the office, I cranked the stereo and turned my conversation with my ex over in my head. The ATF only handled accidents when they involved certain chemical spills, and as far as I knew diamonds were way outside their area of interest. And even if they weren't, something like that didn't need the attention of a bigshot.

I tapped the power button on my computer, still no closer to why Kyle had been at the accident scene. Dialing St. Vincent's media relations office for an update on the victims from the jewelry store, I skimmed my notes from the scene again as I waited for a hospital PR person to pick up the phone.

"Those boots hadn't ever seen a field," I said aloud as I read the clerk's words and pictured her rolling green eyes.

A tobacco field, maybe? Powhatan was full of them. I'd bet my favorite sapphire Louboutins I was right. Kyle didn't give a damn about diamonds. He was there because of the farmer.

6

I hammered out the jewelry store report in record time and plunged straight from that into the feature, with Eunice's three o'clock deadline looming. One hour. I could write a feature in an hour. I thought, anyway.

Troy Wright and his older brother, Darryl, grew up in the same house, went to the same schools, and had the devotion of a mother who loves her sons more than life itself. In a part of Richmond that sees more than its fair share of violence, where schools are underfunded and drugs and crime a part of everyday life for many, Troy Wright is a contender for a prestigious academic award and an honor student at Kingston High School, with dreams of studying broadcast journalism at Virginia Tech or UVA.

Darryl was a convicted drug dealer, found shot in the head in his own home in June.

I lost myself in the rhythm of the keystrokes, the rest of the newsroom falling away until I closed with a quote from Joyce about how proud she was of her son and checked the clock. Three-thirty. Eunice wouldn't be too upset at a half-hour tardy after the day I'd had. Thank God it was her waiting for the piece and not Les.

Unable to ignore my stomach any longer, I sent Eunice the story and went to the break room in search of something edible and a caffeine fix. I hoped Eunice had been in the mood to cook the night before, and that the sports desk hadn't already demolished whatever she'd brought in. But the fridge held only a half-eaten Taco Bell burrito and a salad with a slimy green coating that didn't look like anything a person should eat.

"Gross," I said, swinging the door shut.

"Nothing good in there?" Parker asked from behind me.

I spun to face him. "I don't think I've ever been that hungry," I said. "I'll suck it up until I get home. I have one more story to do, which will make four for today. I'm going to sleep until Monday."

"Damn. And I thought my days were busy when I had a column and a game story," he said. "Anything good?"

"My feature came out great." I spun the bottle cap between my fingers and sipped my Coke, then smiled at him. "Speaking of my feature, I need a favor."

"Anything. I'll owe you 'til the end of time for convincing me to ask Mel out. She's..." He shrugged, flashing a grin with more lovesick than star power behind it. "She's turned my life upside-down. And I love it."

I grinned back. I'd spent years dismissing Parker—an almost-major-league pitcher who looked like an underwear model—as an egotistical jerk who'd gotten his cushy star-columnist job on account of his baseball fame. But he really was a good guy, and a damned fine writer. I didn't often dip a toe into matchmaking, but the better I got to know him, the more I saw that my friend Melanie at the city desk was the perfect balance to his personality. She was smart, serious, and pretty in a non-beer-commercial way. I'd pitched it to him as trying something different than his notch-on-the-bedpost approach to dating, and they'd been fairly inseparable since.

"The kid I did the story on, the one whose brother was the murdered drug dealer from June?" I set the bottle on the counter. "Do you remember any of this?"

"The drug dealer you thought I killed?"

I nodded. "That's the one. His kid brother is a National Merit Finalist and wants to study broadcast sports journalism. And he thinks you're a celebrity. So I sort of told him that maybe you'd let him shadow you for a day. He's a really great kid."

"I am a celebrity." Parker flashed the grin that made the female population of the greater Richmond area call for smelling salts. "But I like you because you don't seem to realize that. When does he want to come in?"

"Monday?"

"Nothing like giving a guy a heads up, Clarke." He dropped three quarters into the soda machine. "But sure. I'll show him around. I can take him out to the park for practice, and to the game, too, if he wants. It's the second to last one of the year."

"Thanks, Parker."

"It's cool. I like kids." He stepped aside when I moved toward the door. "Just get me the address and tell him I'll be there to get him about ten."

"I will." I patted his arm as I passed him. "I have a ton of stuff to do, but I'll see you around. And really, thank you."

"You bet. Have a good weekend, Clarke."

"Thanks. You and Mel doing something fun?"

"Dinner. Movie. I think we might take a picnic out to the country tomorrow. We're getting boring. It's fantastic."

"The great Grant Parker has been domesticated." His happiness was positively infectious, and knowing I was responsible for it gave me warm-fuzzies. I scrolled through police reports until I found the one on the break-in I'd overheard Detective Frustrated talking about that morning. I clicked to another screen and typed the address into Google Maps.

"Holy square footage, Batman," I said, looking at the satellite view of a roof that was easily five times the size of mine. It sat right on Monument, too. A house that big, in that part of town, meant one of two things: old money, or new power. I snatched up the phone and dialed the police department, waiting impatiently for Aaron to pick up.

Voicemail. Damn.

"Hey Aaron, it's Nichelle," I said after the beep. "I'm sorry to be a pain in your ass, but you know you love me anyway. I have a couple of questions about this break-in in the Fan last night, and I'm pushing deadline so hard it's about to push back. Pretty please, could you give me a call as soon as you have a second?"

I cradled the handset and turned back to the computer screen, searching the city tax records for the property address. Maybe I should have bugged Aaron about it at the jewelry store. But with nothing to ask specific questions about, I wouldn't have gotten much, anyway.

The tax record loaded.

"You've got to be shitting me," I breathed, sitting back in the chair. No wonder Detective Frustrated had been so apologetic, and Aaron was dodging my calls.

The latest house on the cat burglar's route belonged to one Theodore Grayson, United States Senator for the Commonwealth of Virginia.

"That is way too much of a coincidence to actually be a coincidence," I said aloud to no one in particular.

"What is?" Bob's voice came from behind me and I clicked the browser window shut and turned around. Technically, every story I'd written was rightfully mine. But digging for something more on Grayson was definitely a gray area. If I found anything else, I'd take it to Trudy. Really. But I didn't want him to tell me I had to yet.

"Not sure," I said. "I have one more story for you today, because people aren't going to be sick enough of my byline by noon tomorrow. There was another burglary in the Fan last night."

"I know," he said. "That's what I came to see you about. Charlie Lewis has a teaser for the early broadcast, and it's already on the web at Channel Four and Channel Ten. I'm not fond of hearing from the TV folks that the home of a United States senator was robbed less than two miles from this building. How the hell did you miss that, Nicey?"

"I didn't miss it," I protested, trying hard to keep the annoyance out of my voice. "I've been busting my ass since six o'clock this morning, running on caffeine and Pop Tarts. I've turned in three stories already and am waiting for Aaron to call back about my fourth. That's not missing anything."

"They had it first," he said. "But if you can get him to talk to you, you'll have it better."

"He didn't give Charlie anything?" I asked.

"No comment from police officials," Bob said. "But Charlie doesn't have your in at the PD. Work it."

"I'm beginning to wonder if I've worked it almost to death," I sighed. "But I'll give it everything I've got. That piece on the hearing I covered this morning has Charlie beat, right?"

"Seven hours ago," he said. "Look, I love having the print exclusive for tomorrow, but it doesn't change the fact that you slipped on this."

"I was writing my feature." I caught his eye and smiled. "It came out really nice. That kid is a National Merit Finalist. He's coming in to shadow Parker on Monday. Wants to be Rick Reilly when he grows up."

The tight line he'd stretched his mouth into softened slightly.

"I'm sure it is," he said. "I'll read it with my coffee on Sunday morning. But you're not a feature writer. Your job is to stay on top of cops and courts. And Les is still pushing Shelby at the guys upstairs. The piece on the hearing is good, but if you want to keep covering both, they all have to be good. The suits wouldn't dream of just handing Shelby your job after the year you've had, but with the recent uptick in readership and ad revenue, your friend the managing editor is pulling for them to split your beat and give half of it to his girlfriend. He says we can afford it now. So just watch it."

"He's trying to get them to steal half my beat because we can afford another reporter thanks to me almost getting killed?" I shook my head. "Only Les. Balls of steel, that guy. Big ones. It's a wonder he can walk upright."

Bob patted my shoulder. "I'd like to not have that picture in my head this close to dinnertime, thanks. Just get me something Charlie hasn't had on the robbery before you go home. Trudy's trying to get an interview with Grayson. He's not commenting, so far, but I swear she has a little black book on those guys. Grayson's campaign is hollering Watergate, and the other guys are denying any part of it. This is leading the front in the morning, and I need it. Right now."

"You got it, Chief."

I clicked the bookmark for the Channel Four website and pulled up Charlie's story.

Damn. She had clearly spent every minute she wasn't at the demolished jewelry store working this robbery, and she'd pretty much knocked it out of the park, for a crime story the police wouldn't comment on. There was footage of RPD uniforms checking every inch of the perimeter of Grayson's house. The story had comments from neighbors, a bit about the history of the house (which included a stint as Confederate spy headquarters during the Civil War), and a long background on other crimes the cat burglar may have committed. Charlie's promo showed the entire yard had been taped off as a crime scene, which was a little odd. I needed Aaron on the phone. It was after four, and I didn't have time to go to Grayson's house before deadline.

I dialed Aaron's cell. Voicemail there, too. So he was either busy, or avoiding me because he knew I was nearly out of time.

I drummed my fingers on the desk, staring at Charlie's story until the letters on my screen blurred. I didn't have time to do all that research, and I'd rather wear saddle shoes for all eternity than quote Charlie Lewis's work in my write-up.

Which left me with what? I flashed onto the detective I'd eavesdropped on that morning. Had he said anything useful?

He had said, "I don't know how they circumvented the security system."

I pulled the police report up again and saw that the Graysons used ADT.

"Except this guy has been careful to skip houses with alarms," I muttered under my breath, pulling a file folder out from under a pile of press releases and flipping through the other burglary reports. That was part of the oddity of the case: the culprit knew which houses had good stuff and no alarm.

I scrolled back through Charlie's report. She'd missed it. I would have, too, if I hadn't managed to overhear the detective talking on the phone.

"So, has the burglar changed his M.O., or was this someone other than the cat burglar?" I mused aloud, thinking about the campaign commercials that were getting nastier every day and Bob's comment about Watergate. I wondered idly if that might be worth a trip by Grayson's campaign office. If I could get the inside scoop on this break-in, it would help make up for losing to Charlie on the first story.

I dialed Trudy's extension to see if she'd gotten anything from Grayson, but she didn't pick up, either.

"It would be so nice if one person would answer the damned phone today," I mumbled, replacing the receiver.

Whatever. There was a difference between this report and all the others no one had pointed out yet, so I'd lead with that.

Richmond Police were quiet about a search for suspects in a seventh robbery in the city's historic Fan district early Friday, but the break-in, at the home of U.S. Sen. Ted Grayson, had one difference from the other six burglaries: the senator's house had a security system.

"Statistics show that a security system is a deterrent to thieves," RPD spokesman Aaron White told the Telegraph *last month, after the third burglary of a home that didn't have a system in place. "These robberies seem to be following a pattern that affirms that."*

Until the break-in at Grayson's home Friday, none of the burglar's targets had a security system. Police reports show that the Graysons have a monitored system through ADT, but the company told police they didn't receive an alert.

Grayson, who has represented Virginia in the U.S. Senate for five years, is in the thick of a hotly contested re-election campaign.

I pulled some details about the campaign from Trudy's coverage, mentioned that there was no list of missing items in the initial police report, and added Trudy's name to the bottom as a contributor, not even reading it over in my haste. Once it was floating through cyberspace to Bob's computer, I thumped my head down on my desk, my stomach gurgling loud enough to be embarrassing, had I been less exhausted or more inclined to care.

Twenty minutes later, I had an "attagirl" from Bob in my email.

My cell phone binged the arrival of a text and I clicked to the message from Jenna: "C has frozen peas. I have pizza and Kool-Aid for my bday dinner."

"Hope he's healed for us to have girls' night next Fri." I tapped back.

"Enjoy your mommy celebration. One more stop, and I'm going to eat, and then straight to bed."

I had just packed up my computer when my desk phone rang.

"Crime desk, this is Clarke, can I help you?"

"Hey there," Kyle said.

"Hey yourself, *Agent* Miller," I said. "Are you liking Virginia so far?"

"Come on, Nicey, don't be that way. I wanted to surprise you."

"Mission accomplished." My lips turned up at the corners. "It was kind of fun to see you with your minions this morning, though. Like an episode of *Where are They Now?* from my actual life."

"Why let the fun stop there? Have dinner with me. I haven't been able to find any decent food in this town, and I know you have to know where it's hiding."

I tapped a pen on my desk. I was tired. But I did need to eat, and Kyle had arrested a high-profile guy for murder that morning. He might be more talkative outside the courthouse and away from his fellow agents.

"What time?" I asked.

"I need about an hour to wrap up here."

I could still run by Grayson's campaign office, then. "Perfect. Tell you what—I made chili the other night, and it's always better when it's been sitting for a while. I'm ready to go home and kick off my shoes, so why don't you meet me at my house at seven?"

"You're inviting me back to your place already?" he said, his tone mischievous.

"I said chili, Kyle. Not lingerie." I gave him my address and hung up, turning for the elevator. So much for my quiet Friday night. But maybe I could trade sleep for some answers.

7

The parking lot was nearly empty at Grayson's tiny storefront campaign office on the northern edge of town. I poked my head in the front door and stepped inside when a striking brunette smiled at me from a banged-up metal desk in the far corner. Posters with larger-than-life images of the senator stared from every wall. He was good-looking, but had that smarmy politician air about him, even in two dimensions.

"Can I help you?" the brunette asked in a bright voice laced with exhaustion.

I smiled. I hoped so. She was young—younger than me. Probably her first job in politics, which meant the important people who worked here likely didn't notice her. "I'm looking for some information on the senator." I kept the smile in place.

"We have brochures and pamphlets over there." She pointed to a folding table just inside the door. "There's a list of upcoming campaign events, too. If you'd like to volunteer to help out with canvassing, I can take your name and put you in the database."

Her hopeful expression told me I'd found a way in.

"I'd like to get to know a little more about Senator Grayson first, but I might be interested in that," I said.

She grinned. "Great! I'll be happy to help you any way I can."

I picked up one of each piece of campaign literature, mostly trying to think up a way to find out something useful without being too obvious. "Here's the thing: I got most of this from the Internet," I said. "I want to know what he's *really* like. I'd like to help him get re-elected. But I'm not sure what to think about most of Washington anymore. What do you think about him? Why do you work here?"

She laughed. "Because I want to work in politics, and I had a foot in the door here. But Senator Grayson is very charismatic. People like him. And he doesn't take any crap from anyone. He's not afraid of a little risk. But I think it's his ability to control most situations that I like best."

"Decisiveness is certainly a rarity in D.C. these days," I said. "That's a good quality for a legislator to have, I think."

She straightened a thick stack of papers and shoved them into a manila envelope. "He doesn't let anyone push him around. Even when people try. I think that kind of conviction is good."

I tipped my head to one side. Who was pushing a sitting senator around? Or trying?

"I agree." I leaned forward. "I imagine it would take guts to tell someone like Senator Grayson what to do. But I guess it took guts for someone to break into his house, too."

Her head snapped up, her blue eyes wide. "I know! Can you imagine knowing someone else was in your home? How violating it would feel?"

"I wonder why someone would do that?" I tried to sound casual.

Either it worked or she was only half-listening. "I wouldn't be surprised if it had something to do with this campaign. I never would have thought politics was so nasty. I was here late one night last week, and then I forgot my purse when I left. I came back to get it, and the senator was in the office." She waved a hand toward a postage-stamp-sized room near the door. Gray mini-blinds covered the window that faced out into the main lobby. "There were two other men in there with him, yelling about getting their money's worth out of him. I know he technically works for the taxpayers, but I thought that was uncalled for. He's already so stressed."

I managed to keep my jaw from dropping, but just barely. Getting their money's worth? She was too naive for national politics. No way that snippet had anything to do with tax money. The photo of Amesworth and Grayson spun through my thoughts. What if this whole thing was a backroom deal gone bad?

"The nerve of some people." I struggled to keep my voice even. "Did you see them?"

"No, I didn't," she said. "I got my bag and left, and they were in there with the door closed."

Damn.

She smiled. "He's a good man. Can you find a couple of nights to come in and work the phones for us?"

Double damn.

Unable to think of a good reason to turn her down, I reached for her sign-up sheet. "I think you've convinced me." I jotted my first name and my personal email address, since I'd left out my job title during our conversation.

"I'll be in touch." She stood when I did and stuck out her hand. "I'm Allison."

"I'll look forward to hearing from you, Allison." It wouldn't hurt to have a source in Grayson's office, even if I couldn't quote her because she didn't know she was talking to the press.

I turned the radio up and rolled the windows down as I drove home, turning what I'd learned over in my head. Last week, she'd said. Amesworth had been killed sometime in the past week, though no one had said when yet. But Kyle had someone in jail for killing Amesworth. I wondered if Billings could have been the third man Allison had overheard. How could I get Kyle to talk about Billings—or Grayson—over dinner?

The kitchen porch light flashed on when I pulled into my driveway, twilight earlier each day as the calendar rolled toward winter. The little red maples that would have been big trees in Texas were dwarfed by the hundred-foot pines, oaks, and Bradford pears in Virginia, and were always the first to change, shading crimson like they'd been painted with a fine-tipped brush.

I loved autumn in Virginia, with cooler air, apples fresh from the orchards in Charlottesville, and earlier evenings. But the six months of bare trees and bitter cold on the way? I didn't care for those.

My toy Pomeranian bounced at the back gate, working her tiny jaw around a battered stuffed squirrel, managing to get a soft squeak out of a long-punctured insert.

I bent to scratch her head, taking the squirrel and tossing it for her each time she retrieved it, my thoughts still swirling around Grayson. Darcy played until the reaches of the yard were dark, then returned without her toy and trotted past me, up the worn wooden steps to the back door.

I barely had time to kick my heels into the corner of the living room before Kyle rang the doorbell.

Darcy yapped and scratched at the door. Kyle knelt and put a hand out for her to sniff when I opened it.

"She's cute. What's her name? Scarlett?" Kyle stood and stepped into the foyer when I moved out of the doorway.

"Darcy," I said, as I smiled and shut the door. I returned his hug, the smell of his familiar cologne making me hold on a few seconds too long, before I spun toward the kitchen.

"That's my girl," he said. "Always with her nose in a book. Good to know some things never change."

I bit my tongue and busied myself reheating chili, making small talk about my house and the city until I carried the bowls to the table. I opened a Dr Pepper for myself and handed Kyle a Corona before I sat down across from him at my tiny kitchen table.

"So, what's new with you, Captain Surprise?" I asked as I picked up my spoon. "Your parents okay with you moving out here?"

"My parents were so thrilled to hear you live here that I'm not sure they noticed anything else. They still think you're the daughter they never had. I've only ever tried to take one other girl home to meet them, and my mother put pictures of you and me on every flat surface in their house before I got there. Granted, that was years ago, but I've been too afraid to try it again since." He smiled wryly.

I couldn't think of a suitable reply, so I scooped more chili into my mouth and hoped he'd keep talking. He watched me over the top of his bottle.

"I was thinking it might be good for more than my career," he said.

Shit. He smiled, and I shoveled another bite into my mouth while I thought out a response.

"There's someone else?" he asked when I opened my mouth to speak.

"N—yes," I said. "There's me. Kyle, I lost myself in you to the point that I almost gave up what I'd wanted most since I was little girl. I've even wondered since if I made the right choice. But I did. I chose me. And I've found a girl who can interview a serial killer and kick some bad guy ass and rock a pair of stilettos, too. I like her. And I don't want to lose her again."

"I'm not saying let's get married tomorrow," he said. "We're not the same people we were. But that doesn't mean we can't like the people we are now."

My stomach flipped a little at the unblinking electric blue gaze. Could we? I dropped my eyes to my bowl. "I don't know, Kyle."

"I'll take that over 'No.'"

I smiled. "The glass is still half full, huh? Let's think about getting to be friends. Slow."

"How slow?"

"As slow as we need," I said with a gentle smile. "That's the best I can do tonight. Let's talk about something else, shall we? Anything interesting going on at work?"

He arched an eyebrow. "Are we off the record, Woodward?"

"Do you see a pen? I'm not always a reporter, Kyle. I can be interested in your job as a friend, too." And I was. But if he happened to say something that might help with my story, so be it.

"Okay." He swirled his spoon in the air to gather stringing cheddar and took a bite, his face thoughtful as he chewed and swallowed. "The press has not been notified of the case I'm working on, but there are some enterprising folks making a pretty penny off the high cigarette taxes in New York."

My brow puckered. Kyle took another bite.

"I think your cooking has gotten even better, Nicey. This is great."

"Thanks. How do crooks make money off taxes?"

"By stealing them. Virginia and North Carolina have the smallest per-pack excise taxes on cigarettes in the country. And we're not that far from New York, where the taxes are high. So these guys buy truckloads of cigarettes wholesale down here, then put counterfeit New York tax stamps on them and sell them at full price up there. It's a major interstate organization. They do a pretty good business, and ninety percent of their customers have no idea they're doing anything illegal."

"Wait. You're saying Joe Smoker doesn't know it's shady to buy cigarettes off a truck instead of in the store? No one is that dense."

Kyle shook his head. "A small percentage of the activity is on the Internet or in back alleys, but most of the sales are being made through convenience stores. I'm pretty sure most of the ones I'm talking about are run by folks who aren't nominees for citizen of the year, so they're getting a cut of the money for providing the outlet. The end consumer thinks they ran to the quickie mart to get a pack, but they're really funding organized crime."

Organized crime? Was that why Joey wanted to talk to me? I brushed the thought aside.

"Wow. That's...crafty. How do people come up with this stuff? It would never occur to me to sell contraband cigarettes to people in New York and pocket the tax money." I dropped my spoon into my bowl and rested my chin on one fist, my hair falling over my left eye.

"I'm afraid you'll never be a criminal mastermind." Kyle's hand fluttered toward my face, like he was going to brush my hair out of it. I smiled at him and shoved the wayward strand behind my ear. He focused his blue lasers on the nearly-empty bowl before he continued. "Anyway, that's what's been occupying my days since I got here."

"Just be careful," I said. "Criminal masterminds have a tendency to hold pretty poor regard for life—especially cops' lives."

He thumped a fist against his chest in a show of bravado and flashed a row of orthodontist-perfect pearly whites. "That's what my friend Kevlar is for. We call him Kev."

Every story I'd ever done on a cop who'd been killed in the line of duty flashed through my mind like lightning. "Kev doesn't protect your head, Kyle."

His eyes softened. "I know that. I'm careful. I'm well-trained. I'm not stupid. I don't want you to worry about me."

"Too late. I have a lot of friends who are cops. I worry about all of you."

Something flared in his eyes, and I found myself unable to look away until the soft flapping of Darcy's dog door broke the spell. She barked once and pawed my bare ankle, demanding a treat. Kyle cleared his throat as he pushed his chair back.

"Let me help you with that," he said, reaching for his bowl.

I set them both in the sink and smiled. "Done. I only use enough dishes to run the dishwasher every few days."

I scratched Darcy's head and gave her a biscuit, sorting through my thoughts. Kyle Miller in my kitchen. After all these years. Would it be so bad to try again? Maybe not. But could I stand losing him again if it didn't work out? My heart hurt just contemplating it.

When Darcy scurried away, I led Kyle into the living room and parked myself strategically on the tufted red chaise lounge, gesturing to the navy sofa opposite my perch.

"Didn't they just pass a law that's going to raise the tax on cigarettes here?" I asked him, remembering a story I'd seen a few weeks before.

"Very good. I guess you're up on the latest news," Kyle said. "My thieves have got to be salivating over that. There are more smokers here in Virginia as a percentage of the population than anywhere else, and the average income isn't nearly what you see in Manhattan, so this tax hike is going to hit a lot of people hard. The crooks will keep buying in North Carolina, and as soon as they figure out how to fake the new Virginia stamps, which even I haven't seen yet, they'll be selling here, too. Not for long, though. We'll catch them."

I nodded, my fingers twisting my hair into knots as I studied the fluffy geometric-print rug under my coffee table. Grayson. Billings. The farmer from the jewelry store. The dead lobbyist. Tobacco seemed to be popping up in my days an awful lot.

"What's up?" Kyle asked.

"Hmm?" I kept my eyes on the red triangle in the carpet.

"Nicey. You're playing with your hair. What are you thinking about?"

When I looked up, Kyle was waving his arms like he was guiding a plane home. I laughed.

"A story. Just trying to figure out what pieces go where in this one."

"Oh, yeah? I'm a pretty smart guy, you know. And the hair tells me there's something you're trying to figure out."

I turned and caught a glimpse of the right side of my head in the dark, flat screen of the TV that hung above my fireplace. There were at least four loops where I'd been bothering my hair as I stared at the floor. I ran my fingers through it and they fell straight again.

"What do you know about Billings?" I asked. "You seemed pretty sure this morning that he was responsible for killing the lobbyist. Why do you think so?"

Kyle leaned forward, studying my face for a moment.

"Off the record, Miss Clarke," he said. "Because I trust you. And I don't think I have to say that if this shows up in the newspaper, I won't make that mistake again, right?"

"Noted."

"I think Billings is paying someone off," he said. "And I have a couple of ideas, though I haven't found enough for an arrest warrant yet. But something went bad. Either the lobbyist grew a conscience, or he threatened to tell, or he asked for a bigger cut. I have a lead on a weapon, and forensics is working on more."

"And who do you think Billings was buying off?"

"That, I can't even tell you as a friend."

I nodded, tugging at my hair again.

He stared, thumb and hooked index finger sliding over the auburn bristles around his mouth a few times. "You think you know the answer to that already, don't you?"

I grinned. "If you're not sharing, neither am I."

"But you're working another angle on this," he said. "Irrespective of what you saw at the courthouse this morning. You're on another trail."

"I can neither confirm nor deny that, agent," I said.

"I don't need you to confirm it. I know you." He sat back and draped one arm over the back of the sofa. "As your friend, let me give you a piece of advice. Watch your step."

"I'm really not investigating anything," I said, turning what he'd said about Billings over in my head and wondering if I was lying to him even as I spoke the words. "But your concern is duly noted. And appreciated."

"Let me know if there's anything I can help you with," he said. "Without actually losing my job, anyway."

"Yeah?" I said, grinning. "Half of getting any story is about who you know. I guess you're a good person to know."

I was kidding, but something I couldn't quite read flitted across his face.

"I like to think so," he smiled, dropping his eyelids halfway and leaning forward.

Oh, I knew that look. It hadn't changed in ten years. Time to go home, Special Agent Bedroom Eyes. No need to test my willpower so soon.

I made a show of eyeballing the clock and yawning, complaining about my long day. He shook his head the tiniest bit, but rose and turned toward the foyer.

"Thanks for dinner." He leaned against the front door and smiled. "I'll give you a call if I come across anything that says I really am a good person for you to know."

I shook my head. "I don't think your worth as a friend is solely dependent on your ability to get me classified ATF information."

"I'm really glad I found you again, Nicey."

"I'm glad you found me, too. My ashes would be scattered all over Shockoe Bottom right now if you hadn't." I feigned horror and he chuckled.

Smiling back, I pulled the door open. And found myself nose-to-nose with Joey.

8

"Hi." The word popped out automatically, and I took a step backward and pushed the door open farther, hiding Kyle behind it.

"I thought we might take that walk." Joey stepped into the entryway, his honey-colored skin particularly attractive against a lavender oxford shirt, sleeves rolled up and tie loose. It was the most informal I'd ever seen him, and I couldn't help noticing how his shoulders pulled at the seams of the cotton. Not enough to classify the shirt as tight, just enough to make my pulse flutter. I felt the corners of my lips tip up in a smile, and his dark eyes lit, crinkling at the corners when he flashed a grin.

It faded when Kyle stepped out from behind the door.

"Thanks for dinner," he said again, laying a hand on my shoulder before he put one arm around me and pulled me into a half-hug.

Joey stared, and my eyes flicked between the two of them, watching them size each other up. Oh, boy.

"I didn't know you had company," Joey said, not moving to leave. "We could go another time."

"Such things happen when you refuse to call before you come by," I chided, ducking out from under Kyle's arm and cutting a warning look in his direction. "Kyle was just leaving. And I could use a walk. It's beautiful outside tonight." Two visits in a week's time was unusual for Joey. He wanted to talk to me, and I wanted to know why.

"I'll call you," Kyle said, turning sideways to slide through the wide doorway. Joey didn't move to make it easier, stepping closer to me only after Kyle was on the porch.

"Thank you, Kyle. It was nice to catch up with an old friend." I hit the last word too hard, and Joey chuckled under his breath. Kyle's smile faltered. I felt a flicker of remorse, but we certainly hadn't been anything more than friends in a long time, and I really wanted him to go before the two of them got into enough of a pissing contest for him to start asking questions about Joey. How would I explain a moonlight walk with a Mafia boss to the ATF?

Not well, that's how.

Kyle nodded and muttered something that sounded like "We'll see about that," turning and jogging down the steps.

I shut the door and flashed a smile at Joey. "Your timing is off. Do you have a fever or something?" I reached up to touch his forehead, and he leaned forward just enough to enter the danger zone in my tiny foyer. I ran my fingers through my own hair instead and laughed shakily, spinning toward the living room.

"Let me get my shoes."

"Preferably some you'll make it farther than a few blocks in," he called after me.

I dug through the basket in the corner of the living room where my less-important footwear lived, unearthing a pair of black ballet flats with purple roses embroidered on the toes. Hurrying back to the door, I found Joey examining my collection of beach glass.

"This is beautiful," he said.

"I love the beach. My mom grew up in California. In Texas, we went to the Gulf coast every year when I was little, and then to Mexico and even the Bahamas when I got older." I pointed to a sapphire piece with violet streaks. "This one came from a place near a coral reef off Grand Bahama Island. I can't come home from a trip without the perfect piece of glass."

I took a deep breath and got more than a faint whiff of a woodsy, musky cologne. He was standing awfully close. And he smelled so good.

"What?" I took a step back and returned his smile.

"You get a look on your face every time you mention your mother," he said, opening the front door. "You must be very close."

"That would have been accurate five years ago. Then she got cancer and I thought I might lose her. The only reason I didn't move back home was that she threatened to disown me if I did. She didn't want me to quit my job."

"She's okay now?"

"She's been in remission for more than four years. I don't close my eyes at night without being thankful for that. So far, so good."

"Good to hear."

We walked in silence, an occasional car passing or pebble scraping under a shoe the only sounds for almost a block.

"So, about your friend back there," Joey said finally. "Is he anyone important?"

Subtle, Joey.

"He's my long-ago ex-boyfriend. Who also happens to be the Richmond ATF office's newest special agent."

"No shit?" He became very interested in the moon, hanging low and blood orange. "How convenient."

I kept my eyes on the stars, which seemed brighter next to the dark harvest moon. Joey and I had chatted a handful of times over the summer, on warm nights when I'd come home to find him on my porch swing holding the dog. But we'd been careful to keep it light, avoiding reference to what we might think of each other outside a bizarre friendship. My stomach flipped at the notion that he might want to be more than friends, but my head warned against the idea. No matter what Freud might say about the dreams I had to the contrary.

"What's up?" Time to talk business.

"Excuse me?" He turned his head to look at me.

"You've been here twice in a week. You want something. I seem to remember you talking about 'using people who purvey information to work around the edges of the law.' So, what is it?"

He slowed his gait.

"You're nosing around Ted Grayson," he said flatly. "I need you to back off. And I'm already sure you won't do it, but I have to ask you. Before some-body decides to tell you."

I spun on one heel to face him.

He met my gaze head-on, looking down slightly because of my flat shoes.

I studied his face for a full minute before I spoke. His mouth was drawn into a tight line, his eyes liquid and pleading. And he wasn't the pleading type. What was Grayson into?

"How the hell do you know that?" I asked finally.

"Men like Grayson have all kinds of connections," Joey said. "And infor-mation is currency. If the right person decides to keep you quiet, you might get hurt. I don't want that." He raised a hand and pushed my wayward lock of hair gently behind my ear, his fingers barely grazing my skin. The simple gesture sent sparks shooting clear to my fingertips. I wanted to lean my cheek into his palm, but instead I tilted my head away. His hand dropped.

"Someone could hurt me?" I asked.

"I don't have say-so over everybody with a gun. Far from it. And this has the potential to get very ugly, Miss Clarke. Let. It. Go. Politics isn't even your game."

"Crime is my game. I think the good senator is up to no good. And you pretty much just confirmed that. I don't do well with letting go."

"Learn," Joey said. "Consider it self-preservation."

"I know you're not threatening me." God, I hoped he wasn't, anyway. But maybe I thought he was sexy because he was more than a little bit danger-ous. "To the casual observer it might sound that way, though. What is your boy Grayson into?"

"He's not my boy," Joey said. "And I'm not telling you a damned thing. The less you can find out, the more likely you are to drop it."

"Have you met me? I am nothing if not tenacious."

"If it weren't for that, I wouldn't be here," he said. "Your ability to dig up dirt is exactly what has me worried." He laid a hand on my arm. "Back off."

"I can't." I stepped past him and started back toward my house, warmth lingering on my skin where his hand had been. "This dead lobbyist could turn out to be the story I've dreamed of my whole life. What if Grayson is the missing piece? I just have to..."

I faltered. The lobbyist's half-eaten face flickered in my memory, right behind an image of Joey standing in my driveway after the discovery of the body, which according to the coroner had only been out there for a few days at the most.

"You were here." My chili threatened to come back up. "Oh, God. Tell me you didn't."

"This would be more fun if you'd stop assuming I killed every dead person in five states." He didn't look away. "I did not hurt anyone. But your dead guy was in over his head. And you're about to get in over yours."

"Kyle already arrested someone for killing the lobbyist," I said. "They had a bond hearing early this morning. I have a story in tomorrow's paper about it."

"Who was it?" Joey's eyes widened slightly, his voice flipping from pleading to tight.

"James Billings. He's a veep over at Raymond Garfield." Puzzle pieces rained into place as I talked, Allison and Kyle echoing in my head. "I think he's the one paying Grayson off, and I think the dead guy was the go-between. Kyle is sure Billings is his man. He got the CA to take on the case himself, and the judge didn't give them the no-bond they asked for, but he made Billings wear an ankle monitor. So they've got to have something compelling."

"I'll be damned." Joey matched his stride to mine, shaking his head slowly.

He kept his head down the rest of the way back to my house, not talking. From his wrinkling brow and twisting mouth, he was either deep in thought or having some kind of internal conflict.

When we turned up my sidewalk, I broke the silence.

"Thanks for coming by," I said. "I'd rather you avoid any more chest thumping competitions with Kyle for obvious reasons, but I really do appreciate your concern."

He stood under the unlit coach lamp next to my front door and leaned one shoulder against the wall.

"I don't want you to get hurt. Follow the Billings story. You'll be safe. And if that agent has a thing for you, you'll stay ahead of your friend at the

TV station, too. An executive going up for murder because of dirty money is a hell of a lead."

"It's not bad, but why do I get the distinct feeling that there's something better here?"

"It's not better if you don't live to see it printed, is it? Make yourself ignore it. You told me once I saved your life. I can't stand the thought of anything happening to you." He snatched my cell phone from my hand and tapped the keys for a few seconds, then handed it back. "Call me if you need me. If your old 'friend' can keep you safe, then that's where I want you to be. Consider it payback: forget you ever heard Grayson's name."

I unlocked the door and opened it.

"I'll be careful," I said.

"Dammit, this isn't a game." He grabbed my arm and spun me around. "Nobody wins if you get yourself killed, and there are people in this up to their eyeballs who won't give a shit if I say to leave you alone once you piss them off. Leave it."

I couldn't concentrate on anything except the feel of his breath on my face and the smell of his cologne, which seemed slightly insane, given the urgency in his eyes. I leaned back against the doorframe. He moved his hand to the wood behind my head, leaning on the wall with his arm alongside my cheekbone. I stared into his eyes for half a second and stumbled backward into the house.

"I won't get hurt," I said. "I swear."

I closed the door before he could say anything else, and watched him go down the walk through the trio of little windows that ran along the top.

Darcy barked behind me and I jumped.

"Talk about playing with fire," I said. "Let's get you a snack and me a cold shower and a good night's sleep, huh, girl?"

Darcy's pawing at the bathroom door popped the broken latch loose before I even got the shower curtain closed. I turned on the water and made a mental note to call the landlord about the doorknob. Standing under the showerhead, I ran back through the conversation with Joey, way too relieved that he hadn't killed the lobbyist. It wasn't until I was halfway through rinsing my hair that I realized what Joey had said without saying it.

James Billings hadn't killed anybody, either.

* * *

Sleep eluded me for the better part of three hours. When I'd tossed and turned to the point that every pillow I owned was scattered on the floor around my cherry four-poster, I threw off the covers and went back to the living room.

Carrying a glass of Moscato to the sofa, I picked up a puzzle piece and turned it every which way, trying to finish the border. But it didn't fit. Closer inspection told that it was one of those they'd cut from the middle with an almost-flat edge, so it wasn't really a border piece.

"Where the hell is the other one?" I muttered, studying the two thousand or so that littered the coffee table, most of them close to the same color. I loved puzzles. The harder the better, so I bought lots of monochromatic ones.

While my eyes searched the pieces on the table, my brain tried to order the week's events into a mental jigsaw.

If Billings didn't kill the lobbyist, who did? Grayson? My gut had sensed the senator was shady for days, and Joey all but confirmed it.

But murder? I shook my head. Not impossible, but I'd put it in the unlikely column at least until I knew more about him. Bribes are one thing. Murder is in a whole different league. I'd met and spoken to more than anyone's fair share of killers, and they are almost always motivated by one of two things: insanity or passion. And Grayson didn't get where he was being ruled by his emotions.

But Joey wouldn't have looked so surprised—or been so damned noncommittal—when I told him about Billings's arrest if he thought the tobacco executive did it. And while I didn't want to think my way-too-sexy mob friend was involved, it was looking like he knew too much about the inner workings of this case.

Kyle's comment about the cigarette taxes floated through my head. Were there federal taxes on cigarettes, too?

I dropped the puzzle piece and reached for my laptop, typing "federal tobacco tax" into the Google bar. Pay dirt: forty-five cents a pack.

I deleted that and typed Grayson's name in again, scrolling past all the same stories I'd seen the first time, looking for a mention of taxes or tobacco.

Halfway down the fourth page, I found something.

In a *Washington Post* article dated the previous October, Grayson's name was mentioned in discussion of a bill that would raise the federal excise tax on cigarettes. The reporter called him a swing vote because he was a moderate who might vote for the higher tax, earmarked for education, a pet project of Grayson's.

I copied the bill number and clicked over to the Senate website, pasting it into the search box.

Oh, shit.

The bill had spent nearly a year bogged down in committee. Until last week, when a retiring senator who was one of the co-authors had forced it onto the voting calendar for a week from Monday.

But I was staring at my screen with a slightly loose jaw because Ted Grayson was the sole dissenting vote on sending the bill to the floor.

The *Post's* analysts had expected Grayson to lean on this bill. Tobacco companies were increasingly unpopular with the public, but they had deep pockets and old friends in D.C. They needed someone on their side, and Grayson was a popular guy on Capitol Hill.

He also represented a fair number of farmers, here in tobacco country. He was the perfect target. And the information in front of me was just enough to make a person curious about why education had suddenly taken a backseat to tobacco. And give me a bad feeling that I already knew.

Allison had said, "Asked what they were paying him for." I sat back in my chair, my eyes on Grayson's Colgate-commercial-perfect smile as my mind clicked puzzle pieces together.

Tobacco was Virginia's biggest agricultural product, and had been since Thomas Jefferson held state office in Richmond. Farmers depended on being able to sell their crops. And the company that turned those crops into marketable product was an industrial giant. I had no trouble believing that either would be willing to pay for votes to stop a new tax that could hurt their sales. But how did the lobbyist end up dead? He was part of Team Tobacco, too, right? Was I looking in the right place? My gut said yes, because Kyle had arrested Billings, who was a tobacco executive.

I clicked last fall's *Post* article back up on my screen, reading the rest of it but finding no mention of the victim, Amesworth, or Raymond Garfield, the tobacco company.

Back to Google.

On page fourteen of my results, Grayson's name popped up in an article about a bill that made it illegal to smoke in restaurants in Virginia—because he'd written the bill. The story on my screen was written by the *Telegraph's* retired opinions editor, praising Grayson's dogged pursuit of the change. Said the Senator's favorite uncle died of lung cancer in his forties, and quoted Grayson as calling Raymond Garfield "Virginia's moneygrubbing, murderous devil."

It made no sense. If he'd flipped on such a major issue, someone would have noticed. A search of the *Post's* editorial archives turned up nothing.

I went back to the senate site and searched for bills concerning tobacco farming, subsidies, taxes, or smoking.

There'd been seven introduced in the past three years. Four that actually made it to the floor for a vote. I held my breath as I clicked into the voting record and scanned for Grayson's name. I found him on the first list and blew the captive air out through my bottom lip, fanning a wayward strand of hair off my forehead. Damn. He didn't vote.

I found him on the second list. Not there that day, either. I clicked quickly to the third. Blank. So was the fourth.

"They're paying him to *not* vote against them?" I shook my head at the screen. Bob would never buy it. But I couldn't shake the feeling that money, tobacco, the dead lobbyist, and Grayson were thicker than Eunice's cream gravy.

"Why would this guy be in bed with the tobacco lobby?" I said under my breath, sitting back in my chair.

My gut said money. It was always money. Well, when it wasn't sex. I clicked back to a picture of Grayson's smiling family, arms raised after his first senate election, and stared.

Why did Ted Grayson need money badly enough to take it from the devil?

I wondered if Agent Evans might be able to find out anything I could use without causing too much of a stir at the Bureau. A crooked senator could have friends God-knows-where, and I didn't want to get Evans in trouble.

With no good answer for that, I slammed the computer shut, turning back to my actual puzzle.

"Dammit, where is the last edge piece?" I grumbled.

I dropped to my knees on the geometric-print rug that lay under my coffee table and poked my head underneath. The puzzle piece was lying next to the carved oak foot of my coffee table, on top of a red Bicycle playing card. I picked both up and clambered back onto the couch.

"King of spades," I mumbled, flipping the card over. "How appropriate."

I snapped the puzzle piece in place and tapped the edge of the card on the table, something tickling the back of my brain.

Of course.

I flipped my computer screen back up, drumming my fingers on the arm of the sofa for the whole three and a half seconds it took the machine to boot up.

Opening the photo file Larry had given me, I clicked onto the image of Amesworth and Grayson. At casino night. Scrolling through the other photos, I watched for the senator's face, finding three shots of him playing cards. Two of them showed a somber, focused Grayson, his brow crunched as he studied his cards like he could will them to change.

"Why so serious, senator?" I whispered, clicking over to Google and holding my breath.

"United States Senators earn a base salary of $174,000 annually. Plus various allowances, speaking honorariums, and other sources of income," I read aloud.

Amazon told me Grayson had written a bestselling book on clean energy policy.

So why does that guy need money—especially money that the Mafia has a hand in? "Cards," I said aloud.

What if Ted Grayson played cards somewhere else—for more than charity chips? What if he was a gambler on an unlucky streak? I couldn't tell if it was brilliant or insane, but it jived with what Allison said about risk, and following hunches had ended well for me in the past.

I made a list of everyone I might be able to wheedle information out of on that front, starting with Allison and ending with Joey. He wouldn't want to tell me, but if I could see his reaction when I asked, it might be all the confirmation I needed.

I gulped the rest of my wine and tried to slow my thoughts. If Ted Grayson was even remotely linked to a murder...that was the kind of story that could make a career.

I just had to make damned sure I was right. And beat Charlie to the headline.

I climbed back under my duvet a little after two, Joey's pleading eyes floating through my brain as I drifted off, swearing I could still smell that cologne.

9

My Saturday started before sunup, thanks to a vivid nightmare about being tied to a table and burned alive. I took Darcy outside for a game of fetch before I scrambled a couple of eggs, hoping a relaxing morning would slow the heart-pounding adrenaline rush that accompanied those dreams.

The sun still hadn't peeked over the eastern horizon when my scanner bleeped off an all-call on a missing person. Which, in and of itself, may not have required my presence. But when four patrol cars, the K-9 unit, and a deputy police chief were on their way to the most exclusive (and expensive) assisted living facility in Richmond at o'dark-thirty on a Saturday, there was bound to be a story.

Thankful I'd showered the night before, I twisted my hair up in a clip and jerked on khakis and a sweater, shoving my feet into eggplant Nicholas Kirkwoods that were almost the same shade as my top.

I stuffed my gym clothes into a bag just in case I made it away from the scene in time for body combat and tapped my fingers on the counter while my Colombian Fair Trade brewed into a mug Jenna's little girl had picked out for my birthday. I added a shot of white mocha syrup and ran out the door.

Skidding my tires on the turn into the nursing home parking lot, I scanned the cars for Aaron's unmarked police sedan.

It was near the doors, just in front of the Channel Four satellite truck. How Charlie could look camera-ready at six a.m. was beyond me, but she managed it on a consistent basis. I hung back and waited for her to finish talking to Aaron, admiring her Donna Karan suit and bright eyes. It was too early to be perky.

"Good morning." Aaron shook his head when he turned toward me.

"How are you, Detective Unavailable?" I asked.

"Come on, Nichelle," he said, raising both hands in mock surrender. "You know how this works. Do you have any idea what kind of shit I'll get into with the feds if I give you anything on this break-in at the Graysons? They're acting like we've got our own little Watergate over in the Fan."

"You could at least call me back and say 'no comment.'" I gave him a half smile, not wanting to fight with him.

"And give you a chance to badger me into saying something I shouldn't?" He laughed. "I'll take my lumps, thanks."

I thumped his shoulder lightly. "Consider yourself chastised. What the hell is going on here?"

"Alzheimer's patient wandered off," he said.

"Bullshit. You're here. I heard Mike say he was on his way. And while I was driving one of the dispatchers said Chief Lowe had called in for a status update." I gestured to the pillared marble entryway on the other side of the open doors, the double staircase straight out of Twelve Oaks. "An Alzheimer's patient who's pretty important has wandered off. And I didn't drag myself out this early and possibly skip my workout for you to give me the runaround. Spill it."

He rolled his baby blue eyes skyward.

"You people and your damned scanners. I have to be careful what I say, though you already know a good bit about it. Remember that hearing you called me about yesterday? James Billings's mother is a resident here. She saw your story when she got up this morning. Apparently a member of the early to bed and early to rise generation. They don't know how she slipped past the staff, but they found the newspaper open on her coffee table and she's gone."

I sucked in a deep breath and looked around. We were just on the outskirts of the city, in a surprisingly rural area. And it was unseasonably cold. Shit. I pulled out a notebook and jotted down Aaron's comments, fighting the urge to join the search party.

"Anything yet?" I asked. "They let him go, you know. He's got an ankle monitor, but he's not in jail anymore. The CA was pretty pissed about that, actually. It was all in the story."

"I know. We'll find her. K-9 is searching the surrounding area. She didn't have more than a half-hour head start."

"Thanks, Aaron."

"They said you can wait inside if you don't want to stand out here in the cold."

I shook my head. "I'm okay."

He stared at me for a second and then patted my arm. "It's not your fault. And we will find her. The good thing about this place being out here is that we're not near a freeway or in a shitty neighborhood like a lot of nursing homes. That's part of the reason they specialize in the care of Alzheimer's patients. K-9 says the dog has a scent. It'll be okay."

I tried to smile as I nodded. Stories can have unforeseen consequences. It was a lousy byproduct of reporting. And Billings wasn't allowed to leave his neighborhood, so he couldn't even come help look for her. Given my suspicion that he hadn't actually killed anyone, that seemed particularly craptastic.

"So, what did you make of Billings?" Aaron asked.

"How come Grayson's security system didn't trip up the intruder?" I countered. "Possibly because it wasn't the cat burglar?"

"Off the record?"

I pretended to consider that for a few seconds. Normally, off the record on a breaking and entering case wouldn't help much. But he didn't need to know I wanted information on Grayson for another reason.

"Why not?" I said.

"Possibly," he said. "A couple of things were unusual about this particular break-in. But we don't know anything for sure yet, and I'll lose my ass for talking about it right now."

"We can't have that. You wouldn't do well sitting on your boat with no ass," I said, my brain spinning through the reasons I could imagine someone would break into Grayson's house. Billings came to mind first because of Joey's comments, but he'd been in jail that night.

What if it was Watergate? And did that make it Trudy's story or mine?

Aaron's radio beeped and he stepped away to talk to the officers in the field. My thoughts wandered back to Grayson. I pulled out my cell phone and tapped my browser open, searching for information on the new tax law I'd talked to Kyle about the night before. Between what he'd said and Joey's ominous warning, I wondered if Joey and his friends were the bad guys Kyle was looking for. I also wondered exactly what the new Virginia law was poised to do to tobacco sales.

"Bingo," I whispered when the results flashed up on my screen.

I was no marketing genius, but given the information in front of me, I'd say the tobacco companies had to be pretty desperate to keep the federal tax from going up. In five states (including this one with the new state tax), the proposed doubling of the federal rates—from forty-seven cents to a dollar a pack—would have people spending $3.50 a pack just on taxes. In this economy, that would price a lot of people out of smoking.

And Grayson was the chairman of the committee holding up the federal bill.

It wasn't a leap to think folks had paid him to stop the bill. It wasn't even a long jump. But I had no proof. And no real idea who killed Amesworth, either.

I looked back inside the grand foyer of the nursing home where Billings's mother spent her days. Marble floors gleamed under elaborate crystal chandeliers that were probably worth more than my car. Whoever said money was the root of all evil was pretty smart.

So, the million-dollar question was: what did Grayson need more money for? If I could find that, it might give me enough to take the story to Bob. I considered my gambling theory. How could I find out if Grayson was a lousy poker player?

A hand on my elbow broke my concentration.

"They found her," Aaron said. "Dressed in her Sunday best, complete with hat and gloves, plodding through the pasture. On her way to the courthouse, she said. But she's fine. All's well that ends well."

I smiled at him, relieved. When I turned for the doors to the building, a round little man with a bad comb-over and a navy suit was taking questions on the front steps. I joined a small huddle of reporters that included Charlie, the still-relatively-new girl from Channel Ten whose name I couldn't remember to save my life, and Erica from the local talk radio station.

I pocketed my cell phone and dug out my notebook and pen again, jotting down his answers to the standard questions about the facility's security, the age of the patient, and the frequency of such incidents.

"Does Mrs. Lansing have family in the area?" Charlie asked.

I looked up.

"Her son," facility administrator Harvey Butters said, pulling at his collar. "He couldn't be here this morning."

"But he was notified?" Charlie asked, perking up. I cringed slightly, knowing she'd picked up a scent. I'd hoped no one else would connect the dots, since Billings and his mother didn't share a last name.

"We called him, of course," Butters said. "He's very concerned, and was happy to hear his mother was safe."

Charlie let it go, but made a beeline for Butters when he was finished, asking, I was sure, for a way to get in touch with Mrs. Lansing's next of kin.

He waved his hands helplessly as he talked, gesturing to the newspaper on the front doormat. Charlie shot me a glance and picked up the paper after Butters hurried inside. I watched as Charlie read, a small smile playing around my lips. She looked up and offered a nod. I waved, calling a goodbye to Aaron and checking my watch. I still had time to get to the gym if I hurried. And then I had a story to write and some answers to find.

* * *

The early body combat class on Saturdays was more advanced than my weekday class, but since I'd missed two during the week, I figured a little extra burn was in order. Particularly after the two (okay, five) of Eunice's white chocolate macadamia cookies I'd smuggled out of the break room on Monday afternoon.

With faster music, quicker punches, more jumps, and a new hooked side kick the perky brunette instructor called a "cheerio chagi" in an unmistakable lowcountry drawl, I felt about as graceful as a grizzly in stilettos. The insecurity bred like bunnies on pheromones, until the footwork that had earned me a spot as one of the best in my regular class was a distant memory. I stumbled sideways into the mirror twice, threw the wrong kick, *ap-chagi*'ed the girl in front of me, and came close to falling too many times to count. I also worked up a sweat that would do a football player running August two-a-days in Texas proud. How much of that was exertion and how much was embarrassment was a tough call, though.

By the time I shoved my gym bag into the back of my little red SUV, Grayson and his reason for needing extra income had pulled my attention from my Three Stooges imitation.

I stopped at my house to shower and toss on a quick face. Then I pulled on some jeans and a turtleneck, jammed my not-so-dainty feet into a pair of pink Manolos, and grabbed a pack of strawberry Pop Tarts out of my tiny pantry on my way to the office.

I stepped out of the elevator, rolling my eyes when Shelby Taylor came out of the hallway that led to the managing editor's office. Her fling with Les had been nothing but a pain in my ass since it began.

"Nichelle!" She grinned and folded her arms over her ample chest, which did not go with her tiny everything else. Shelby reminded me of a pixie Barbie with black hair. But jealousy had no hand in why I disliked her. She gave me plenty of reasons that had nothing to do with her appearance. Like the Splenda that coated every word she spoke to me, for instance. Shelby didn't know how to make a comment that didn't have razor edges. "Trying to get a jump on Charlie by sneaking in on a Saturday? She thumped you pretty good on the burglary yesterday. Did your scanner break?"

"My scanner was working fine yesterday, and this morning, when it tipped me to a missing person call at five-thirty. You really ought to be careful what you wish for, Shelby. I don't think my hours would be good for your boinking the boss. But good morning to you, too. Nice to see you're as sweet and sincere as ever. Now if you'll excuse me, I have a story to write. You remember what that's like, don't you?" I imitated her fake smile.

"I remember doing it better than you have lately." Shelby sneered, turning toward the copy desk. "Keep losing to Charlie, and I won't even need Les."

She sashayed off before I could say anything else, and I hurried to my cube, fuming and more determined to find out what the hell was going on with Grayson.

Today's deadline first, though. I flipped my computer open, digging in my bag for my notes from the nursing home. The woman's identity was definitely the most important thing about the story, given that her son had been arrested for murder less than forty-eight hours before.

I checked my notes and started typing.

Richmond police found an Alzheimer's patient who wandered away from Jefferson Meadows Assisted Living before dawn Saturday in less than an hour, returning Elizabeth Lansing to her home without incident.

Lansing's son, James Billings, was arrested Friday in connection with the murder of Henrico attorney Daniel Amesworth, twenty-nine. Officials said when Mrs. Lansing learned of her son's situation, she was determined to see him, even if it meant going on foot.

"They don't know how she slipped past the staff," Det. Aaron White, RPD public information officer, said at the scene.

Harvey Butters, the chief administrator at Jefferson Meadows, said Mrs. Lansing was unharmed and resting in her room by sunup Saturday.

I read back through the story twice before I sent it to Les, sure he'd find something to complain about anyway. And if he didn't, Shelby would.

"Can't please everyone," I mumbled, trying to channel my mom's bubbly self-confidence as I clicked my web browser open.

I didn't even have time to figure out what I was looking for before Les emailed me back.

"It'd be nice if I hadn't seen every word of this on Channel Four twenty minutes ago. Charlie's up by two in two days. Don't worry about the typos. Shelby will catch them."

"At least he's consistent," I muttered, turning my thoughts back to Grayson.

Before I could type Grayson's name into Google again, I had an idea. I checked the files I'd saved on him already and dialed my prosecutor girlfriend's cell number.

"It's Saturday," DonnaJo said when she answered. "I have fuzzy pink flowered pajama pants, coffee, and a new mystery novel. Unless you want a coffee book club meeting, I'm not talking to you."

"I wish," I said. "I'm at the office. Your Saturday sounds much more relaxing. One quick question?"

"Go home, Nichelle. The bad guys will still be there Monday."

"I will. I just need to ask you something first." I said, clicking my pen and fanning my notebook to an empty page.

She sighed. "What?"

"Do you know anyone who knows Ted Grayson?"

"Not anyone who can get him to talk to you about that break-in at his house."

Perfect.

"Damn," I tried to sound convincingly disappointed. "What about someone who can get me some background on his political opposition?"

"Can't your D.C. reporter get you that?"

"She's not here today." It came out a little too quickly.

"Uh-huh." DonnaJo was quiet for a minute. "I have an old friend who served in the House of Delegates with Grayson. He used to be a prosecutor. I'll give you his number, but leave me out of this. Ted Grayson has a lot of friends, and if you're nosing around, I don't want to be caught in the fallout."

"Got it." I smiled as I jotted the guy's name and number down. "Thanks, doll. Enjoy your book."

I dialed the number I'd just written down. Leon Casey picked up on the second ring.

"I'm working on a story about Senator Ted Grayson," I said in my most earnest tone after I introduced myself. "I ran across your name in my research. You're a former colleague?"

"You could say that," Casey said, his voice so smooth I expected honey to drip from the receiver. "Ted and I go way back. But I'm not in the loop about this election, if that's what you're looking for."

"I'm just trying to find general background information," I said. "Do you have time to answer a couple of questions?"

"If I can," he said. "I'm not sure how much help I'll be."

I asked about how they knew each other (school, and then the state house) Casey's career (prosecutor, politician, now private attorney handling mostly family cases in a poor part of town) and Grayson's family (married, one son studying computer science at William and Mary) before I got to the restaurant smoking bill.

"That was some fancy footwork on Ted's part." Casey laughed. "Can you imagine? He announced he was going after tobacco in Virginia and I thought he'd just sunk his political career."

I nodded. "I'm sure you weren't alone."

"That's for sure. The whole capitol building was in an uproar. Ted even got death threats. They had to hire bodyguards," Casey said. "It was crazy. But he was determined, and he's a charmer. He talked people whose great-grandaddies used to farm tobacco into voting for that bill. You ever heard the saying 'he could sell ice to eskimos?' Ted Grayson could sell heroin to Nancy Reagan."

My hand flew across the page, not missing a word. Something I'd seen online tapped at the back of my brain.

"Thank you so much for your time, Mr. Casey," I said. "I have one last question: what's your favorite non-work memory of the Senator? Is there a house of delegates guys' night?"

The question was vague to avoid raising suspicion, but I crossed my fingers under the desk. Boys' night and poker games go together like coffee and cream.

"Oh, I don't know," Casey said. "We didn't know each other well in school, but we had some mutual friends. We did play cards occasionally. Just friendly games, but Ted was pretty good. He has that way about him. You can't even be mad at him when he's taking your money."

I wouldn't bet on that. Maybe Casey couldn't, but plenty of people could. Maybe mad enough to make the senator desperate. I thanked Casey for his time.

I pulled up the Internet research I'd done on Grayson and scrolled through the voting lists on the tobacco-related bills again. Opening a new window, I went back to the story about the committee trouble with the cigarette tax bill.

Three other senators were listed as swing votes in the *Post's* article on the tax. They were all on Grayson's committee. And they had all voted in favor of the tobacco industry on bills Grayson had skipped out on.

Charming and popular.

"He's very charismatic," Allison had said.

"Are they paying him to deliver votes?" I mused, tapping a pen on the desk. "He skips out to escape questions about why his record has flipped, and then he gets the other guys to vote the way he wants them to on the bill?"

I shook my head at the screen. Maybe, but I needed solid proof.

Before I could figure out how to go about getting that, the phone rang. Who knew I was here on Saturday morning? I was tempted to let it go, but I have a mental block that renders me unable to ignore a ringing phone. I raised it to my ear.

"Crime desk, this is Clarke," I said.

"Remember how you went poking around in our body dump site the other night?" Aaron.

"Yeah," I said. "You still haven't told me why Officer Charming felt the need to tattle on me."

"Officer Charming?"

"Oops. Was that out loud? Sorry," I said. "He was…less than thrilled to see me. Didn't even thank me for pointing out that paper scrap."

"Well, consider yourself thanked," Aaron said. "The report says the lab results were forwarded to the ATF, and it doesn't say what the paper is, except that it's not any ordinary kind of paper. I don't know how our recovery guys missed it, but if you hadn't seen it, it would still be out there in the dirt."

"I think this is the first time in history that a cop has called a reporter to thank them for being nosy," I said, scribbling his comment fast.

"Thought the heads up was the least I could do, since you found the thing. You scratch my back, and all that," Aaron said. "It's all been added to the report, so it'll be fair game first thing in the morning, but if you can do anything with a half-day lead, you got it."

"I'll give it my best shot."

"Have fun. I'm going fishing. Right now, before anything else can require my attention."

"Have a drink for me." I clicked off the call and dialed Kyle's cell number, hoping he wasn't still a fan of sleeping in on Saturday mornings.

"Miller," he said, not sounding like I'd woken him.

"So, what kind of paper was that I found at the Amesworth body recovery site?" I asked.

"Good morning to you, too, old friend," he stressed the last word. "Have a nice walk with your new friend last night?"

All right. I held my tongue to keep from firing back a smartass retort. I needed him to tell me something no one else at the ATF would be willing to share, so I couldn't afford to piss him off. I had a feeling a bruised ego and a touch of hurt feelings were behind the sarcasm I was hearing, so I tried to soften the blow.

"You were awfully territorial for a guy I haven't heard from in a decade," I said. "You know you'll always have a special place in my heart, Kyle. But we're different people than we were then. Slow, remember? Can't we be friends? See where it goes?"

"Who was that guy?" He sounded less tense.

"A friend." That I'm not telling you anything else about. "And I didn't mean to hurt your feelings." Every word true, even if there were a few I'd carefully omitted.

"What do you mean, 'paper you found?' " He sighed, a more conversational, if guarded, tone replacing the injured one.

"I mean, paper I found." I said. "I was poking around after the coroner's team left, and I saw something in the soil and waved over the RPD uniform in case it was important. A little birdie tells me that it might be. So what kind of special paper is it?"

"The kind that could be material to my investigation, and is not public information at this time," he said.

That was just a shade shy of "no comment." I sighed. I wanted to know what it was, but I didn't want to get Kyle in trouble at work. "You wouldn't have it if I hadn't found it," I said finally. "What if I promise that we're off the record?" If he'd tell me what it was, it might lead me to something else I could print.

"I'm sorry, Miss Clarke," he said, all business. "It's evidence in an open investigation."

"Didn't you already make an arrest?"

"The investigation doesn't have to stop when the arrest is made," Kyle said. "How long have you covered crime?"

He was right, though that didn't happen very often. Normal police involvement in a case almost always ends when an arrest is made. But in something like this, they spend the time between booking and trial shoring up the case for the prosecutors. Tagging a guy like Billings for murder would require Kyle to have all his proverbial ducks lined up laser-straight. Defense attorneys who make the right kind of money can unravel a case quicker than a kitten can tear through a closet full of cashmere.

"All right," I said. "I give up. Thanks for your time. And for dinner last night. It really was fun."

"It was." I could hear the smile in his voice. "We should do it again sometime. When your other friend is otherwise occupied."

"That could be nice," I said. "As long as we have an understanding about expectations."

"Such as?"

"Such as I'm not hopping into the sack with you because you buy me a steak and a nice bottle of merlot."

"How about good enchiladas and a couple of margaritas?"

"Hardy-har-har, Kyle. Not even empanadas and tequila shots." I leaned back in my chair. "But we could get to know each other again." I couldn't deny that I'd felt something the night before, at the dinner table. I wanted to know if it was first love nostalgia or leftover gratitude for saving my life or something else. Something that might be worthwhile. Kyle presented his own set of challenges, but they certainly weren't the same ones I faced with Joey.

My heart didn't race in close quarters with Kyle like it did around Joey. And technically, they had both killed people. Sweet cartwheeling Jesus. From the life of a nun with cuter shoes to raining sexy men in a matter of months.

I promised to call him later and cradled the phone.

Flipping through the stack of message slips on my desk, I found a number for Agent Evans at the FBI. If he'd known about Billings's arrest, maybe he knew something about the paper scrap. But it was only his office number, and he wasn't there. I left him a message and blew out a short breath, drumming my fingers on the keyboard and thinking of Grayson playing cards. Where could I find information on card games—ones with the sort of stakes that a guy like Grayson would be interested in? I'd covered a couple of floating poker games that the police department's major crimes unit had blown open, but I generally only knew about such things after they'd been broken up by the cops.

Aaron and the guys at the PD wouldn't give me anything on a gambling ring they hadn't busted. And while the Mafia was an obvious angle for information on illegal gambling, Joey had made it clear the night before that he wanted me to keep my nose out of whatever I was trying to stick it into.

It's funny how hard it is to follow good advice.

10

I was hauling a case of canned Purina Pro Plan into my grocery cart when it hit me.

If I wanted information on gambling, I didn't need to talk to the cops. I needed to talk to a gambler.

I scrambled to keep hold of the dog food, so startled by my epiphany I nearly lost my grip on the 24-can value pack—and a toe to my furry princess's beloved beef and carrots.

I hefted Darcy's food into the cart and took off for the checkout, tossing in a couple of cans of soup on the way so I wouldn't starve. Groceries stowed in the back of the car, I sped toward the office and ran to my desk, where I pawed through my file drawer in search of information on a trial I'd covered back in March.

I wriggled the manila folder free and flipped it open, paging through the police reports on a gambling ring that had been operating in basements on the Richmond American University campus for years, aided by a former professor, a baseball coach, and a security guard.

I checked the dates and clicked my laptop on, searching the *Telegraph's* archives for my story. The security guard had only been taking cash to keep his mouth shut and look the other way. He'd been fired, but wasn't in jail.

The professor and the coach were a different story. I scanned the text for something I thought I remembered.

"Bingo," I mumbled.

The coach, one Peter Esparza, age forty, had also been nailed for fixing games for local bookies. And bookies were the kind of folks who might have dirt on high-stakes card games.

A quick search of the department of corrections website told me he was in cellblock six at Cold Springs, which was a little more than an hour away. I nearly lost a heel off my shoe sprinting back to the elevator.

The September breeze and just-turning leaves made it a lovely day for a drive. Halfway to the prison, I was still wondering how I'd get Esparza to talk. Fishing my cell phone out of my bag, I dialed Parker's cell phone.

"What's up, Lois?" he said when he answered.

"What do you know about Peter Esparza?" I asked.

"That he got fired and he's in jail," he said. "Which I believe I learned from a story you wrote, didn't I?"

"C'mon, Parker," I said. "You know everyone involved with sports in this town. You have nothing to offer me on this guy?"

He laughed. "I appreciate the vote of confidence, but I'm not sure I know anything that's useful to the crime desk. Has there been a new development in that case? I thought Esparza was convicted and serving time."

"No, there hasn't been, and yes, he was," I said. "But I need to talk to him. Tell me what he's like. Is he a dick, or am I going to get anywhere with him?"

"What the hell do you need with a mediocre has-been baseball coach?" he asked.

"I have a hunch," I said. "I'll fill you in later if I'm right."

There was a pause so long I wondered if I'd passed through a dead zone.

"Parker?" I said finally.

"Yeah. Sorry," he said. "Esparza's all right. Not the guy I would have pegged for fixing games and helping kids get into gambling. He's pretty full of himself, but he's not an asshole."

"Anything that might make him inclined to talk to me? Other than the fact that he probably doesn't see many breasts these days?"

"That could be enough," Parker said.

"Thanks. Tell Mel I said hi." I clicked off the call.

I pulled up outside the gates of the prison and handed my identification to the guard in the little stone shack. I gave him Esparza's name and he directed me to the visitors' parking area.

By the time I made it through security, issued a placard that told me which hallway to take and told them where I was supposed to be going, visiting hours were growing short. I tried to subtly adjust my bra as I walked, Parker's words ringing in my ears. A bra can only work with what's there, though. Maybe Esparza was a leg man.

I passed the placard through a thick plastic window at the end of the hallway. The guard on the other side looked at it, plucked a phone handset from the wall, and said something I couldn't make out into the receiver. Two minutes later, a buzzer worthy of a game show set sounded in stereo and the heavy steel door to my left clicked and swung open. Silent Jim the prison guard waved me inside.

The gray hallway smelled so strongly of ammonia, my nostrils stung. I followed it to a tiny interview room where a series of three little desks mirrored each other on a wall of the same thick plexiglass the guard sat behind. A slight man with olive skin and bushy, graying hair sat at the desk in the middle. The other two were empty. When I walked into the room, he stood. That was new. I'd been to Cold Springs a few times, though usually I was down at cellblock nine interviewing a killer who was some flavor of crazy and about to be put to death by the good people of the commonwealth for his (or her, once) crime. The murderers usually didn't stand when I came into the room.

Esparza watched me walk to the desk on my side of the glass.

I lifted the telephone receiver, wishing I had a Clorox wipe. I don't generally worry about germs, but the handset was nothing short of slimy, a film over the black plastic consisting of God-only-knows-what making me reluctant to put it near my face. The thing was heavy and there was no way to hold it gingerly. Esparza picked up his handset and I tried to forget about the sticky, bacteria-laden plastic, pressing mine to my ear and pasting a smile on my face.

"Have we met?" he asked in a light Spanish accent before I could introduce myself.

"We have not," I said, betting that Parker knew the guy at least in passing and hoping a little name-dropping would help. "I'm a friend of Grant Parker's, actually—I work with him at the *Telegraph*. I'm working on a story I think you can help me with."

"Unless it's about the state of the showers in this joint, I can't imagine how." He flashed a bright white smile, but his brown eyes didn't light.

"Not exactly." I took a deep breath, cutting my eyes to the guard in the corner, playing a game on his phone. "I'm working on a story I think may involve gambling, and I was hoping you might help me out."

He stared through the plexiglass and I held his gaze without blinking.

"Why would I want to do something like that?" he asked. "If there's one thing this place has taught me, it's that doing other people favors is for suckers. You go off and splash a card game or a dogfight across the front page, the guys who run it end up in here, and I might end up on the wrong end of a shiv."

The tough guy act was so obviously put on, it was almost funny. But laughing wasn't going to help me get what I wanted. Nearly seven years of interviewing the best and worst of society had given me a decent asshole radar. This guy wasn't a hardened criminal. I just needed to convince him to help me.

"I have no intention of telling anyone where I got my information," I said, still looking him straight in the eye. "Not only that, but I don't really care about the operation itself. I care who's playing."

"Why?"

"Research," I said, shrugging and opting for honesty. "Right now, I don't have a story assignment. I think I've got a lead on a dirty politician, but finding anything concrete on this guy is harder than salsa dancing in stilettos."

He stared for a good thirty seconds, and I stared right back, not blinking. His dark eyes softened a touch and he turned his head slowly and checked the guard, who appeared invested in killing all the bad fruit, or whatever else required one to frantically wave a finger back and forth over an iPhone screen.

"A dirty politician," he said slowly. "Someone important enough to get me the hell out of here?"

"I don't know," I said. "Maybe. While I can't imagine that the Governor and my guy share too many political ideals, I'm not sure how well they know each other. Or if they like each other."

His shoulders dropped. "I see."

"I could lie and tell you absolutely," I said after a minute. "But the best I have is maybe. I really don't know."

The corners of his lips tipped up in a half-smile. "Maybe is better than no, right?"

I nodded, trying to keep my expression neutral.

"I don't know much," he said. "But there are some political types around here who like to play cards. A lot of the games float. What you're asking about is big business, but it's also a relatively small circle of people." He paused, shaking his head. "Look, I've done some things I'm not proud of. If you were to stop by the sports dorm at RAU, you might find a pitcher who's in over his pretty-boy head. But I doubt he'll talk to you."

Maybe not, but I knew someone he might talk to.

I smiled and thanked Esparza, wondering as I watched him hang up his phone how this man had taken a turn so wrong it had landed him in this place. He obviously didn't fit in with most of the prison population.

I checked out and climbed back into my car as the sun was sinking in the western sky.

I punched the talk button on my cell phone twice so it would redial, and laughed when Parker asked if Esparza had fallen victim to my feminine wiles.

"I wouldn't know a wile if it bit me in the ass, so I'm going with no," I said. "What are you up to tonight?"

"Being boring." He sighed. "I was supposed to have a date, but Mel bailed on me about a half-hour ago. Her sister went into labor. Why?"

Perfect. I made a mental note to send balloons.

"Esparza would say I'm on a lucky streak," I said. "I need to borrow your star power. Put on something that looks expensive and meet me at Capital Ale in half an hour. I'll fill you in when I get there."

"Am I going to get shot at?" he asked.

"God, I hope not." I laughed. "But you told me once I could ask you for help if I needed it. So this is me asking."

"You really more told me than asked me, but that's cool," he said. "Going to work with you isn't as boring as sitting here watching *Die Hard* alone."

"How could young Bruce Willis and terrorists be boring?" I asked.

"Careful, you might talk yourself out of a partner."

"Point taken. Strike that."

"Expensive like coat and tie, or expensive like tux?" he asked.

"We're not going to the Oscars. I just want you to look like a celebrity. But no old baseball uniforms," I said.

"You got it." He hung up.

About to pass my exit, I jerked the steering wheel and drove home, my brain jumping from Senator Grayson to Billings the tobacco executive and back again. There was a connection. There had to be. But the sticking point hadn't changed: how had the lobbyist I was almost positive had been their go-between ended up dead? If Amesworth was in cahoots with the bad guys, like Kyle thought, then why would they kill him?

Patting Darcy's head and filling her food bowl on my way through the kitchen, I thought about Joey. He was worried about me. But it wasn't like I was going off alone to chase a criminal. I was going to a well-populated place, and taking Parker with me.

Ten minutes later, I climbed carefully back into the car in my go-anywhere black sheath dress and a pair of blood red patent leather Manolos I'd had since college. They were the first pair I'd ever bought, after spending much of my teenage years slouching to hide the height that made me different from the other girls. My five-foot-three Syracuse roommate had wealthy parents and a love of stilettos that had rubbed off on me after years of watching her wear shoes that could double as works of art while I slogged around in boots and sneakers.

I beat Parker to the restaurant and ordered a Midori sour.

Waiting in a corner booth with a good view of the door, I stirred my drink and wondered if it was smart to pull Parker into this.

When he walked in, nearly every female head in the place turned to follow his progress toward me. I had to admit, he looked the part: his tall, athletic frame was the perfect showcase for the dark chinos, emerald shirt, and leather coat that made him look like he'd just stepped out of GQ.

I returned his smile and gestured to the seat across from me.

"Thanks for coming."

"Bob might fire me if I let you get shot at again." He flashed the million-dollar grin. "So, what's up? Am I playing Hardy Boys to your Nancy Drew?"

I put my glass on the table and leveled a serious gaze at him. "Indeed. I need some dirt on RAU baseball."

"You made me get dressed up to ask me about work?"

"Specifically, I need to know about the pitchers. And who might be into gambling."

"Esparza." He nodded slowly. "Care to share what he told you?"

"He didn't say much, except that there's a pitcher I need to talk to."

"But he didn't give you a name?"

"Nope. That's where you come in."

"You don't need star power for that," he said. "Reading the stat sheets could give you a bead on who you need to talk to. Someone's record tanked halfway through the season."

"Why haven't I seen this in your column?"

"I have a suspicion, Clarke. Nothing I can prove, and certainly nothing you can print. He's a good kid in a bad situation. Assuming I'm right, anyway."

"I'm not looking to print it. I need information, not to bust a kid who's been stupid." I said as I grinned. "And reading through a billion pages of numbers sounds way less fun than getting dressed up and hauling you to a party."

"Party?" He looked around. "You need to take a powder, Clarke. I can't keep up with you tonight."

"It's Saturday night. I like the odds of a party going on at the jock dorm." I downed the last of my drink and grabbed the little black clutch I'd stuffed a handful of essentials into, unsnapping it and tossing a few bills on the table. "And a drunk pitcher is more likely to spill his guts to a celebrity than a sober one is to talk to a reporter. Let's go, superstar."

* * *

Rothschild Hall on the RAU campus is the biggest, most state-of-the-art of the school's dorms, housing the student athletes. A back-to-campus party was in full swing.

Parker strode through the doors like the building was called "Grant Parker is the Shit Dormitory," smiling and nodding at the coeds brave enough to make eye contact with him and not even flinching when at least two of them pinched his ass as he moved through the crowd. I tried to stay behind him, but the size and enthusiasm of the group made that next to impossible.

Two different boys handed me two different kinds of beer within three minutes of when I walked through the front doors, and I nodded a polite thanks and tried to keep my eyes on Parker's perfectly-tousled blond head as he scanned the giggling coeds and desperate-to-get-laid jocks, looking for whoever his statistics told him was suspect.

Music blared into the hallway from several of the rooms, and students darted in and out of the suites with drinks and food in their hands. A group of girls with their hair in pigtails strutted down the hallway in a conga line, trying to add to their train as they went.

"Conga!" A freckled blonde with purple glitter eyeshadow squealed, letting go of her friend's hip to grab my hand as she danced past. "Come on!"

Feeling suddenly more dated than a pair of battered Doc Martens, I smiled and shook my head, waiting for them to pass before I charged after Parker. By the time I caught up to him, he'd been surrounded by a knot of college kids who were hanging on his every word as he told a story about digging his team out of a ninth-inning, three-run deficit with three three-and-outs in a row followed by a grand slam.

I laid two fingers on his elbow and he slid his eyes to me. He didn't miss a beat in his tale as he nodded subtly to a tall, dark-haired kid across the circle from him.

They erupted into spontaneous applause when he recounted crossing home plate and he laughed.

"It was fun," he said. "I played because I loved the game. Stick with that, and you'll never be unhappy."

He kept his eyes on the dark-haired kid as he spoke, and the boy suddenly became very interested in his shoes.

Bingo.

Parker shook hands all around, easily dismissing everyone except the dark-haired kid. When it was just the three of us, Parker flashed his best sports columnist grin and threw an arm around the younger pitcher's broad shoulders.

"Willis Hunt, this is Nichelle Clarke," he said. "Nichelle, this is Willis. He's going to go pro in the next couple of years, if he can get his arm under control."

The boy smiled a beer-addled smile and shook my hand sloppily.

"Thanks, Mr. Parker. I don't know about that."

"Call me Grant," Parker said, steering Willis toward a hallway that wasn't stuffed with gyrating bodies. I followed, keeping quiet and hanging on every word.

"You had one hell of a season last year," Parker said, stopping in a little alcove and sitting on a wide bench, gesturing to the simple gold sofa across from him. Willis flopped onto it. I perched on the edge of the bench next to Parker and tried to look unobtrusive.

"I did alright, I guess," Willis said.

"You had the best record in the east for the first half," Parker said.

"Half doesn't make a season," Willis mumbled, staring at his hands. "My dad and the coach told me that enough times that I won't ever forget it."

"It's a lot of pressure." Parker leaned forward and rested his elbows on his knees. "And a lot of people who want to tell you what to do. I remember."

"You were great," Willis said. "You should be a three-time Cy Young winner on your way to the Hall of Fame, man. I loved watching you play when I was a kid. My dad is a UVA alum."

"Thanks," Parker said. "Sometimes things don't go the way we think they will, do they?"

Willis raised his eyes, his dark irises sober as a preacher on Sunday. "They don't."

"You have amazing control for a kid your age," Parker said softly, holding Willis' gaze. "It was really something to watch. Then all of a sudden you're throwing wild pitches and hitting batters left and right."

"I got the jitters, I guess." Willis didn't look away, and his expression screamed that he was desperate to spill his guts. I tried not to breathe too loudly.

"But only when the odds were astronomically in your favor going into the game?" Parker arched an eyebrow.

"Mr. Parker, they'll kick me out of school," Willis whispered, conflict plain on his face. "I won't ever play again."

"You can only throw the nervous rookie thing for so long before you won't be playing anymore, anyway." Parker's deep tenor verged on hypnotic. "What happened? You owe somebody money?'"

Willis sighed, staring past Parker at the beige wall. "After my freshman season, people started to notice me. Some guys I met at a club took me to a card game one night. There were girls, an open bar, the whole deal. Just like out of a movie. I won over a thousand dollars, and I couldn't believe it was really my life."

He continued. "I went back the next weekend and the one after that, and I just kept winning. They started calling me Lucky Sixteen, you know, for my jersey number. It was a great time."

"Until you stopped winning," Parker said.

"I thought I'd get it back. They said I could have credit with them so I could keep playing. I thought I could turn it around."

"And then you ran out of credit."

Willis hitched in a deep breath and drug the back of his hand across his face. "Yeah. They said I had to pay up, and my family doesn't have that kind of cash."

"How much are you in for?" Parker asked.

"Almost thirty grand."

Holy shit, kid. I bit my tongue to keep the words from slipping out, my eyes flashing from Parker to Willis and back. Parker closed his eyes and shook his head.

"So they said you could work it off by throwing games."

"Please, Mr. Parker." A tear rolled down Willis' cheek. "If you put this in the newspaper, my career will be over."

"I have no intention of doing that." Parker shook his head. "You've been had, kid."

"They'll rat me out if I don't do what they want," Willis said. "I don't know what to do."

"Ratting you out rats them out, too," Parker said. "But this is a hell of a corner you've backed yourself into."

Willis dropped his head into his hands. "I know." The words were muffled.

Poor kid. I felt bad for him. Parker did, too.

"Let me talk to them," Parker said.

Willis raised his head slowly. "What?"

"Let me talk to them. Where are the games?"

Willis stared for a long minute.

"Why?"

"Because you're a decent kid," Parker said. "I like you. You have a chance at a future I missed. Tell me where to find a game."

"They move around," Willis said. "But one of the bartenders at the Tuscany always knows. Short guy, bald head."

Parker stood, pulling a card from his wallet and handing it to Willis. "Call if you need to talk. I know the pressure. But play your A game, kid. Your career will be over if you don't, anyway. Play every game like you might never get to play again, and you won't have any regrets."

A hitch in his voice caught my attention. Was Grant Parker tearing up?

I jumped to my feet and scooted out of the way. Parker moved back toward the front door, leaving Willis Hunt on the gold couch nodding and mumbling about dreams under his breath. I hurried after Parker, throwing a sad look at Willis over my shoulder. He was young to be in that much hot water.

"Where are we going?" I asked, following Parker back into the chilly evening air. My stomach flipped with equal parts excitement and fear.

"To a card game." Parker jerked the driver's door of my car open and slid behind the wheel. "These assholes have screwed with the wrong sport."

11

The Tuscany was across town from the university. On a Saturday night, we were in for at least a half-hour drive.

I studied Parker's jawline as he wove the car in and out of traffic. "Tell me about it," I said.

"'Bout what?" he asked as he slowed for a red light.

"About baseball. What do you miss? What did you love about it? What was your best game? Freud would have a field day with that bit you just gave Willis about regret."

"I haven't talked to anyone about me and baseball in a long time."

"Talk to me."

He sighed. "Baseball was all I ever wanted to do. My dad started me in little league when I was four, and I fell in love with the way the bat rang in my hands when it connected with the ball. When other kids were going swimming in the summer, I was at the batting cages. I always got to pitching practice early and stayed late. I was varsity all through high school and my pitching got better every year."

Aside from Parker not running over anything or anyone, I wouldn't have known he even saw the other cars in front of him. His eyes stared straight ahead.

"By the time I was a senior we had won two big school state titles and the scouts were coming to every game," he continued. "I graduated with a full scholarship to UVA, and my freshman year, I made the travel team, pitching against juniors and seniors. My sophomore year, I was the star. We won every game I started and I struck out a hundred and seventy-nine hitters that year.

"About halfway through that season, the pro scouts started showing up. I spent the rest of that year focusing on baseball. I breathed it, I dreamed it —I don't remember anything about those four months but practices and games and trying to impress the scouts. And I did. I went into the draft in June and the Angels picked me in the fourth round. The *fourth round*. I was going to get to play baseball for a living. My dreams were all coming true."

"You're left-handed," I said. "That's good when you're a pitcher, right?"

He glanced at me and smiled. "Yep."

"How fast could you pitch?"

"My second year in the minors, I was throwing ninety-six mile-an-hour fastballs."

I whistled. "Wow. That's fast."

"The faster I threw, the harder time I had hitting the strike zone. I worked my ass off getting a handle on that in double-A. I started the next season in Salt Lake City with the triple-A team, sure I'd get to the show by the end of summer. I wanted to play for the Generals, and getting called up was the first step to getting traded home. I never went out after the games. I got my sleep; I ate as well as I could living on the bus and in shittier motels than I remembered from my tournament days. I wanted it."

"But you got hurt," I said.

"In July, just after the fourth." His hand drifted to his left shoulder as his face twisted at the memory. "We had a four-night rotation, and my game two nights before was tough: I threw over a hundred pitches. I shouldn't have played that night, but it was the last game of a big series, and the bull pen was having a rough time. They just needed me for one hitter. Of course I went in. I was twenty-one years old and I was invincible." The hard laugh sounded alien coming from Parker.

"I can still remember the pain. It felt like my arm was being ripped right off. The ball hit the dirt. I fell. The crowd got so quiet. I laid there and stared up at the lights and cried, because I knew it was over.

"That's pretty much it," he said, rotating his left arm. "Four surgeries later, it doesn't hurt anymore, but baseball is still a part of my past."

"Wow, Parker..." I floundered for the words that would banish the hurt I saw on his face. I wasn't positive there were any. "That well and truly sucks."

He chuckled.

"It was ten years ago," he said, turning into the Tuscany's full parking lot. "I survived. I'm okay, most of the time. But a kid with Willis Hunt's talent doesn't deserve to have the same fate because of one dumbass mistake."

"Agreed." I opened my door. "Maybe we can help Willis out of a jam and find a hell of a headline, too."

The bald bartender parted with the location of the game about three and a half seconds after Parker flashed a wad of fifties.

"Enjoy your game, pal." He waved a dismissal at us and turned to a striking redhead who wanted a glass of Shiraz.

Parker glanced at his watch when we got back to the car. "It's not even ten yet. You ever played cards?"

"Nothing racier than Go Fish," I said. "How about you?"

"Twice a month with the guys from photo for four years running." He grinned. "Much smaller stakes, but I hold my own."

"You're just damned handy to have around today."

"I do my best."

A few minutes later, we stopped outside what looked like an abandoned strip mall.

"There's no one here," I said, surveying the parking lot. "You think we're the ones who've been had?"

"Oh, ye of little faith." Parker pulled around back, where the lot was awfully crowded for such a dark building.

"Nice," I said.

We walked along the sidewalk in silence, stopping when we reached the door near the far end of the building.

"Assuming the place isn't haunted, there's a party going on in there," I whispered. Parker raised a fist to rap on the door.

A lock squealed inside the door and it opened a crack.

"Looking for a card game," Parker said, cash in hand. He laid an easy arm across my shoulders and I stiffened, then attempted to feign boredom. The door opened wider and a squat, broad man with a hawk nose gave us the once over.

"Seven-fifty cover," he said.

Parker didn't bat an eye, pulling fifteen bills off the stack and handing them over. Well, there went the cash I was hoarding for Louboutin's spring collection.

The man moved aside and I stayed close to Parker, my stomach lurching slightly as the door slammed shut behind us. Now what?

The room looked like a gentleman's study out of an old movie: rich, wood-paneled walls, a long bar with shiny brass fittings, and thick, felt-topped tables scattered over the cherry floors. I scanned the faces at the tables, looking for Grayson and trying not to sigh when I didn't see him.

A tall, thin man with graying temples pointed Parker to an empty seat in the far corner, and I followed.

"Hey!" A debonair guy with a Sean Connery vibe looked up from his hand and laid his cigar in a marble ashtray. "You're Grant Parker!"

I sucked in a deep breath, waiting for Squatty the doorman to come throw us out on our asses. Parker flashed the million-dollar grin and offered a hand.

"Guilty. Mind if I sit in?"

"Hell, no." The man stuck the cigar back in the corner of his mouth and shook Parker's hand. "Not every day I get to play cards with a star pitcher."

"Isn't it?" Parker spoke so softly I wasn't sure I heard him, and I really hoped no one else did. He pulled out the empty chair, folding his long frame into it. I stood behind him, a disinterested half-smile fixed on my face. Captain Cigar glanced at me as he dealt Parker in.

"You don't want to play, sweetheart?" he asked.

"No thanks," I said, winking. "I've been told I have a lousy poker face."

I turned, looking around at the fifty or so faces hunched over cards and hoping to pick out Ted Grayson's features. Still no luck.

I made my way around the room, chatting up the doorman, catching dirty looks from a few of the players who shielded their cards when I walked by, and coming up with diddly squat.

Reaching the bar, I boosted myself onto a stool, and ordered a glass of

Riesling. I studied my six female barmates. All pretty. All dressed well. All young. What were they doing hanging out here? I caught a snippet of the conversation two stools over, where a blonde was carrying on about the miracle of Botox.

"Nice shoes," a voice from my left shoulder said. "Kirkwood?"

"Manolo," I said with a grin. "And thanks. I've had these a long time."

My eyes met large, dark ones set perfectly in deep olive skin. The woman leaning on the bar next to me had flowing jet tresses that were thicker than mine, a straight nose, full lips, and eyelashes most women would trade a kidney for in a heartbeat.

"They're timeless," she said. "And you're new. Please tell me you don't give a shit about having someone shoot poison into your face."

I laughed.

"I'd rather spend my money on shoes."

"My kind of girl." Her teeth flashed white against her dark skin. "I'm Lakshmi."

"Nichelle," I said. "Nice to meet you."

"Likewise," she said. "Who'd you come with?"

I pointed to Parker.

"Nice," she said.

"What about you?" I asked.

She gestured to a goateed man with thin shoulders and dark hair.

"He's a brilliant doctor, but he sucks at cards," she said. "I'm still not sure why he likes for me to hang around and watch him play, but at least he's not the only one." She nodded and raised her glass when the man winked at her.

I eyeballed the women in the room and figured they were walking trophies for these guys, but returned her smile.

"Me, either," I lied. "A doctor, huh? What kind?"

"Neurosurgeon," she said. "He also teaches at RAU Medical School. I'm a grad student at the university."

"Studying what?" I asked.

"Statistics and Political Science," she said. "I'm going to be the next Nate Silver."

"Oh, yeah?" I grinned. I liked her. "What do you make of the Senate race?"

"Grayson by two, two and a half," she said, confidence radiating off her in waves. "He won't hang on by much, but he's not in any real danger. Numbers don't lie."

"Have you ever seen him here?" I hoped the question sounded more casual than it felt.

"Ted? Playing poker?" Lakshmi threw back her head and laughed. "No. There are too many people here. He wouldn't risk it getting out."

Damn. I took another swig of my drink. Now I owed Parker seven hundred and fifty dollars, and I'd struck out.

She stood and excused herself to go to the restroom as I set the glass back on the bar, turning toward Parker. He was grinning while Captain Cigar was sweating buckets across the table.

He nodded in my direction and I smiled. At least one of us was having fun.

The blonde with the Botox addiction let out a high, squealing laugh that smacked of too much wine, and I turned toward her. She was chatting with a petite redhead, who was grinning at Lakshmi's doctor friend. The blonde leaned her chin on her friend's shoulder and giggled. "I hope he's winning. You know he's spending a pretty penny to have her sit here and watch him play cards. Maybe he'll get his money's worth later. I will never understand why men pay for sex. Isn't it cheaper to buy a girl a piece of jewelry and a nice dinner every once in a while?"

Oh. My. God. I gulped my wine so I'd have a reason to keep my mouth from falling open. Maybe I hadn't wasted my evening, after all. That could be a hell of a story.

Lakshmi walked back into the room and I pasted a smile on my face. We talked for an hour, about her brilliant statistics professor, shoes, and everything else but politics. When she'd had a third glass of merlot, I steered the conversation to more personal things.

"Where're you from?" I asked.

"D.C." Her words were starting to slur. "I lived there the longest, anyway. My dad was military intelligence. He works for the state department, now."

"So you come by your interest in politics honestly?" I smiled.

"I guess so," she said. "It's hard to not be cynical about politics when you know politicians, though. They're mostly weasels."

I stared for a second, her laughter at the idea of Grayson playing poker popping up in my thoughts.

No way.

But she'd used his first name. Could she know him? Like, in the Biblical sense?

"Do you know very many politicians?" My voice was too high. I cleared my throat and took a deep breath. "How about Senator Grayson?"

"He's an asshole. Everyone thinks he's so charming, such an upstanding family man." Lakshmi put her glass on the table and shook her head, snapping her mouth shut like she'd thought better of what she was going to say.

I stayed quiet.

"Well." She flashed a crooked smile and it was easy to see why men would pay to be with her. She looked like she belonged in a painting. "If people only knew."

Christ on a cracker, as Eunice would say. Not cards. Call girls.

The photo of Grayson's family flashed up from my memory and I pictured his short, round wife with her mousy eighties mom hair standing next to Lakshmi.

My gut said I'd found where the money was going.

If I was right about it coming from Billings, I just needed the filler pieces of my puzzle. Was Amesworth their go-between? And how and why had he ended up in a shallow grave?

"I think I'm done with the wine," Lakshmi said, standing.

"It was nice to meet you," I said. "Good luck."

"I make my own luck," she said. "It gives me the best probability of getting what I want."

I watched Lakshmi stumble toward her doctor friend, who was saying his goodnights, and wondered: was Grayson being bribed and blackmailed at the same time? Hookers, no matter their looks or price, are never good for political careers. What if Grayson had killed Amesworth to keep his secret?

Why was it that every time I found an answer, three new questions popped up? It was like an exhausting game of mental whack-a-mole. I pulled out my cell phone and checked my email. Nothing interesting. And it was after midnight already.

I looked up, and Parker caught my eye. The other men were trickling out. I nodded slightly and he stood, sweeping a stack of bills off the tabletop.

He shook hands with the other men at his table, bending over Captain Cigar from earlier and looking toward the door. A tall, thin man with platinum hair and an expensive suit had joined our doorman to bid everyone goodnight.

Parker held a finger up at me and made his way to the door. I followed, lagging behind a few steps as he took the guy aside and moved quickly from pleasantries to serious conversation. The man shook his head, holding his hands up. Parker took half a step closer, his easy smile fading, and said something else. I had a pretty good feeling he'd found who Willis Hunt owed money to.

Pulling out a roll of bills, Parker peeled several off and pressed them into the other man's palm, an uncharacteristically serious gaze causing his green eyes to narrow. The other man pocketed the cash and nodded.

Parker turned and caught my elbow. "Ready?"

"Am I ever," I muttered. "Do I even have to ask what you just did?"

He steered me out the door, smiling a goodnight at people we passed and muttering out of the corner of his mouth. "Probably not, but give me a second and I'll tell you, anyway."

I took my keys from him and jumped into the driver's seat, starting the car before he even had his door closed.

"Where's the fire? It's after midnight, you know," he said, clicking his seatbelt into place.

"Time doesn't matter to the news," I said. "I just got the scoop of the century. Now I have to prove it."

"Sound like a good time was had by all." He grinned. "Willis is even. As long as he stays away. I promised to keep their game out of the paper and left my winnings there."

"About that. I'll pay you back if you'll just let me know how much," I said.

He pulled out the cash roll.

"Zero," he said. "I told you I was good. I won my seven-fifty plus another grand, which I left with our host."

"Nice," I said, thankful I didn't owe him my shoe money. "Thanks, Parker."

"Thank you. I've known Willis was in trouble for months, and you gave me a way to get him out. Besides, this was definitely better than watching a movie alone."

"Indeed," I said under my breath, turning the radio up and pressing the accelerator harder. With an even juicier possible reason for Grayson being on the take, I was doubly anxious to get some research in before I crashed after a very long day.

The silent ride back to Parker's motorcycle was short.

I waved goodnight and pointed my car toward the Fan. Four blocks from home, I decided to take a small detour past Grayson's house and see what I could see.

12

The house was a gorgeous Georgian restoration with soaring ivory columns juxtaposed against deep red brick, the entire front lit by floodlights so bright that even at two ticks 'til one, it was noon in the Graysons' front yard. The Graysons had to be gone. Who could sleep through that?

I tapped my fingers on the steering wheel, debating for half a second before I climbed out and walked the length of the yard on the opposite side of the street. I wanted a closer look, but wasn't stupid enough to go traipsing around outside a home which had been recently burglarized.

I studied the front of the house as I walked, assuming I wouldn't see anything out of the ordinary.

Call girls. The guy had a wife, a kid, and a voter base that didn't look kindly on philandering. So to keep the wife from finding out he was cheating, he was taking bribes. Seemed reasonable enough.

Still didn't give me a why on a break-in or a dead guy.

Turning on my heel, I started back up the street, looking at a large window that faced a ten-foot wall of hedges on the south side of the house. A window that appeared to have a hastily-patched hole in it.

Shit. I stepped closer to the middle of the street, peering into the darkness. I still wasn't going over there, but by squinting I could see duct tape crisscrossing a full pane of that window.

That, plus the presence of a security system meant this was almost certainly not the work of the catburglar. That guy got in and out of houses without a trace. He was the Criss Angel of breaking and entering. No way he punched out a window.

And no way a broken window doesn't set off the alarm. Right?

I climbed back into my car, trying to remember what Aaron had said that morning and wondering for the millionth time if the robbery was a political ploy or the key to this whole damned thing.

My headlights hit off a shadow on my front porch when I turned into the driveway, and I squinted into the darkness again. I'd taken all the summer flowerpots down already, but it looked like there was something hanging from the ceiling.

I hopped out of the car and hurried toward the sidewalk, a small, puffy shape coming into focus as I got closer to the steps.

"No." I stopped, my hand flying to my mouth, stomach churning.

A small furry shape. Hanging from a thick cord. My legs felt rooted to the sidewalk. I needed to see and didn't want to know, both with such over-whelming urgency that I couldn't move. I tried to scream, and finally was able to form a word. "Darcy!"

An explosion of yipping came from behind the closed front door, followed by unmistakeable scratching on the wood.

"What the hell?" A sob escaped my throat at the familiar bark, safely inside the house.

I ran up to the porch, poking the macabre new decor. Stuffed. I snatched it down and examined it. It was a toy. A stuffed toy Pomeranian dog. A piece of paper poked out of the collar.

I glanced around, hugging the doll to my chest and unlocking the door as quickly as the pitch dark and my fumbling fingers would allow.

Safely inside with the deadbolt and chain fastened behind me, I slumped to the floor and scooped my very alive, very hyper dog into my arms, burying my face in her fur and sobbing until she started to wriggle and whine.

"I'm so very glad to see you, princess," I said, wiping my eyes with one hand and ruffling the fur behind her ears with the other. She yipped, then bounced out of my lap and down the hall toward the kitchen. I got up to follow, turning on lights as I walked, the skin-crawly feeling I'd had on the porch returning when I pulled the note from the fake dog's collar.

Dear Nosy Nichelle, Next time it won't be a prop. BACK OFF.

Darcy barked, and I found her in the kitchen, tapping her food bowl with her foot.

"It's not dinnertime, girl. You ate already," I said.

She tapped again, and I turned for the pantry. "I've never been so glad to have to feed you in the middle of the night, that's for damned sure," I said, my hands shaking as I opened the can.

She gobbled her food while I unknotted the bungee cord around the toy's neck and examined it in the light. Nothing special: blue with black flecks, available at a million hardware stores and every Wal-Mart.

I stared at it, knowing I'd likely wrecked any fingerprints anyone might be able to lift from it and wondering who would do something so heinous. And how they knew what kind of dog I had.

I shoved the toy dog, cord, and note deep into the kitchen garbage can, covering them with tossed-out food and used tissues and shuddering when I slammed the lid. Walking through the house, I checked locks and debated calling someone.

Jenna and my mom were my go-tos with problems, but this would only worry them. I finally had Joey's number, but he'd probably hire me a body-guard if I told him about this, and I didn't even know for sure it had anything to do with Amesworth's murder. Fifty people had seen me at the card game just an hour ago: what if someone had recognized me? Or what if the cat burglar was tired of being in the news?

As hard as I tried, I couldn't shake the creeped-out feeling. I checked the locks twice more, looked in all the closets and behind the shower curtain, and flipped every light in the house on.

I picked up the phone to call Kyle three times, but the years apart and the late hour stopped me before I pushed send. Antsy, I flipped through TV channels until I found a *Friends* rerun and turned the volume up too loud. I paced. I ran back through my week, wondering if there was anything I'd missed.

"I hope Aaron doesn't have plans for Monday morning," I finally told

Darcy. "Because I'll be waiting with a cup of Starbucks Pike Place and a long list of not so fun questions when he gets to work."

I was afraid to take her outside, but she seemed to enjoy indoor fetch just as much, and I tossed her worn out old squirrel for twice as long as usual.

By the time she was played out and curled into a russet pompom in her bed, I had a decent list of questions for my favorite detective. I couldn't bring myself to turn the lights off, and fell asleep wondering if I'd still be Aaron's favorite reporter by lunchtime Monday.

My mishmash nightmares were full of dangling dogs and burning warehouses.

* * *

Aaron was happy to see the coffee when he got to work Monday, but he didn't look thrilled to see me. He faked it pretty well, covering his startled expression with a grin and waving me into his office.

"You going to start making a habit of dropping by unannounced?" He flipped the light on and gestured to one of the worn black plastic office chairs. "Because I could get you a key."

"No thanks," I said, taking the seat and crossing my left knee over my right. "Just in case anything ever goes missing out of the lockup again, I'd rather not be on the suspect list."

"Let's hope we don't have to worry about that." He settled into his rolling chair, shooting me a look that very clearly said "cut the shit and tell me what you want."

"The robbery at the Grayson house," I said. "There are several things that don't add up."

"Nichelle, you know as well as I do that there are B-and-Es and then there are B-and-Es." he sighed. "If I tell you anything beyond what's in the report, Grayson will have my badge. That guy may have a perfect smile, but he's a mean bastard when you cross him. It's hard to get to that level in national politics without being a certain kind of prick."

"It wasn't the cat burglar," I said, putting a hand up when he opened his mouth just in case it was to argue. I really didn't want Aaron to lie to me. "I know it wasn't the cat burglar, because not only does the alarm system not fit, but there was a hole in one of the downstairs windows. That was conveniently left out of the report."

He closed his eyes. "I know."

I studied him for a second. "Remember that favor you promised me several months ago? I think I want to call it in. What the hell is going on here?"

He shook his head. "I'm not sure you want to do that. Because I really, honest-to-God don't know. Off the record?"

"Do I get comments any other way lately?"

"We left the window out of the report on purpose. Like I told you Saturday, the general consensus is that this crime was not related, but we want whoever did do it to assume we think it's the cat burglar. The Graysons swear nothing of value is missing, that their maids came in and turned off the alarm system, but whoever broke in was watching for that and went in after it was deactivated. The crew was cleaning upstairs and someone heard a noise and came down, and the would-be thief took off."

Something tickled the back of my brain.

"No one saw the intruder?"

Aaron flipped open a file folder and read something for a second.

"Maid insisted the sound she heard came from the back of the house, which is where the senator's private study is," Aaron said. "But Grayson was very particular about the officers not going in there to check for prints."

"I bet he was," I said, finally connecting the nagging feeling to my memory.

Troy Wright's mother was a maid.

And she'd said her crew cleaned a senator's house.

I bounced in my seat.

"We have no idea what might actually have been missing," Aaron continued. "The damned campaign people are hollering that it's political— which it may very well be—but when the victims in a case like this don't want to cooperate, we find ourselves in a very awkward situation. He's a high-profile guy, so it's big news. If you print what I'm allowed to give you on the record right now, we're going to look like the goddamned Keystone Cops."

"Good thing you don't have to run for office." I grinned.

"True enough. But if we're going to look like third-rate nincompoops, I'd rather it be because we actually screwed something up."

"Fair enough," I said. "What do you make of the Billings case?" I asked, changing the subject.

"The ATF is running that show," he said, leaning back in the chair and lacing his hands behind his head. "I heard a rumor that you have an old friend who has recently joined their ranks over there. I bet you know more about it than I do."

"I doubt that. I know Kyle's convinced he's got his man. I'm not so sure."

"Oh, yeah?" Aaron raised his eyebrows. "What makes you say that?"

"A hunch, mostly. I don't have anything concrete."

"Always go with the gut. Mine has rarely steered me wrong. But I'm not in much of a position to help you with that. Not unless I want a pissing contest with the new special agent at the ATF, which I really, really don't. Good luck, though. Don't get shot at any more."

I laughed. "Thanks, Aaron. Sorry I ambushed you."

"You brought coffee. We're good."

* * *

Sitting in my parked car in front of police headquarters, I dialed Joyce Wright, certain she wasn't home, but hoping I could leave her a message. She picked up on the second ring.

"Joyce!" I said, so startled at her soft "hello" I almost dropped the phone. "Good morning! I thought you'd be at work. It's Nichelle Clarke from the *Telegraph*. Do you have a few minutes to talk to me?"

"I got all day for you." Her voice caught. "That story that was in the newspaper yesterday about my boy—there's no way I can ever repay you for that."

A warm flush flowed from the pit of my stomach, putting a smile on my face. Eunice had done a beautiful job with the pages, starting the story on the front of the "Richmond Lives" section with a collage of the photos Joyce had loaned me and running several more with the jump copy. I didn't often write stories that touched people the way Joyce's voice told me this one had touched her.

"I'm so glad you liked it." I had obsessed over it to the point of irritating the hell out of Eunice, who assured me it was lovely and the woman wouldn't be able to help being happy with it. I was glad she was right.

"It's beautiful," she said. "That sports reporter came by here early and picked Troy up to take him to the baseball stadium. He was more excited than I've seen him since the Christmas he got his first bike. You're good people, Miss Clarke, as my grandmomma would have said."

"Nichelle," I corrected. "And thank you. I have a question for you: you said the other day that you work in the Fan. Do you work in Senator Grayson's home, by any chance?"

She chuckled. "I do," she said. "I read your story about that break-in. Did the police tell you that nonsense? Because it wasn't in the middle of the night. It was after seven in the morning, and I had just gotten there. They said me coming downstairs scared the damned thief away."

"So I have learned, though not on the record," I said, thinking that an exclusive with Joyce would be a coup, but might get her into trouble if Grayson didn't want the real story in the press. And with what Aaron had said about wanting to keep the fact that it wasn't the cat burglar under wraps, it could muck up the PD's investigation and get me on their shit list as a bonus. That wasn't a good place for the newspaper's crime reporter to be.

"Joyce, do you have time for a cup of coffee?" I asked, checking the clock. I'd already missed three-quarters of the morning news budget meeting by going to see Aaron, which meant I'd have some explaining to do when I got to the office if I didn't want to end up in trouble with Bob. But as long as I didn't tell him everything, the idea of an exclusive might keep me out of hot water, and just because she told me what happened didn't mean I had to run it. She might know something about Grayson that would help me figure out what he was up to.

"I have to have the decaf these days on account of my blood pressure," she said. "It's hell, getting old. But why not? I been suspended from work. They say I can't come back until they know for sure I didn't break that window at the Grayson house and call the police to cover it up."

I almost dropped my phone for the second time in five minutes.

"Are you serious?" My thoughts ran to the aging furniture in the tiny living room and the boy with the electric smile who wanted to go to college. It wasn't a good time for his single mom to be out of work. "What is this, 1955?"

She laughed.

"I guess things don't change as much as people like to think, Miss Clarke. I got family and some savings. As long as they don't take too long about figuring out who did do it, we'll get along."

I asked her to meet me at Thompson's on Cary Street in half an hour as I pulled into the office garage. I stepped off the elevator and headed straight to Bob's open door, mostly because I knew he'd only get more pissed off if I tried to avoid him.

He glared when I tapped on his door frame, rolling his chair away from his computer and waving me into his office. Thunder rumbled through a wall of low, gray clouds outside the window, mother nature chiming in with her annoyance. I dropped into my usual orange-velour-upholstered wing chair and met the glare head on. Crossing my legs, I bounced my dangling left foot so much that my pink slingback Jimmy Choo slipped right off my heel and dropped to the floor.

"I wouldn't get too comfortable, Nicey," Bob practically growled. I grimaced. He didn't get mad at me very often. "You missed the news budget meeting for the second time in as many weeks, and this time I didn't even get the courtesy of a warning phone call. You're a good reporter, kid, and you know I've got a soft spot for you, but Les is angling to give Shelby half your job already. You really don't need to force me into his corner. What the hell is going on with you lately?"

"I'm working on a story," I began then halted, still not sure how to tell him enough to get me out of this jam, but not tell him so much as to get me into another one. There were two people on our reporting staff Bob held in higher regard than me: Grant Parker and Trudy Montgomery. And I was desperate to avoid the appearance of pulling a Shelby with Trudy's beat. I really didn't think that was what I was doing, but I was terrified Bob would see it that way. I took a deep breath. Just the facts, Nichelle.

"I went by Ted Grayson's house the other night, and the break-in there was not the work of the cat burglar," I said. "The PD is keeping that all hush-hush because they don't want to piss off the senator—at least not while he still is the senator—but there's something fishy going on there, Bob. I can feel it. I just need a little time to figure out what it is."

He sat back in the chair and heaved a heavy sigh.

"Ted Grayson, huh? Have you talked to Trudy?"

"No," I said, and his eyebrows went up. "So far, what I'm dealing with is clearly a crime story. I didn't see the need to bother her during election season. She's already up to her neck in deadlines."

Bob studied me carefully for a long minute, then finally shook his head at me.

"What else have you got? You were unusually productive last week, but I need copy from you for today. Since you missed the meeting, I have no idea what you have coming in."

"I may have something on this robbery, actually," I said. "Aaron couldn't give me anything on the record, but the Graysons' maid was the one who called the cops, and she's meeting me for coffee in a little while."

"Nice." He nodded. "Not to turn you away from a good lead, but I know you, Nicey. It hasn't occurred to you that the maid could get fired for talking to you?"

"I don't have to print what I get from her," I said. "Besides, they already suspended her. They say she can't come back to work until the break-in is solved. It's ridiculous. If someone doesn't figure this out soon, she'll be looking for a new job anyway, and that's unfair. She might be able to point me to something I can get on the record, though."

"I see. So you have to find out who broke into the senator's house so she can go back to work?"

"Something like that. The more noble the cause, the more determined I am."

"Why do I have a bad feeling about this?" Bob leaned forward, resting his elbows on his knees. "Oh, wait; because the last time you decided to play Woodward and Bernstein, you almost got yourself killed."

"I remember. But I'm not investigating anything this time." I hoped the lie was convincing as it slid through my teeth. "I'm taking a source on a robbery story for coffee because she's a nice woman and I like her. That's all. If I can make more of a story than a day two out of it without getting her in trouble, I will."

"You're a lousy liar and you know it," he said. "But I trust you enough to let you go with it. I also need a follow on the thing with the jewelry store today. Les tells me that story went viral on Facebook—thirty thousand shares in one day—so the number crunchers want you to stay on top of it."

"I suppose it's not every day there's a pickup buried in the side of a building. I'm glad I had one that shut him up for a day."

"You didn't shut him up," he said. "Les is like a dog with a bone when he wants something. And he thinks putting Shelby on the courthouse would be the best thing to happen to journalism since moveable type. All your Facebook popularity did was strengthen his case that you're the best cops reporter in town and we should let you focus on the PD."

He looked up. "You want to think about it?" Bob's voice softened. "It would give you more free time and it would get Les off your ass."

"No. I wouldn't know what to do with free time if I had it, anyway." I didn't want to give up the courthouse because the trial stories were often juicier and wider-read than the initial crime reports. Which was exactly why Shelby wanted it. "And before you ask, no, I'm not handing the PD over to Shelby, either. I have sources there who skate dangerously close to being friends, and I don't want to give that up."

"I respect the hell out of your ambition, kid. Just take some advice from an old man: don't put one shiny heel out of line," Bob said. "Also, don't piss Ted Grayson off. I know he has some friends upstairs, and I know they would not hesitate to can you if he asked them to."

Great.

"Yes, sir." I stood and smoothed my skirt. "Anything else?"

"Other than don't get yourself killed, which should be obvious, but in your case seems to bear repeating?" Bob asked with a wry smile. "Just one thing: if your gut tells you to ask Trudy about the Grayson thing, do it. I don't need you ladies in some sort of standoff because she thinks you're bigfooting her territory. And don't miss the meeting tomorrow."

"You got it, chief," I said, flashing a grin and turning for the door.

* * *

I just barely beat Joyce to the coffee shop, and when I'd ordered myself a skinny white mocha and her a decaf caramel macchiato, we settled into overstuffed armchairs in the corner.

"It took me fifteen minutes to get over here," she said, staring at the line of brake lights on West Cary. "Silly little storm pops up and folks around here drive like they ain't never seen a raindrop."

I grinned. "That they do. But I'm guilty of holing up in my house like the zombie apocalypse is coming when there are more than three flakes of snow on the ground, so I can't say too much. Except that in my defense, I'm from Texas. Everything shuts down when it snows."

I studied Joyce's kind face and soft, honest eyes. Hardworking. Forthright. Her canary yellow shoulder-padded suit looked like it had walked out of a 1989 Sears catalog, but it was clean and pressed. I couldn't believe she'd done anything wrong.

If I was right about this, was I right about Billings, too? Kyle clearly thought he had his man, and while Billings might not be a stand-up guy, there was a difference between being a greedy asshole in business and being a murderer. Like, a life prison sentence.

"Joyce, did you see anyone at the Graysons' house on Friday morning?" I asked.

She met my eyes straight on and shook her head slowly.

"I was upstairs cleaning the bathroom, and I heard a noise downstairs. I thought it was Mrs. Grayson, coming in early from her trip. She goes to New York to shop all the time now, and I wanted to ask her if she was ready for me to change out the linens to the winter sets, so I went down the back stairs, calling to her. I heard footsteps, and when I got down there, the door was standing open. I peeked into the senator's office and saw the broken window, but I didn't go in there because he's very particular about no one being in that room but him. I closed the door, called the police and Mrs. Grayson, and then waited for someone to show up."

"What kind of footsteps did you hear?" I asked.

She furrowed her brow. "I'm not sure I follow you."

"Were they light, sharp, loud?" I asked. "If you think about what different kinds of shoes sound like on wood flooring, what do you think the person was wearing, and do you see them as large or small?"

She tipped her head to one side and twisted her mouth, considering that for a second before her lips popped into a perfect O.

"I know who it was," she whispered, her left hand flying to her mouth. "Oh, Jesus, Miss Clarke, I think I know who it was."

"Who?" I leaned forward in my seat.

"I don't know the man's name, but I've seen him," Joyce said. "He's come to talk to the senator a handful of times here lately. He dresses like a western movie and drives a big pickup truck, and those boots he wears clomp on that floor in the back hall something terrible. That's why I heard him from the other corner of the house. But why would he break in? He'd been invited over plenty of times."

She lost me at "big pickup truck" and "boots." I stared at her, my brain reeling quickly through different pieces of my week. I dug in my bag for my cell phone and pulled up the *Telegraph's* mobile site, searching for my story on the jewelry store.

"This pickup truck?" I said, flipping the screen around.

She studied the photo on the screen for what seemed like a long time. "I think so, yes, though I can't see the front of this one, and I never paid attention to his plates," she said, handing the phone back. "Did he hurt himself?"

"No." I laid the phone on the table and stared at the photo. "He hurt some other people, though. How sure are you that his boots are what you heard?"

"As sure as I can be, given that I didn't see him."

"Did you tell the police about this man?"

"I didn't even think to," she said. "It hadn't occurred to me, about how the shoes sounded, until you asked me that question. They didn't ask me that. Do you know who drives this pickup, Miss Clarke? Maybe I can go back to work soon, after all.'"

"I sure hope so, Joyce," I said, locking the phone and tucking it back into my bag. "I would love to visit with you more, but I have to get back to the office and see what I can find out about this. Thank you so much for your time."

"Of course. Miss Clarke?"

I stopped mid-stride and turned back to her.

"The detective I spoke to gave me a card. Should I tell him about this? What you asked me about the shoes?"

I nodded. I wasn't sure they'd run down a lead based on faraway footfalls, but it couldn't hurt for her to call and tell them.

I darted to the car without bothering to open my umbrella, my brain rushing a hundred miles an hour through what I knew about this story. It got sexier—and more convoluted—by the minute.

Driving back to my office as fast as traffic would allow, I shivered a little in the chill that had come with the storm and cranked up the heat, wishing I'd thought to check the weather and grab a jacket on my way out to accost Aaron. I ticked off what I knew in time to the swishing of the windshield wipers as I waited for the light to turn green.

The girl at the jewelry store said the guy who ran into the building was a tobacco farmer. Kyle was probably looking for this farmer. James Billings, the VP at Raymond Garfield, and Amesworth, the dead lobbyist, were funneling money to Senator Grayson through the tobacco lobby to pay for his secret sexual escapades. And Joyce seemed pretty sure the farmer had broken into Grayson's private study. Which meant there was something in there he wanted, and if she spooked him, he might not have gotten it.

Parking in the garage, I glimpsed Trudy Montgomery's shiny convertible a few slots down. The nagging feeling I needed to talk to her was too strong to ignore.

I glanced at the clock. Just past noon. I had four hours to get Bob his stories. Plenty of time to have a heart-to-heart with the *Telegraph's* resident political insider.

13

"I've always admired your knowledge of the inner workings of D.C." I smiled at Trudy from her office doorway, sipping plain coffee because the last of my white chocolate syrup had disappeared. "Bob is right. You know more about the players up there than anyone this side of the beltway."

Trudy cocked her head to one side, turning her chair toward me. "Thank you. I think. Why do I feel a 'but' coming on here, Nichelle?"

I took a deep breath. I liked Trudy. I respected her work. I needed her to tell me what she knew about Grayson, but more than that, I really hoped she didn't know what I knew. It's easy to get close to sources when you work a beat for a long time, and I didn't want to think Trudy might be looking past Senator Grayson's transgressions because she liked him. But it wasn't impossible.

"Not a 'but.' A 'so.' " I said. "So—how is it that you don't know Ted Grayson is taking bribes?"

"What in the pea-picking hell are you talking about? Ted Grayson's one of the straightest arrows on Capitol Hill. He wouldn't take a bribe if his life depended on it."

"Only if his sex life depended on it," I muttered.

"Pardon?" She arched an eyebrow.

"Nothing." I waved a hand. "You really don't know anything about this? No one in the opposing campaign has anything on it?"

"I don't have the first clue what you're talking about," she said, never breaking eye contact. "Why don't you step in here and have a seat and let's figure it out, shall we?"

I obliged, shutting the door behind me and settling into the chair opposite her.

"I went by the campaign office Friday night, looking for information on the robbery at the Grayson house," I said.

"There some reason you didn't just ask me?" She leaned back in her chair.

"You didn't answer your phone."

"What did you find in your visit to the campaign office that makes you think Grayson is on the take? Was there a confession letter taped to the front door?"

"I talked to a girl who works there. She said she overheard him arguing with two other men who asked him what they were paying him for. I've been running my ass off chasing this murder story on the lobbyist, and Grayson's name just keeps coming up. If he's the straightest arrow on the hill, we're in serious trouble."

"Do you have anyone to corroborate this story? Or any other proof?"

"Grayson is taking bribe money from Raymond Garfield tobacco and who knows who else. Trust me. You want my notes?"

"I think I can do my own research, doll. And I will. In November." Trudy ignored me when I opened my mouth to protest. "Do you have any idea the lengths a campaign can go to plant information? The Internet is a powerful tool. If you have the right people doing it, you can make anyone look guilty of anything. This has been the single nastiest race I've ever covered, and it's not even October yet. Unless you've got a photo of Grayson standing over the corpse with a weapon and blood on his hands, you have nothing I'm interested in. And even then, I want the negative."

"Trudy, I've covered cops for a long time—" I began.

"I know, and you could be on to something. Or you could be looking too hard for something that's not there in an effort to get catch the eye of a certain section editor at the *Washington Post*. That's immaterial to me, really.

If Grayson's dirty, which I would have a hard time believing, then he'll be dirty when the election's over, too. And I'll trust your information a lot more the second week of November."

Her computer beeped and she turned her attention to the screen.

"The new *Post* poll has Grayson by two." She glanced at me.

"I can't let this go," I said. "I have a dead guy and a man in prison I'm almost positive shouldn't be. And I'm not sure that's even all of it."

She stared at me. "I believe you. At least, I believe you believe what you're saying. But you really ought to drop it. I am not risking my reputation based on your gut. You're a big girl. If you must chase it, go on. What do I care? If you dig something up on him, you're that much more valuable at cops and courts. Or maybe someone in D.C. will notice you. If you don't, it's your job on the line, not mine. Just watch it. If you're dealing with Calhoun's campaign, he'll come at you harder after this poll. You'll have a helluva time knowing who to trust."

I nodded, pushing myself out of the chair and turning for the door. "Thanks, Trudy." I paused and looked back at her. "You don't know anyone else in the newsroom who likes white mochas, do you?"

"I'm a hot tea girl, myself," she said. "Why?"

"No reason." I let myself out, thinking about my deadlines and Joyce and wondering if I could pump Aaron on the farmer without him knowing what I was up to.

* * *

I dialed Aaron's cell phone, tapping a pen on my desk blotter.

Why didn't Trudy want a story this big? Bob was right—she knew everything about everyone inside the beltway. I replayed her nonchalant dismissal in my head. She couldn't possibly want me walking such a close line with a big story on her beat. Did she know something she wasn't letting on? It hadn't seemed like she was lying, but she was obviously tight with Grayson. Could she be trying to throw me off to cover for him?

"What now?" Aaron barked when he picked up.

"Did you guys hold that farmer who ran into the jewelry store over for a hearing?" I asked, unfazed by his annoyance. I was fairly sure a guy flashing wads of cash around the jewelry store would have easily made bail, but it didn't hurt to ask.

"He was out in two hours," Aaron said. "Hearing is tomorrow morning. Why?"

"Bob wants a follow on the story today." I twisted my fingers into my hair. It wasn't a lie, because Bob had asked me for a story, but it still felt a little smarmy. "I can tease the hearing. I'll pop in and write it up for Wednesday, too." An evidence hearing wouldn't get thirty thousand Facebook shares in a hundred years, but it would make Bob happy. And at least remove one of Les' reasons for bitching.

I thanked Aaron and hung up, drumming my fingers on the handset and staring at the cream wall of my cubicle before I flipped my computer open and searched for the police report on the accident at the jewelry store. I copied down the farmer's address and grabbed my bag, hurrying back to the elevator. While calling would certainly be faster, I'd get a better read on whether the guy was lying to me if we were face to face. I wasn't sure if or where he fit into my larger story, but the possibility of getting Joyce back to work was enough to make the drive out to Powhatan worth it.

Virginia's early-autumn splashes of warm reds and bright yellows blurred with the green that still clung to most of the trees as I laid on the accelerator outside the city, my thoughts racing through everything I'd seen and heard at the jewelry store. Lots of cash. Big, loud guy. Looking for obnoxious diamonds. A showoff with a heavy foot, too, if he'd intended to peel his big red bubba truck out backward as fast as he must have been going to plow into the store as he had. Which all added up to this: he probably wasn't going to want to talk to me. Playing the bimbo and using flattery would be my two surest ways to get his jaw flapping. I detested both and wasn't good at either.

I slowed the car and turned onto a narrow gravel road, then took a left into a driveway flanked by stone lions guarding an open wrought-iron gate. The drive wound through a grove of manicured magnolias that were just losing their blooms to the early fall chill, the soft slope of the hills in the surrounding fields golden brown with tobacco plants. I flipped the radio off and rolled the windows down, the *whir-chug* of a combine coming from somewhere I couldn't see.

A majestic, whitewashed house with black shutters appeared, the closest thing to Tara I'd ever seen in real life, making me catch my breath.

"Jesus," I whispered as I stopped the car, staring at soaring white columns that lined a portico built for hoopskirts and mint juleps. "Welcome to Dixie." The house was so far from the suburban tract home where I'd grown up it was positively intimidating.

Squaring my shoulders and trying to shake the feeling that I didn't belong, I hitched my bag over one shoulder and climbed out of the car. There was a stable-sized garage to my right, but no other vehicles in sight.

In place of a regular, push-button doorbell, there was a heavy, braided cord with a tassel on the end. I shook my head slightly and yanked, bells chiming over my head like Saint Luke's on Sunday morning. An honest-to-God plantation. And from the looks of the fields and the sound of the combine, the folks who owned it had fared just fine with paid labor.

One of the eight-foot, black double doors swung inward, and a petite woman with a sweet smile and skin as pale as her uniform smiled at me. The flush in her cheeks just made her look that much paler.

"Can I help you, darlin'?" she asked in an accent that spoke more of the Appalachian mountains of West Virginia than it did of Richmond.

I flashed my widest smile.

"I'm here to see William Eckersly. My name is Nichelle Clarke, and I'm a reporter at the *Richmond Telegraph*. I was wondering if he might be able to help me with an article I'm working on?"

She shook her head.

"Mister Will isn't here this morning," she said. "He had business to attend to in town. But if you'd like to leave a calling card, I can make sure he gets it when he comes home."

"Who is it, Doreen?" A voice that was impossibly wispy and gravelly at the same time came from deeper in the house, and even before the slip of a woman it belonged to rolled her wheelchair into my line of sight, I had a mental picture of a little old grandma who was once the formidable lady of this enormous house.

"Miss Lucinda! You're supposed to be resting." The maid shot a chastising glare. "This here is a reporter who wants to talk to Mister Will."

"I'll have time enough to rest when I'm dead," Lucinda Eckersly took a long draw on a mask attached to a green metal oxygen tank that rode alongside her chair in a little rack. "Lord only knows what my son has done to drag our name through the mud now. Because losing his family to that whore of his wasn't enough. What can we do for you, young lady?"

She leveled a gaze at me that could have terrified a professional linebacker into doing exactly as she said, and waved me into the foyer.

"Doreen, show Miss?" Lucinda arched an eyebrow at me.

"Clarke," I said. "Nichelle Clarke."

"Are you kin to the Prince William County Clarkes?" Lucinda's head snapped up, a gleam in her watery blue eyes. I smiled. Plantations, feuds, uniformed servants and pull chain doorbells. I began to wonder if I'd driven through a space-time vortex on my way out to the country.

"No, ma'am. I grew up in Texas, and my family's from California."

"Well then," she said, giving me a critical once-over. "Follow Doreen to the sitting room, and I'll be with you directly. I need a new tank."

I followed Doreen, trying not to let my jaw drop at the massive works of art that lined the foyer walls, interspersed with swords, framed papers, and dark, heavy, very antique-looking furniture. Jenna would bust something to get a look at some of this stuff. A painting I was pretty sure (from having an artist like Jenna as a friend) was an actual Chegal hung just inside the front door. A wardrobe that would have taken up half my living room sat along the wall opposite the polished staircase that rose to the second floor. My shoes clicked on the hardwood, the sound echoing through the cavernous hallway.

"Nice shoes," Lucinda called behind me. "I used to be a high heels girl myself, before I got too old to walk in them anymore."

"Indeed she was," Doreen said, stopping in front of a set of rich, golden wood double doors. "Miss Lucinda was a beauty in her day. Belle of the county. Richest husband, biggest house. To look at her now, you wouldn't know it, but she was quite a lady."

"I believe it," I said, stepping through the doors into a dim, silent room with an oversized rectangular piano in one corner and a pair of sculpted wood and silk sofas flanking a fireplace in the other. The musty smell said it wasn't used too often anymore. Doreen pulled heavy drapes back from the floor-to-ceiling windows and tied them with thick cord, flooding the space with sunlight. Dust motes, no doubt from the drapes, danced in the beams. I perched on the high-backed settee facing the window, crossing my legs.

My eyes fell on a framed photo on a wooden side table: A burly man in camouflage and a neon-orange vest with one foot on the ribcage of a humongous buck. Twisting the deer's head up by an antler with one hand, he brandished an ornate, old-fashioned looking rifle with the other. William?

"How long have you worked here?" I asked Doreen as she fussed with the drapery cords and straightened the music books on the piano.

"Forty-one years in November," she said, not looking up from her work. "I was the first person Miss Lucinda hired when she married Mister Harold, God rest his soul. My momma kicked me out when I was sixteen and I came east looking for a better life than coal mines and dirt floor shacks. I found it here. Miss Lucinda has been through a lot. But she's a good woman. A real blessing to me and my family."

She raised her eyes to meet mine at last, and something serious in her stare sent a chill through me, sunshine be damned. I smiled and nodded, but before I could ask any more questions, the door creaked open and Lucinda wheeled herself into the room, preceded by the distinct odor of a burning cigarette.

"Sorry to keep you waiting, Miss Clarke," Mrs.Eckersly said, a Virginia Slim dangling from her lower lip. She rolled herself to an opening in the furniture arrangement opposite me and cut a defiant glance at Doreen, who shook her head as she shut the door behind her, but didn't say a word.

I tried to keep my features arranged in a neutral expression, but my eyes locked on Lucinda's oxygen tank, which was full, according to what she'd said, then flitted to the lit cigarette. I was pretty sure I was suddenly in mortal danger, sitting and chatting with a little old lady in the middle of the afternoon.

On one hand, I wanted her to talk to me about her son, and I was pretty sure she wanted to talk, too. On the other, I was fond of remaining in one piece, and she was going to blow herself right the hell up, sitting there smoking with an oxygen tank strapped to her. I couldn't tell if she got points for stubbornness, or lost them for stupidity.

"Would you like a smoke?" she asked in her gravelly half-whisper as if on cue, fishing the pack and a pink Bic lighter out of her flowing blue satin housedress.

I sucked in such a sharp breath that I dissolved into a coughing fit, trying to smile. I desperately wished I'd paid more attention in science class. How far would an explosion from a liter or two of oxygen be lethal? If we combusted, would I walk away in blackened Louboutins, or maybe just lose a hand?

"No, thank you," I said.

"I know." She flashed a tight grin, her wrinkled lips parting over nicotine-yellow teeth. "You youngsters think tobacco is bad for people. I'm seventy-nine, and I've smoked since I was fourteen. I like it and it makes my family a good living, so I'm not quitting. There's lots of folks like me who won't quit, either. No matter how much they want to charge in taxes. But you didn't come here to listen to me prattle about that. What has my Billy done now?"

I tilted my head to one side and studied her before I answered, assessing quickly that this momma was no fool, and "her Billy" probably thought he got away with more than he actually did.

"I think you know way more about that than I do, Mrs. Eckersly." I folded my hands in my lap, trying not to flinch as she flicked burning ashes directly over the oxygen tank. "More than William thinks you do, too, don't you?"

"He doesn't pay any more attention to me than he does those paintings out there," she chuckled, and it sounded like rocks rattling in a box. "Too wrapped up in following his libido, not paying near enough attention to the things he should. This place has been Eckersly land since Jefferson's day. But times are changing. The economy is different. And my son likes beautiful women who like him to buy them expensive things."

"Does your son have a girlfriend?" I asked.

She took a long drag off her cigarette, staring at me as she blew the smoke out slowly. I stifled a cough.

"My son has a whore," she said. "Not the kind that hangs out at bars looking for a good time, but an honest-to-God member of the oldest profession. She likes diamonds, and furs, and shoes like those ones you're wearing. She's young. She's pretty. She's got Billy acting like a fool. I'm glad you came by today, Miss Clarke, because I'm tired of talking at my son. I'll be damned if he's going to run this farm into the ground over a good piece of ass. So, how can I help you?"

I studied her determined gaze, wondering why she wanted to help me at all. I wasn't asking, because she might think better of talking to me. I considered her words. Money. Prostitution. Lakshmi. Grayson. What if the farmer and the senator shared a call girl?

"You said William's girlfriend is pretty," I said, trying to keep the raw excitement out of my voice. "What does she look like?"

"Dark hair. Pretty face. Prettier than my daughter-in-law, sure, and Lord knows men aren't always faithful, but this has become more than a little boyish fun. My grandsons will have their legacy." She lost the last word in a coughing fit. Holding up one finger, she fumbled for her mask, taking several deep pulls on it before she put it down.

The steely determination in her rheumy eyes was jarring, and I found myself wondering for a second if I suspected the wrong Eckersly. But studying the frail frame that was swallowed in the dressing gown and watching her cough at the slightest excitement dismissed the thought. This woman didn't overpower a twenty-something attorney who played ball three nights a week and just finished a triathlon.

But her son—depending on how dire his financial situation was— certainly might have. If Joyce was right and Eckersly had broken into Grayson's place, what if he'd shot Amesworth like the deer in the photo? Joyce could go back to work and I would have the second story of the year. Third, too, counting Grayson's call girl.

Charlie would have a hard time covering jealousy green with makeup.

Lucinda stared past me, at something I couldn't see. "I love my son. I don't want my family name dragged through the mud. But I cannot let him lose this farm. He won't turn it over to me or hire an overseer no matter how much I beg him. He's into some things he shouldn't be. Besides the girl. I'm not sure about what or how, but he whispers a lot, on the phone. Maybe you can help me, too. If Billy's done enough wrong to go to jail, I've got a power of attorney that turns the farm over to me."

I studied her face, sadness and disappointment plain in every line.

"Is there anything else you can think of that might help me?" I asked. "Is your son active in politics?"

She laughed. "Billy's not the public service type."

"Does he know a James Billings? He's—"

"A bigwig at Raymond Garfield," Lucinda finished my sentence. "Of course we know him. This industry is a pretty small one."

Hmmm. So maybe a small lead, but still nothing I could print. I sighed. I needed more details, and it was obvious she didn't have them.

She pulled another cigarette from the pack.

"Thank you, ma'am." I jumped to my feet before Lucinda could light up again. "It was so nice to meet you, Mrs. Eckersly, but I have to scoot back to my office."

She nodded in dismissal, dropping the cigarette pack in her lap.

I hurried from the room, the sound of the Bic clicking making my steps faster. Letting myself out without bidding Doreen goodbye, I hoped her employer didn't blow them both to kingdom come.

Back at my desk, I fired off a follow-up to the jewelry store story, quoting Aaron about the bail and the hearing and recapping the details of the accident. A quick phone call to the store's manager got me a comment about the structural damage, which was irreparable. They were waiting for the insurance check to clear and hiring a contractor to raze the premises and build a new store.

"This one will have kevlar in the walls if they do such a thing." She laughed.

"I understand the customer who was driving the truck had just bought a rather expensive piece," I said, trying to remember if Lakshmi had been wearing a bracelet and failing. "Had you seen him in the store before?"

"Not that I remember," she said.

"Was there anything unusual about the bracelet he bought?" I asked.

"It was big. And pretty. Why do you ask?"

"Just curious," I said. "It goes with the job."

"Is there anything else I can help you with?"

"Not that I can think of." I thanked her and hung up.

I sent the story to Bob just before four and wandered to the break room, hunting for a Diet Coke.

Halfway there, I heard a round of hearty laughter pouring from Parker's office.

Sticking my head around the doorframe, I felt my face stretch into a grin when I saw Troy, spinning Parker's seat back and forth and holding court with half the sports desk. He looked so happy it was positively infectious.

"So, what do you lead your story with?" Parker asked, gesturing to the computer and pushing a notebook across the desk at Troy. "You interviewed the coach. There's one game left in the season. Give me your lead."

I shot Parker a smile and mouthed a "thank you" when he glanced at me. He nodded and focused on Troy, who was studying his notes with a furrowed brow.

"I guess I'd say to start with the comment he made about focusing on pitching in the draft this year?"

"Yes and no." Parker grinned. "Nice job picking out the most important thing. But you write the lead. You don't start with his comment."

Troy tilted his head to one side, and I could almost see the sponge soaking up every detail. "Why?"

"Clarke?" Parker turned toward me and I stepped through the door and waved at Troy. "Care to explain the whys and wherefores?"

"Your lead is supposed to catch your reader's attention and summarize your most important point, and very rarely does someone say something that captures the most important part of a story more succinctly than you can write it," I said. "My favorite prof in college had a saying in a frame over his desk: every journalist gets to lead a story with a quote twice in their career. Once when they're too green to know any better, and again when the Pope says 'fuck.' "

"Hear, hear! I'm totally framing that and putting it over my desk," Spence said from the black metal chair in the corner. "And I'm giving Bob one for Christmas."

"I always thought that'd be such a great story to write," I said, leaning on the edge of the desk and cutting a glance at Troy. He probably heard worse before first period, if I remembered high school right. "Can you see it? 'Vatican City, AP: 'Fuck,' the Pope said Friday. 'Just fuck it all.' Bishops were stunned speechless when his holiness erupted in a string of swear-words during morning mass. The Associated Press has learned the Pope was frustrated with level 15 of Angry Birds. In a statement released this afternoon, the Vatican apologized. 'It was not intended to be said aloud,' the press release reads."

"Damn, Clarke, you missed your calling." Parker grinned. "You ought to be writing for the Onion."

"I'll take that as praise." I turned to Troy. "Have you had a good day?"

"The best!" He bounced in his seat. "Mr. Parker took me to the ballpark and then over to RAU to watch football practice. He even listened to me practice calling plays and gave me pointers, and he let me interview the baseball coach and took me to eat barbecue for lunch, and he said I could help with his column." The words spilled out so fast I could hardly keep up, and that was saying something. Taking Troy's notes, I flipped through at least twenty pages.

"Jeez, kid, you don't need shorthand lessons," I said. "These are pretty detailed."

"I want to make sure I don't forget anything," Troy said. "Thank you so much, Miss Clarke."

"Did they win you over to the print side of the world?"

"I still want to be on TV," he said. "But I never knew newspapers were so much fun. It wouldn't be a bad place to start."

"A backup plan is a good thing to have," I said with a smile.

"All right, y'all," Parker boomed, shooing everyone toward the door. "If Spence wants my column today, Troy and I have some work to do."

"Have fun," I told Troy, smiling when he gushed another thank you.

"Thanks again," I told Parker as I slipped out the door. "I owe you one."

"Nah. Setting me up with Mel is worth a few favors. Her sister had a girl. Cute little thing," he said. "What were we looking for the other night, anyhow? You find anything on your lead?"

I shrugged. "I'm still working on it." The fewer people who knew about my suspicions until they were more than suspicions, the better. Especially given what I'd just heard from Trudy.

He cocked his head, leaning on the doorjamb. "You're really not going to tell me? You don't think I killed somebody else, do you?"

I laughed. "You're never going to let that go, are you? I'm not entirely sure what it is that I'm into, and I don't want to talk about it until I am."

"Into? You playing Lois Lane again?"

"No." I took a step backward.

"Liar." Parker shook his head. "Does Bob know what you're doing, at least?"

"Part of it. Really, I'm playing it safe." I shoved the toy dog and Joey's warning to a vault in the back of my brain.

"Uh-huh. I'm buying you a handgun for Christmas."

"My shoes seem to work pretty well, thanks."

"I have to get to work or I'm going to miss deadline." He moved to close the door. "Stay out of trouble."

I rounded the corner into the break room, and the empty syrup bottle in the garbage can inside the door caught my eye. I scowled. What I really wanted was more coffee, though the Coke had fewer calories. And in the grand scheme of things, the mystery of the disappearing syrup was less important than a dead man and a crooked politician.

I jammed quarters into the Coke machine a little too hard and gulped half the bottle on my way back to my desk.

My cell phone binged the arrival of a text as I plopped into my chair.

"Miss you, baby girl."

My mom. I snatched up the phone and dialed her number, checking my email as it rang. Nothing from Bob yet.

"Hey, sweetheart," she said when she picked up. "Are you busy?"

"I can squeeze you in," I said. "I miss you. What's going on there?"

"Have you ever seen that TV show *Bridezillas*?" She sighed. "Those broads have nothing on this woman I'm working for. My God, Nicey. It's all I can do to refrain from slapping her about. Nothing and no one is ever right or good enough, and she's such a little snot; she insisted that I meet her for coffee on Thursday, and hand to God, she snapped her fingers at that poor server no less than ten times in half an hour. She's like that with everyone. The biggest part of the hours I've spent on this wedding so far have been running interference with other businesses for the bride, because she's so hateful people don't want to work for her."

"Then why are you working for her?"

"Because her grandfather's last name is on a few buildings downtown. Big ones. And I thought she was nice the first time she came in. I was wrong. It's like peeling an onion. The closer it gets to her wedding, the more layers of nasty there are to her. But her stuff is almost done, and I'll be rid of her soon. Thank God."

I laughed. "If anyone can get a Bridezilla safely down the aisle, it's you," I said. "What kind of flowers will she have?"

My mom's love of plants had led her to start a tiny flower shop when I was a kid, and it had grown into a thriving wedding-planning boutique. That was irony for you: my mother, who held the deepest disdain for marriage of anyone I'd ever met, made a living helping people do, in her estimation, something foolish.

"I used lilies, white roses, and orchids when I made the test bouquet last week," she said. "It came out lovely. It's a waterfall style with a lace handkerchief that belonged to her grandmother around the base. At least, she said it was her grandmother's. I'm beginning to think she escaped from some hell dimension."

I laughed. "It sounds lovely. Hang in there. When's the big day?"

"Next Friday," she said. "Twelve more days, and one more box of antacids. I think I can, I think I can."

I shook my head, waking the computer and smiling when I saw a thumbs up from Bob in my email. He also okay'd my request to cut out of the staff meeting early the next morning, so I could make it to the court-house for the Eckersly hearing.

I glossed over my week, telling my mom about the jewelry store and relating the tale of Lucinda Eckersly, former grande dame of Powhatan County and current explosive hazard.

"It makes me smile to hear you so happy," my mom said. "I sure do love you, kiddo. Any chance you'll head this way anytime soon?"

"I love you, too," I said, shutting my computer down and closing the lid. "I'll be there for Christmas, which will be here before you know it. How many holiday weddings are there this year?"

"Three. And if you're really coming, I won't book any more." Her voice brightened considerably.

"Put it on the calendar." I smiled back. "I'll be there with bells on my Manolos."

I hung up and shoved my computer and charger into my bag, my gurgling stomach reminding me that I hadn't had time for lunch once again.

I ducked into the deli across the street. I ordered a turkey and smoked cheddar panini with tomato mustard on sourdough and carried it to a corner table when it was ready, crunching homemade potato chips that were perfectly seasoned with salt, pepper, garlic, and something else I could never place.

I watched Anderson Cooper as I ate, surprised to see a Virginia map flash up on the wall behind him a few minutes into his show.

It took the captions a minute to catch up.

"The new state tax, combined with a federal tax hike that has strong support in the house, would make the capital of the nation's tobacco industry the most expensive place in America to buy cigarettes."

I froze with a chip halfway to my mouth.

"They'll reverse their operation in Virginia." Kyle.

"No matter what they do with taxes." Lucinda Eckersly.

"Fake the tax stamps." Kyle.

"There are people in this who won't give a damn if I say to leave you alone." Joey.

What if Grayson wasn't just selling his vote (or, his friends' votes, as the case may be)? Could the dead lobbyist have been expendable because the senator had known the vote wasn't going to go his way, seen his hooker money slipping away, and decided to sell something else? Like stamp designs?

I looked out the window.

It was getting dark outside.

Suddenly focused on something much more important, I wolfed down my sandwich and ran out the door, wondering how many years I could spend in prison for breaking into Ted Grayson's house.

14

I spent the entire ten-minute drive home making a mental list of the reasons my plan was a) insane, b) unlikely to work, and c) very likely to get me arrested. The fact that Charlie would have a tickertape parade and crack a bottle of champagne with that story was my most compelling reason for going home and sinking into a hot bath, but my gut was convinced Eckersly had, in fact, broken into Grayson's study. Whatever he'd been looking for was likely still there, according to Joyce.

And according to the police and the campaign, the family had been in D.C. since the break-in.

My transmission squealed a protest when I threw the car into park in my driveway before it had stopped moving forward. I snagged the first-aid kit from under my seat, grabbed the latex gloves, and jumped out, unsure what to do next. Darcy yapped from the other side of the kitchen door, scratching at the wood when I didn't go inside right away. I'd blocked the doggie door and left her inside with puppy mats on the floor, which she disliked, because I was afraid to have her outside without me after the warning I'd gotten.

The nice thing about the Fan was that tiny cottages like mine sat side-by-side with million-dollar antebellum homes like Grayson's. It wasn't a terribly long walk, and I'd skipped the gym that morning. I glanced down at my pink Jimmy Choos, the peep toes cute, but impractical.

Scurrying into the house, I let Darcy out for just long enough to do her business and caught a glare when I called her inside.

"Sorry, girl. We'll play later," I said, stooping to scratch her ears.

I changed into black yoga pants and a black tee, slipping my feet into soft-soled leather flats and hurrying back outside before I could chicken out. Stuffing the gloves into my pocket, I turned toward the cracked old sidewalk and started walking.

The sun had officially disappeared, the chill that settled over the bricks of Monument Avenue with the late September evening air making me wish I'd grabbed a sweater. I shoved my hands into my pockets and ducked my head against the breeze, walking faster.

By the time I reached the drive alley that ran behind the Grayson home, I'd worked out a plan. Since the house faced a busy street, and the police had the front yard lit up like Rockefeller Center, I turned up the drive. Katherine Grayson seemed like the kind of detail-focused woman who'd have one of those stone plates with the family crest on it at the entrance to her driveway, even though it was behind the house.

I dug out my tiny pink flashlight, pointing it at each fence opening as I passed, and was beginning to wonder if I'd guessed wrong when the beam bounced off a polished marble plaque bearing the house number and the senator's name. Bingo.

I knew as sure as I knew my shoe size (nine US, forty European) there was no one inside, but I was nervous. I stood there, warring with myself over the insanity of this idea. Breaking into the private home of a United States senator was very different than anything else I'd ever done in the name of research—even the things that had bent the law. I shushed the little voice that detailed what could happen to me if I got caught.

Just when I'd resolved to go in, a crash came from my left and I jumped nearly out of my skin. Claws on pavement, then aluminum. A raccoon, probably. I gulped a steadying breath and stepped toward the house.

"Don't do that, Miss Clarke." The smooth voice was in front of me, and in the still darkness of the alley it carried easily. I scanned the fence line around Grayson's house, but Joey was better than me at keeping hidden. To be fair, he'd had more practice.

He stepped out of the shadows at the foot of the drive, debonair as ever in a charcoal suit and wingtips that glinted even in the moonlight.

"Go home. Stay out of this. This guy is so much bigger than you know."

I strode across the alley, arching an eyebrow when he laid a restraining hand on my arm.

"What the hell are you doing here?" I asked. "And cut the bullshit about trying to protect me, because I don't buy it. You're either protecting yourself, or your buddy Grayson, or the both of you."

"I was in town and came by to check on you. Hoping you'd taken my advice. I had a bad feeling when you took off on foot, and I was right. Tell me something: when have I ever steered you wrong?" He let go of my arm, the place where his fingers had rested tingling in the cool air, and I stared into his brown eyes. He didn't look like he was lying. His gaze was so intense I had to drop it after a minute when my stomach flipped like I'd gotten a side of jumping beans with my panini. Damn him and his gorgeous jawline. Why did he have to be a crook?

"It's not that easy," I began.

"Sure it is," he said, his voice soft and deep at the same time. "I can't recall ever having given you a personal reason to distrust me. I care about you. Maybe more than I'd like. Certainly more than is convenient with the sky falling around your boy here, and you refusing to listen to reason."

His eyelids dropped a fraction of an inch and he reached for my arm again. I stepped backward.

"I can't," I whispered. "Kyle's got an innocent man going up on a murder charge, and you know it as well as I do. I'm going to find out what the hell's going on here. Grayson's up to his Hermes necktie in hookers and bribes, and he may not have killed that lobbyist, but there's something in that house that's going to get me closer to figuring out who did. Someone else wanted it badly enough to break in, but I don't think they got it. I'm going to find it. So unless you want to share what you know, get out of my way."

He stared silently for a long minute. I drew myself up to my full height, nearly six feet even without stilettos, and stuck out my chin for good measure.

"Do you even know how to pick a lock?" He sighed.

"I'll figure it out," I said.

"You'll set off the alarm and get yourself arrested. Come on."

He crossed the backyard in a dozen strides, keeping to the shadows seemingly by second nature, and stopped in front of a door I wouldn't have even noticed on the far right corner of the house.

I managed to keep up without my heels to unsteady me on the emerald turf. Joey pulled a thin scrap of metal from his wallet and what looked like a tiny screwdriver with a funny curved end on it from inside his jacket.

He cut his dark eyes at me as he worked the tool around, first in the deadbolt and then in the button lock on the handle. When the second one clicked loose I gave an involuntary gasp of awe.

"My undesirable skill set suddenly isn't so undesirable, is it?" He flashed a tight grin.

I didn't answer, trying not to breathe too deep, every fiber of my being acutely aware that he was very close, and he smelled unbelievably good. Cologne, yes, but something else, too. Not aftershave, or hair gel, I didn't think. I couldn't place it, but it was downright magical, and making it damned near impossible to concentrate on anything else. There was nothing undesirable about Joey, no matter how hard I tried to remind myself there should be.

A tiny click pulled my focus away from the hollow alongside his Adam's apple. Whatever he'd been doing now allowed him to open the door enough for us to slip through.

"No siren?" I asked.

"Magnets," he said. "Most of the security systems in these places were installed in the eighties, and not many of them have been updated. There's a magnet in the doorframe that tells the alarm system the door is closed. As long as the connection isn't broken, ADT will never know we're here."

The little piece of metal was stuck to the inside of the doorframe about halfway between the lock and the top.

"I'll be damned," I whispered, filing that away as very useful information I hoped I'd never need again.

I slid through the doorway and felt him tense when I brushed against him, fighting to keep a smile off my lips. At least it wasn't just me.

"Where are we?" I asked.

"What used to be the maid's quarters," he said. "Behind the kitchen, usually."

I flicked my little flashlight back on and crept down the hallway into the house, cracking a big set of double doors on my left.

"Laundry room," I said, the smell of Tide giving it away before I could make out the outline of the huge, front-loading washer and dryer alongside the sink on the opposite wall. White breadboard cabinets lined the perimeter of the room, three drying racks folded into the wall above the sink. "Damn. Martha Stewart's laundry room."

Two feet further and across the hall, I hit pay dirt.

"Study," I whispered, peeking through the French doors. The heavy scent of good cigars and better scotch was probably as much a part of these walls as chemicals were a part of the photo cave at my office.

Joey waved a "ladies first" gesture and I ducked inside, completely unsure why I was whispering and tiptoeing, but doing it just the same.

"I'll take the desk," I said, reaching into my pocket for the latex gloves and offering him one. "Put this on and look in the cabinets."

He pulled a pair of black leather driving gloves from inside his jacket and grinned. "Thanks, but I've done this before. What am I looking for?"

"You don't know?" I raised an eyebrow.

"I'll rephrase. What are you looking for?"

"Something that proves Grayson is dirty. I'll know it when I see it," I said.

"Good plan." Joey chuckled and turned to the cabinet.

I opened drawers and flipped through files, closing them when I didn't see anything promising.

In the very back of the second drawer, I spied a familiar name.

"Billings," I breathed. I wriggled the folder loose and opened it.

Spreadsheets full of six-digit numbers. Dollar amounts? I turned and laid them on the copier that was enclosed in the handsome cherry secretary behind the matching desk. A slip of thick paper fluttered from between the sheets and landed face down on the deep red and beige Oriental rug.

"What are you talking to yourself about over here?" Joey asked from directly behind my shoulder.

"A file on Billings," I said, picking up the slip, which was printed with a pattern of little curlicue doodles and numbers. Was that what a tax stamp looked like? Not being a smoker myself, I had zero frame of reference, but it looked promising. "What is this?"

Joey yanked the chain on the desk lamp and studied the paper before he sighed and thrust it back at me.

"What you came here for," he said. "Let's go."

I opened my mouth to object, pointing to the stack of documents. I froze when the floor started to vibrate.

"Garage door," Joey said. "Do you trust me?"

He held my gaze for a very long second.

"More than a rational person would," I said.

"Then move."

I did, crossing to the door silently.

Through the open door I heard a woman giggling and a deep voice I couldn't make out enough to recognize.

"He's supposed to be in D.C.," I whispered involuntarily. "Cheating weasel."

"Who says he's not in D.C.? He's not the only one cheating," Joey breathed in my ear, putting one hand on the small of my back and steering me through the dark hallway to the open door. He flipped the metal piece loose as he followed me out, since Mrs. Grayson and her friend had disarmed the alarm system. Turning the knob, Joey pulled the door shut silently, scanning the yard before he nodded an all clear and waved me off the patio.

I stuffed the gloves into my pocket and hurried toward the driveway, anxious to get home with the slip of paper and check Google for cigarette tax stamp pictures. Two steps into the lawn, my foot clipped a buried sprinkler head and my ankle turned under me. I bit my lip hard, but managed to avoid yelping. Joey's arm shot around my waist before I could fall, and I gripped his shoulder and leaned into him, hobbling silently to the alley. I blinked away tears and cleared my throat, my searing ankle feeling twice as big as usual.

"Are you alright?"

"I don't even have my good shoes on," I said. "What kind of shit is that? I can run in stilettos, but in flats, not so much."

"Look at it this way," Joey said with a barely-suppressed chuckle. "You might have broken it in the heels. Hobble this way, and I'll drive you home."

After a few steps I made out the outline of his Lincoln, parked under a willow three houses down.

He helped me into the passenger seat and rounded the front of the car, sliding behind the wheel.

I bent forward and probed my ankle gingerly, sucking in a sharp breath. It was swollen, and very tender.

"Do you need to go to the ER again?" Joey asked, concern clear in his tone.

"I don't think so," I said. "I will tomorrow if it gets worse, but I think some ice will be okay for tonight."

"What are you going to do with those stamps?" he asked tightly, laying an arm along the top of my seat as he turned to back the car up.

"Stamps?" I asked, playing dumb.

"The tax stamps you found in the file," he said.

Pay dirt. I reached into my pocket and patted the slip, sure it meant Grayson was going down, but unsure exactly why that was.

"What's Grayson doing with them?" I blurted the question, but after I said it I wondered if he was distracted or annoyed enough to fire an answer back.

Joey kept silent, studying the road as he turned up Monument toward my house. Fine. I could figure that out for myself. I stared at his jawline, trying not to imagine what the faint stubble there would feel like under my fingers as hard as I was trying not to care if he was caught up in whatever dirty dealings Grayson was doing. His arm had felt so natural around my waist, warmth lingering there even with the cool leather of the seat against my back.

But the truth was my goal, no matter what. Right?

He stopped in my driveway and shut off the engine, turning to face me.

"You're not going to let this go, are you?" he asked.

"I can't," I said.

"Billings is no angel."

"But he's not a murderer, is he?" Resting an elbow on the console, I twisted in the seat, trying to configure my throbbing ankle into a more comfortable position.

"No. But these are not nice people, Miss Clarke."

"Nichelle, for the eleventy thousandth time. And I've held my own so far." I didn't move my eyes from his, though I'd always been hesitant to hold his gaze for long in close quarters.

"You're flirting with danger." He leaned closer, his eyelids simmering.

"I'm well aware of that." My breath stopped. My sexy mobster friend was about to kiss me.

At least, I hoped he was. Because I was sure as hell going to kiss him, criminal status be damned.

It was fast and slow all at the same time. I wasn't sure who kissed who, only that suddenly his lips were on mine, and what he did or didn't do outside of that didn't matter one little bit.

I wouldn't even admit to Jenna how many times I'd fantasized about this moment, and the reality was so much better: sweet, rich, and forbidden. Like eating an entire box of Godiva white raspberry truffles when you're supposed to be on a diet. And surprising—Joey was an intimidating, do-as-I-say guy, but his mouth was soft against mine. Hesitant. His palm cradled my cheek the way a collector might hold a Fabergé egg.

I curled my fingers into his thick, dark hair and pulled him closer, parting my lips and pressing them harder against his.

He swept the tip of his tongue along the line of my lower lip and I gasped, dropping my hands to clutch his shoulders, certain I was about to melt into a puddle on the black leather seat.

Oh. My. God.

He tightened his arm, his hand between my shoulder blades pulling me to him, but kept the kiss gentle. My ribs protested melding with the console, but I didn't care. Electricity skated up my spine with every thump of my heart and flick of his tongue.

When I pulled away, his fingertips lingered on my jaw, his thumb streaking sparks across my cheekbone as he stroked it with the lightest touch.

It took everything in me to refrain from inviting him in. I leaned away instead, opening the car door.

"Goodnight, Joey," I whispered. "Please, please, if you're involved in whatever Grayson's doing, disappear before I find out."

"I have no intention of going anywhere, Nichelle," he said. I wanted to believe it was an answer, not an argument. "Sweet dreams."

I eased out of the car, gripping the top edge of the door as I tested my ankle. It hurt, but the kiss was working like morphine. I could feel the pain, but I truly did not give one damn.

I watched as he backed out of the drive, then turned for the door when he flickered the high beams at me.

I took Darcy out back and leaned on the wall as I threw her squirrel, then checked her food bowl, tucking the stamps into my utensil drawer as I limped through the kitchen. Dropping clothes on my way into the bathroom, I pulled a clean t-shirt from the dryer on my way out. I needed to ice my ankle, but I was too drained. It would still be swollen in the morning.

What kind of worms am I going to find in this can? I wondered, trying to think about anything but Joey's toe-curling sweet kiss. As if that were even possible. Folding the cloud-soft duvet back, I climbed into my big cherry four-poster, Joey's jawline waiting on the backs of my eyelids.

15

Sleep was fitful, thanks to my ankle and a drawn-out dream that would've made a porn star blush. By the time first light peeped through my shades, I was ready to hobble to the kitchen for some coffee and an ice pack.

A little rummaging in the far reaches of my linen closet produced an ace bandage I'd used on a sprained knee that had ended my brief Venus Williams phase. I wrapped my ankle tightly, dropping a few ice cubes in a Ziploc and propping my foot on a stack of throw pillows while I sipped a homemade white mocha.

I picked up the stamps by the edges and studied them in the lamplight. The paper was an odd, linen-type adhesive variety, and the strip was scored for easy tearing. The mark itself was a curlicue design with an alphanumeric code printed underneath, and *Commonwealth of Virginia* printed across the top in bitsy letters.

Grayson was definitely dirty. Joey's cryptic non-information and the paper in my hand proved that much.

"Are they fakes?" I wondered aloud, trying to remember exactly what Kyle had told me about the huge case he was working on. "Why would Grayson have fake state tax stamps if he's taking bribes to keep the federal taxes lower?"

Darcy yipped from her bed in the corner, and I looked over at her.

"What do you think, girl? How did the senator get ahold of these?"

I laid them on the table and picked up my coffee, still thinking about Grayson. All the work he'd done at the state level for tighter regulations and banning smoking in public places didn't jive with any of this. And how did the dead guy fit in?

Hold on. The dead guy.

I snatched the stamps off the table and peered at the edge. Not paper, exactly, but like paper. With an odd sheen because of the adhesive.

"Ten to one the scrap I found near the body is this same kind of paper, Darcy," I said, knocking the ice to the floor in my haste to get to my feet. I grabbed my cell phone and pulled up the photos I'd taken at the scene, but I couldn't tell anything definitive from them. It looked promising, though. "I wonder what Kyle's up to this morning."

I limped to the bathroom, the ice, the bandage, and a double dose of Advil keeping the throbbing to a minimum.

Scrubbing my face with a wet cloth, I smiled at the determined flash in the violet eyes that stared back at me from the mirror. If the paper had come from the stamps, Kyle would have to at least acknowledge the possibility that he was wrong. I brushed my teeth and twisted my hair up into a messy bun, finger-combing a few strands around my face. A touch of makeup, and I debated which shoes would accommodate my bandaged foot.

I settled on a pair of Tory Burch pumps I'd picked up at a Salvation Army sale in July because I couldn't pass up the price even if they were a half-size too big. Stuffing Kleenex in the toe of the right one, I slipped it on my uninjured foot and paired the turquoise suede shoes with cream slacks and a canary wrap sweater. Professional, but cute enough to hold Kyle's attention.

I walked gingerly until I got the hang of slightly limping in heels, then climbed in the car and flipped on my scanner.

"Female, approximately twenty-two years old. Forensics is picking through the dumpster now."

A body.

Between the math building and the student union at RAU.

Having just covered a horrific murder case involving students there over the spring and summer, my stomach turned at the idea of another dead coed. Writing about murder is hard enough without tragically young victims.

I started the engine, fishing for my cell phone to call Bob.

"I'm really not trying to piss you off, Chief," I said when he picked up. "But I'm going to be late. There's a dead girl in a dumpster at RAU this morning."

"Really?" He was the only person in the world who could sound perky in response that statement and not come off as a creep. "Shot? Stabbed?"

"Don't know. They're not saying much on the scanner and I'm still in the car. But I'm on my way over there to see what I can see."

"Stay with it as long as you have to," he said. "Good thing I'm not the only person you're standing up."

"I'd never—" I began, but stopped when I remembered that I was supposed to go to the courthouse at eight-thirty. "Shit. The jewelry store hearing."

"Ding ding ding! It was in your copy last night. Early hearing. Any big reason you need to be there?" He meant was there any reason for him to send someone else; in this case "someone else" would likely be Shelby Taylor.

"Not really. I just wanted to get a look at the guy," I lied. I wanted much more than a look at William Eckersly. "It's just a bond hearing."

"I can send photo," he said. "It won't hurt to have a shot of that guy in a courtroom on file. Let me see if we've got anyone available."

"Thanks, Chief." I clicked off the call, thinking he had no clue just how handy that picture might be.

I turned onto the campus, a half-dozen RPD cars, an ambulance, and forensics, coroner's, and TV vans making it even more difficult than usual to find a parking place.

Finally double-parking next to the Channel Four van, I hurried around the student union to a sidewalk looking out on a picturesque courtyard. Students stood clustered in groups, whispering and staring toward a large blue dumpster. A thirty-foot radius was blocked off by crime scene tape, the grass between the sidewalk and the dumpster hidden beneath the feet of better than fifty reporters, cops, medical examiners, and suit-and-tie university administrators.

I found Aaron at the center of a circle of microphones, giving the first media briefing of the day.

"...pending notification of next of kin," he was saying when I walked up, and I dug for a notebook and pen. "The remains were discovered when a university employee came outside to dump the garbage early this morning."

I scribbled, looking around for a traumatized janitor while Aaron talked about the forensics team's deconstruction of the dumpster's contents.

When he offered a thank you and turned back toward the crime scene tape, I spotted a woman who was sitting by herself on the back steps of the union building, her arms wrapped tightly around her knees, her RAU-gold apron barely visible the way she was hunched over.

"Late to the party this morning, Clarke," Charlie Lewis purred from behind my left shoulder, and I shifted my attention to a group of students standing on the opposite side of the sidewalk for her benefit, not wanting to clue her in to the possibility that the woman who'd found the dead girl might be available for an interview.

"Some of us need our beauty sleep," I grinned, turning to face her. "We don't all fall out of bed HD-ready like you do, Charlie."

She rolled her green eyes and shook her head, her perfectly-coiffed bob not swaying. "Flattery will get you nowhere," she said. "I have a lead on this girl you won't believe. And you can see it at noon with everyone else."

"Fabulous. That gives me plenty of time to run down something better before press time," I said, watching Aaron over her shoulder. He cut the tape and motioned for the crowd to stay put. They were moving the body.

"Speaking of," I said, stepping around her. "Excuse me for a second."

I hobbled quickly to the back end of the coroner's van, craning my neck for a glimpse of the stretcher. Peering at corpses wasn't my favorite thing about my job, but was sometimes a necessary evil. Without a name to attach to the story, I needed to be able to describe the victim.

I saw dark hair, matted and strewn with something that looked like shredded lettuce.

Then the medical examiners lifted the gurney and the early-morning sunlight flashed off a large bracelet on her wrist. Who kills a coed and doesn't steal her oversized bling?

Wait—a big flashy bracelet. Like the one Eckersly bought his girlfriend?

I elbowed past the cameraman from Channel Ten, not caring about catching a glare and a muttered curse in reply. I managed to get a good look at the victim's face.

Holy shit.

Allison. The girl from the campaign office.

"No." The word popped out before I could stop it and I bit my tongue, staring at the paramedic who'd stepped up to the back of the ambulance and obstructed my view like his midsection might suddenly sprout a window.

I closed my eyes, trying to erase the image of the girl's expressionless face from the backs of my eyelids. I'd only met her the one time. Maybe I was wrong. But my gut said I wasn't. Why was a Grayson campaign intern dead in a RAU dumpster?

I spun on my heel and winced when my ankle protested, steadying myself for a second and starting back toward the steps where I'd seen the woman I suspected had found the body.

When she wasn't there, I sighed, but then saw her white and gold baseball cap disappearing through a door further down the side of the building. I hobbled faster, trying to catch up.

Checking over my shoulder, I could see Charlie with her mic in a medical examiner's face. Channel Ten was talking to the kids gathered on the quad. I pulled the door open and ducked inside, finding myself in a large room with a fireplace on one wall and several groupings of overstuffed furniture that had probably survived the Reagan era. I saw the woman huddled in a ball in the corner of a sofa next to the fireplace.

I slowed my steps as I approached her, experience telling me she might startle easily after such a traumatic experience.

"Hi," I said, my press credentials in my hand, but dangling at my side. "I'm Nichelle. That was a pretty terrible thing to see. Did you find her?"

Upon closer inspection, I put her age closer to the girl in the dumpster's than my own. Jesus. She was probably a student, too, doing work-study at the union.

She didn't answer me at first, hugging her knees with her legs crossed at the ankle, whimpering so softly I wasn't sure if I imagined it.

"I just opened the door to put the bags in," she said. "I can't reach the lid. And her hand fell out. Her hand. I touched it and she was so cold. I screamed and screamed, and someone came to call the police. She was so pale. They pulled her out. Her neck had a funny bruise. Just a purple line. She wasn't even wearing a coat. Just her tank top and jeans and that tacky bracelet. And it was cold this morning. So cold." She stopped and let her head drop to her knees. "I wish I could reach the lid."

"The bracelet was a little on the gaudy side," I said, wondering if she'd gotten a good look at it and making a note to ask Aaron about the bruising around the victim's neck.

"The bracelet didn't go," she mumbled. "Why would a girl that classy wear fake diamonds?"

"Fake?" I eased myself down onto the edge of the sofa. My ankle wasn't complaining much, but it needed a rest.

"As a Rolex hanging in a trenchcoat," she looked up.

"You're sure?"

"My father has worked for the Rothschild family for almost thirty years. That bracelet was fake. What does it matter? Her arm fell out of the dumpster! Right in my face. Someone killed her. Maybe right here on campus."

She resumed rocking and whimpering, and I pondered that. Eckersly hadn't given her a fake bracelet, so scratch that. But why would a girl like Allison have a gaudy fake tennis bracelet on? Did someone kill her for the bracelet and leave it when they got a better look at it? I shoved the thought aside. I was more likely to get a personal one-of-a-kind masterpiece from Christian Louboutin himself than that was to be true. Way too coincidental.

I asked for the girl's name and jotted it down, not sure I'd need it. She'd been through enough for one day. Most of what she'd told me I'd have to confirm elsewhere. It had been chilly that morning, which meant a scantily-clad corpse would be cold no matter if it had been in the dumpster thirty minutes or twelve hours. I'd have to wait for the autopsy report to get time of death.

I thanked her and headed back outside, nearly walking into Charlie when I opened the door.

"There you are!" she practically shouted. "Would you mind moving your heap out of my way? Some of us have actual work to do today."

Oops. I'd figured she'd hang around for a while getting extra footage.

"Sorry, Charlie." I hobbled toward my car. Her camera guy was in the van's driver's seat, and he looked irritated, too.

"What were you doing in there?" She kept pace with me, arching an eyebrow at my limp, but not asking about it.

"Bathroom," I said.

"Bullshit." She laughed. "You are a lousy liar, Clarke. But keep all the secrets you want. You've got nothing on me today. Just don't miss the noon broadcast."

"We'll see." I knew Allison worked for the Grayson campaign already, but I wasn't telling her that. And I had bigger things to worry about if Charlie was onto the senator. Shit.

I peeled out of the parking space. I'd have to be in the office in front of a TV at noon. Just in case.

Checking the clock, I knew I had better than three hours to get the body discovery ready to go on the website. What else could I find out in the meantime? The dead girl was connected to Grayson, and Grayson was connected to Kyle's case. I was sure of it.

I rummaged in my bag for my cell phone and called Kyle, really grateful for the first time to have my ex in Richmond. No way I'd have an ATF agent's cell number under any other circumstance.

"What's up?" he said when he picked up.

"You have time for coffee?" I asked, thinking about the stamp thingies I'd hidden under the loose floorboard in my coat closet that morning. I was glad I'd never gotten around to reporting that to my landlord. It was damned handy for keeping things hidden. Better than a safe.

"Actually, yes. IT is working a bug out of our computer system this morning, so I'm staring at papers and twiddling my thumbs," he said. "You hear any more from your walking buddy?"

"Give it a rest, Kyle," I said. "It's unattractive, this territorial thing. Who I walk or do anything else with is just big fat none of your business. But I need to talk to you. You're sure Billings is your guy on the Amesworth murder?"

"You heard Corry ask for them to no-bond him, right? How often does that happen?"

"Almost never." But even if Senator Grayson didn't kill the lobbyist, he was into something he shouldn't be. Possibly more so than the rest of his cohorts on Capitol Hill, though who could really tell about that? Maybe he was just dumb enough to get caught. My gut was surer every hour that all this had something to do with Kyle's big contraband cigarette investigation, though.

But how was I supposed to convince Kyle of that without confessing to a federal agent that I'd broken into a senator's house?

"Just come meet me at Thompson's—it's a little coffee shop on West Cary," I said. "Ten minutes?" I'd figure something out.

"Twenty."

I hung up and shoved the phone back into my bag.

What did I know? Nothing I could prove.

What was I pretty sure of? That Allison, a volunteer on Senator Grayson's campaign, was not dead in a dumpster because of a failed robbery or a random coed slaying. I'd bet my favorite Manolos on that. But why was she dead, and who killed her? I had a feeling that was the key to this whole mess. And I had no idea what Charlie was so excited about, so I needed to find the answer quickly.

I flipped through mental notecards on the case, beginning with Amesworth, the lobbyist. On the surface, suspecting that he was killed by someone involved in bribing Grayson didn't make sense, because all the players should have been on the same team. So something went wrong. That was plausible. Maybe Grayson wanted out. Maybe Amesworth was shaking James Billings, the tobacco company executive, down for more money to support the lifestyle the *Telegraph's* photo library told me Amesworth enjoyed. Except Joey didn't think Billings was the killer, and neither did I, really. Plus, he was on house arrest. If he'd killed the girl, Kyle would be able to place him at the scene.

Then there was Eckersly, the tobacco farmer who shared a proclivity for expensive call girls with the senator.

I parked in the coffee shop lot fifteen minutes early, blowing out a frustrated sigh. I knew just enough to know there was something there, but I needed the middle piece of my puzzle that would pull it all together.

Hopefully Kyle had it, and I could convince him to share.

* * *

Kyle looked good. My stomach gave an involuntary flip when his ice blue eyes met mine across the coffee shop. I tried not to notice the biceps ringed by the sleeves of his fitted blue Polo, or the way his torso tapered at the waist like a cartoon superhero's, and I squelched the little voice singsonging a reminder that he seemed more than a little interested in picking up where we'd left off. I didn't date cops. And Joey was a way better kisser than I remembered Kyle being. Though one kiss wasn't exactly picking out china; not to mention his occupation not being exactly desirable.

Kyle ordered his coffee and I watched, not liking the way his eyes lit when he spun from the counter and saw that I'd been staring at his tight ass in his khakis.

"Enjoying the view?"

"Knock it off. Old habits die hard."

"Sure they do. Especially when old habits have a bitch of a fitness test for work every three months and spend hours in the gym every day." He sat down in the chair across from me and not-so-subtly flexed a bicep as he sipped his latte. "Is ogling all you wanted me for, or can I do something else for you?"

"Your head has definitely gotten bigger," I said.

"It's not the only thing."

"Oh my God, Kyle," I thumped my cup down on the table and laughed in spite of myself. "Are you twelve? Shut up. No, don't shut up; tell me about Billings."

He sat back in the chair and laced his hands together behind his head.

"I'm afraid I can't go on the record with the press about an open investigation, Miss Clarke." He winked.

His ability to push my buttons had not changed.

"Dammit, Kyle," I said. "I have a ton of work to do, two different bosses breathing down my neck, and a story that has more rabbit trails than Mr.

MacGregor's garden. I don't need it on the record today. I just need to know why you're so sure it's him."

He stared for a long minute, not saying a word.

"He's part of the other thing you were telling me about, too, isn't he?" I asked. "The contraband stuff and the stamps. That's why you picked him up so fast." He twisted his mouth to one side, and I knew I was onto something.

"Just tell me!" I didn't really mean to shout that. People turned to look and I ducked my head. "I heard you had a weapon. Do you have positive ballistics? Any other evidence? I need to know whether or not to believe you before I have a stroke."

"Same old Nicey." He laughed. "Off the record?"

"Sure." I made a show of tucking my pen and my cell phone back into my bag.

"The bullet that killed Amesworth was fired from a very special gun. A Sharps eighteen-fifty-nine Confederate Carbine rifle. It's a piece that was used by Civil War sharpshooters. Very expensive to manufacture back then, and consequently very rare. Like, there were only about two thousand of them made a hundred and fifty years ago."

"And Billings has one of these rifles?"

"He does, but it's missing from the rack in his office where he keeps it. He says he loaned it out, but won't say to whom. He hasn't filed an insurance claim on it, either."

Hmmm. Rare gun. Suddenly missing.

"That's pretty damning," I said. "But why the hell would anyone use a gun like that to murder someone?"

"This guy is a real bastard," Kyle leaned his elbows on the table. "I've been working this contraband case since before I left Dallas. It's one of the reasons they transferred me here."

"He's the vice president of a company that makes money off of a product that kills people," I said. "He's not supposed to be a stand-up guy. That doesn't mean he murdered someone."

"You have a better explanation for his gun vanishing just after someone was shot with one just like it?"

I considered that for a second.

"No. But how did you know he had one, anyway?" I asked. "Guns don't have to be registered in Virginia."

"I got a lucky break. The new family smoking prevention law says the FDA has oversight of tobacco manufacturing. I sat down with the inspector who'd been over to Raymond Garfield a few days before Amesworth was killed, and we got to talking about guns. His father was a collector. He was telling me about this beauty in Billings's office, and then this guy turns up, shot with the very same antique gun. After years of work, I finally have Billings on something."

"That's a lucky break." It sure sounded like he had Billings on the weapon. But Grayson had those stamps. I sipped my coffee, mulling that over.

What if Billings was telling the truth? If the gun really had been loaned to someone, why wouldn't he just cough up their name to save his ass? Because the someone was Senator Grayson and it might make the ATF wonder why they were so buddy-buddy?

"What do you know about Ted Grayson?" I asked.

He raised his eyebrows.

"United States Senator for the Commonwealth of Virginia, fairly middle of the road politically, historically not a fan of guns or cigarettes."

"Thank you, Wikipedia," I said. "But I've been poking around in his backroom dealings, and there's something fishy."

"What do you have on him?"

"Nothing concrete," I said, unable to come up with a single possible way that I should know he had those stamps. "I think he's taking bribe money. I've been wondering if it's from Billings. But everything about this is so convoluted, I'm not sure of anything. My gut says there's something more here, though. I don't think Billings is your murderer." I sipped my coffee.

"Well, I'm very glad all your years of training in criminal investigation have led you to that conclusion." He didn't even have the decency to sound annoyed. He sounded amused.

"I'm sorry, have we forgotten my ability to channel Nancy Drew?" I asked.

"Beginner's luck." He waved a hand.

Asshole. I folded my arms over my chest and glared.

"You're pretty sure of yourself for a guy with no murder weapon," I said. "Don't you even think it's worth looking into anything else?"

"I'm looking into plenty else," he said. "My guys are checking the tire tracks from the body dump against Billings's cars as we speak. I'm almost certain Billings had a couple of folks from the House of Delegates on his payroll, and I think that's why Amesworth is dead. But come on, Nicey. How am I going to go back to the office and open a file on a sitting U.S. senator—one who's in a smackdown of a reelection campaign at the moment, let's not forget—because my ex-girlfriend told me she has a hunch? You're going to get me laughed right out to the podunk sheriff's department."

"I'm not asking you to open a file. I just think you should consider the possibility that you've got the wrong guy. He might be an asshole, and he might well be a criminal. I don't know what you've got on him with the cigarette case, but think about it, Kyle: what does contraband tobacco carry? Five years? If he's not a murderer, he doesn't deserve to be called one."

"I've been doing this for a while now, Nicey," he said, softening his voice. "If he wasn't a murderer, he'd give us the gun."

"I think you're wrong." I sounded petulant, and I wasn't proud of it, but I couldn't really tell him why, either. I wasn't sure I knew myself. "But I'm not going to convince you of that, am I?"

"Not based on your gut, you're not," he said.

"Thanks for coming to meet me." I stood.

"Have dinner with me tomorrow night," he said, getting to his feet and gesturing for me to walk ahead of him to the door.

"I have work to do," I said.

"Come on, Nicey, don't be that way. I'll buy. Anywhere you want to go. I still need you to show me where they have good food around here."

He pushed the door open and I walked through it, sighing as I looked back at him. He was a good friend to have. And he did fill out those khakis nicely.

"Bring me what you have on Billings," I said.

"Do what?"

"I'll have dinner with you, but I want copies of your file," I said. "I won't run it, and no one will know I have it. I'll even give them back. I can't shake this feeling, though. So prove me wrong. Let me see what you've got."

He stood on the sidewalk in front of the coffee shop, shading his eyes and staring at me for a long minute.

"It's been a long time," he said. "How can I be sure you won't throw away my career for a scoop?"

"You can't," I said. "But you want me to believe you. Believe me."

He shook his head. "I'll pick you up at six-thirty."

"I'll be ready for some after-dinner reading."

I unlocked the car, annoyed that I'd spent a half hour and had nothing on my new murder victim to show for it.

I climbed behind the wheel and dug my cell phone out. I had four texts and three missed calls from Bob.

I clicked the messages open.

"Your dead girl was a prostitute. Channel Four just blew the top off a college call girl ring. Where the hell are you?"

Double shit. Charlie had dropped the noon time slot into conversation twice. I should have known she was lying. And Bob hated nothing worse than losing to the TV folks on a big story.

16

"Tell me one more time why you were busy with the ATF and a murder case the CA himself is calling a slam dunk while Charlie Lewis was digging up a call girl ring that makes sorority row look like the goddamned Chicken Ranch?" Bob's face was nearly purple, and despite cringing because his anger was almost never directed at me, I worried about his blood pressure and his heart.

"I'm sorry," I said, wondering how Charlie had known that and whether she was closer on my heels than I wanted to think. I dismissed the thought quicker than I usually would, largely because Charlie was the least of my problems. "I didn't know."

"Except that we pay you to know," Bob practically roared. "Dammit, Nichelle! Do you have any idea how stupid it makes me look when I spend months—*months*—going to bat for you with the suits upstairs and you turn right around and drop a ball the size of Mercury? Les was practically glowing when Andrews gave him the go-ahead to send Shelby over to the campus to knock on doors. They even made Parker go with her because he knows so many people on the faculty over there."

I closed my eyes for a long minute, inhaling for a ten count.

"Bob, I'm working on something," I said, holding my voice in check and hoping it would calm him down. "When have I ever let you down?"

"Today." He sat back in the chair and sighed. "This morning, you let me down. If Charlie knows it, you could know it, too. Nobody in this town is better at covering cops than you are, kiddo. But you're only as good as what you're getting for me next, and you know it. You're not the only one Les is gunning for."

I nodded. The *Telegraph* was Bob's entire reason for getting up the morning, but he lived under constant threat of being forced out by Les, who was as smarmy and backstabbing as they come. I couldn't imagine the newsroom without Bob, and it wouldn't be a place I wanted to work.

"I'll apologize to Andrews myself," I said. "But you have to believe me. Grayson is crooked. And I am *thisclose*," I said, holding up my thumb and index finger, barely touching them together, "to finding something that pulls all this together. The girl, too, possibly."

"No." Bob shook his head and leveled a don't-fuck-with-me-on-this glare at me. "Ted Grayson is a politician. Rick Andrews, who happens to be the publisher of this newspaper, is one of his biggest campaign contributors, which you would know if you'd asked our actual politics reporter for information about him. You will back off of Grayson this minute. You will throw yourself into the call girl scandal and find me something that will redeem us both for today. You will work with Shelby for the duration of the story, since she's already been assigned to it. And you will not put another toe out of line, or Shelby Taylor will be my new courts reporter. Are we clear?"

I returned the stare, biting my lip to stave off the pricking in the backs of my eyes that meant tears were threatening.

"Yes, sir."

"Get to work." He turned to his computer screen and flipped it on, dismissing me.

I walked out of his office and saw the back of Les' balding head bobbing through the cubicles toward the break room, but managed to keep myself from chasing him down and delivering a swift *ap-chagi* to his ass. I couldn't even tell if I was madder that he was still trying to help Shelby get my job or that he was after Bob's. I could probably go somewhere else, but Bob...If Les managed to convince Andrews that Bob wasn't still at the top of his game, he'd be pushed into retirement. I didn't think Bob would last long without the newspaper.

I limped to my desk, determined to dig up something on the call girl ring. Shelby could run around RAU banging on doors with Parker all day long, and she could sleep her way into my byline, but she didn't have my connections. I snatched up the phone, feeling stupid for not figuring it out sooner. Lakshmi had told me she was a grad student there, for Christ's sake. Apparently, so was Allison. She also worked for Grayson's campaign, which tied him to it at least marginally. But was her earnest admiration of the senator professional, or had she fallen for her client?

I called Aaron first, and left him a message begging for any five minutes he had that day.

Next, I dialed the head of security at the campus, who, not surprisingly, was in a meeting. But he'd always seemed to like me well enough, and he was an old-school guy who preferred print to TV.

I called Evans at the FBI next. He answered.

"Are you the only law enforcement agency in town who isn't working on the call girl thing?" I asked.

"Not federal jurisdiction, as far as I can see, but it is quite a story," he said. "What can I do for you today, Miss Clarke?"

"Why did you call to tip me off about Billings's arrest?" I asked.

"I thought you'd be interested in it," he said. "You called me asking for information about the dead lobbyist and bribery investigations."

"You know about the bribes, right?" I asked, tired of skirting the issue and in desperate need of an answer. Though I wasn't sure what I'd do with it if I got it. Bob and I had a special bond, but he didn't love anything more than he loved the paper. He would absolutely hand Shelby my job if something I did put his in jeopardy.

"What do you know?" Evans asked.

"I don't have time for this," I said. "You're on Grayson, Kyle Miller at the ATF is on Billings. Got it. But there's something here that ties the two of them together, and it has to do with these two corpses."

"Which two corpses? The lobbyist and the call girl? What's the girl got to do with anything?"

"I was hoping you could tell me that." I sighed. "Look, I don't have a positive I.D., but I'm nearly a hundred percent sure that she's an intern on the Grayson campaign, and she tipped me off about the bribes, though she didn't realize she was doing it. I also hear there's a good chance Grayson's name might be in the call girls' little black book. And he's in the middle of a fight for his career. That's entirely too coincidental, don't you think?"

"Where'd you get that?" Evans asked, his voice suddenly tight. "About Grayson and the call girl?"

"I pieced it together from a couple of interviews."

I didn't know if Grayson was sleeping with Allison or Lakshmi or both, and I wasn't sure I could trust anything, given that my earnest-campaign-worker source had turned out to be a prostitute. And was now dead. The only person I knew hadn't done it was Lucinda Eckersly, because if she strangled a young, athletic girl, I'd deliver my beat to Shelby on a platter and probably never get out of bed again.

Evans was silent for a long minute.

"Let me see what I can find," he said. "I won't talk to another reporter before I talk to you, but this could take a while."

Thanking him for his time, I hung up. Fabulous. Except I didn't have a while.

"Dammit." I grabbed my bag and hurried to the elevator, ignoring my ankle and trying to remember if I had any Advil stashed in the car.

"Where are you off to?" Eunice asked as I stepped onto the elevator. "I thought Bob was going to bust something when he couldn't find you this morning."

"I've got to save my job from Shelby Taylor," I said. "And somewhere around here, there's a murderer who needs catching."

"You leave the murderers to the police, huh, sugar?" she called as the doors closed and saved me from having to reply.

"They think they've got him already," I muttered, pulling my cell phone out of my pocket and tapping out a text to Parker. I paused to send it as I pulled the car out of the garage and got my signal back.

"Keep Shelby away from the math building."

There was a call girl in the statistics department I wanted to get some answers from. My phone binged.

"Chasing her up and down Greek row," his reply read. "This is bullshit. She's waving her press badge under their noses. No one's talking."

"Let her go," I tapped back. "Sorry you're wasting your day. I'll fill you in later."

"Better be a hell of a story. You can buy drinks."

"Capital Ale @ 7. Bring Mel."

If I didn't find something by the time Charlie went on the air again at six, I'd be toasting my new job at the copy desk—or my outright unemployment.

* * *

I scanned the office directory in the math building for the professor Lakshmi had mentioned, hoping he'd know where I could find her. Three-oh-six. Stairs. Yay.

My ankle protested the whole way up, but I found the office, door ajar.

I tapped lightly.

"Come in," a gruff man's voice called.

I poked my head around the doorframe, smiling at the gray-haired, tweed-clad man I assumed was Professor Gaskins.

"Can I help you?" he asked.

"I'm looking for a student of yours, actually, and I could swear she told me she works in your office," I fibbed. "Lakshmi?"

He smiled. "She's my teaching assistant. One of the most brilliant grad students I've ever taught."

"Do you know where I might be able to find her?" I asked. "It's kind of important that I talk to her."

"She usually teaches a freshman course for me this time of day," he said. "Something tells me it might not be packed today, though. It's downstairs in the auditorium."

"Thanks."

I limped back down and opened the lecture hall door, Lakshmi's sweet-as-bells voice ringing clear in the empty hallway. She smiled confused recognition as I slipped into a seat in the back row. There were three students down front, all boys, hanging on her every word.

"Well," she said. "I think that's enough for today, guys. I'll see you Thursday."

"Do you remember me?" I asked once we were alone and face to face.

"From the card game, right?" she asked. "I didn't know you were a student here."

"I'm not." I held her gaze. "I'm a reporter at the *Telegraph*, and I'm working on a story about the call girl who was found in the dumpster outside this morning. I think you might be able to tell me something about that."

Her expression faltered for a split second before she stretched her lips into a thin line and started gathering up her books. "I have no idea what you're talking about."

"I think you do," I said. "I heard your friend the other night making some rather snide comments about your companion and how much he was paying you. I think other people are paying you, too. And I think some of the same people might have been involved with the victim of last night's murder. How do you know you're not next?" Nothing like a healthy dose of terror to make people spill their guts. "I won't use your name. But if the cops get to whoever's behind this, you might live to get your Master's. Talk to me."

Lakshmi shoved the books into a canvas bag and sighed, her eyes on the desk. When she looked up at me, they were full of tears.

"My dad left the government to work in experimental energy. His company went under two years ago," she said. "I would have gotten kicked out of school because we couldn't pay the tuition. He made too much the year before for me to qualify for any aid, and they didn't care that he'd lost everything. Allison offered me a way to stay on campus. She made it sound like fun, and the money was amazing."

"She was in charge?"

"I don't think so, really. She was president of the Delta Kappas when we were undergrads. I took her the money at the end of the night. But I got the idea she was fronting for someone."

I pulled out a notebook and jotted that down.

"Was Senator Grayson a client?"

Lakshmi nodded. "My client, for a while. Allison thought it was funny, because of my major."

"So you were the only girl Grayson saw?"

"A lot of the clients had certain girls they liked, and they liked the girls to be 'theirs,' too, so we had to be careful about what we said. Some of the guys are real bigshots. But either they were old and bald and wanted a young, pretty girl on their arm for some function, or they had wives who weren't into the same things they were in the bedroom. Mostly, I got those guys."

"Ted Grayson?" I guessed.

"He likes his women bound, gagged, and in a little bit of pain, for the most part."

My eyebrows went up.

"Pain?"

"Not torture, or even really heavy masochism," she said. "But he likes to pull hair, hit you, push you around. Pretty tame stuff, on the whole, but still nothing he wanted anyone to know. He pays a pretty penny to have that secret kept."

"How much?"

"Five thousand a night," she said. "I kept three, took two to Allison. I don't know where any of it went after that."

I nodded and kept scribbling. Two thousand dollars a night and multiple girls, it sounded like. So what the hell was with the fake diamonds?

"How often did you see Grayson?" I asked.

"Once a week or so," she said. "Until he got tired of me. I don't miss him. He was creepy. Treated me like I was his property. About the only thing he ever did talk to me about was how beautiful a prize I was, and how I had to stay 'unspoiled' for him."

I jotted her words down, but the other half of my brain was spinning through the numbers. Twenty thousand dollars a month wouldn't exactly be easy to hide. So Grayson sold his vote to the devil to feed his sexual fantasies. And Allison knew this, yet still worked in his campaign office. Blackmail? Was that why she was dead?

"You don't happen to know who got Grayson as a client after you, do you?" I asked.

"I think Allison did." Lakshmi shook her head. "You don't think Ted has anything to do with her death, do you?"

"She was strangled," I said, another thought popping through my head. "Did he go for the bedroom asphyxiation bit?"

"Not with me," Lakshmi said. "But I wouldn't say it's impossible."

I scribbled. Holy shit.

"What am I going to do?" Lakshmi dropped her head into her hands and sobbed, and I wasn't sure she was even talking to me. "I was getting out. My parents are back on their feet and I don't need the cash anymore, and I was going to cut ties with the whole thing after Christmas. Now my whole life is ruined."

"As far as I'm concerned, you're a confidential source," I said. "I'm not the only reporter in town who knows Allison was a prostitute, but if I were you? I'd get suddenly ill, take the rest of the semester off, and hope no one turns your name in. Allison's dead, right? Lay low for a while. It might have the bonus effect of keeping you alive."

She nodded. "What's one semester?"

"Not much compared to a lifetime," I said. "Thanks, Lakshmi. I wasn't kidding when I said I liked you. Good luck."

"You won't print my name?"

"You have my word."

"Consider me gone." She grabbed the bag and headed out the door.

Grayson was taking bribes from Billings. Evans had all but confirmed it. And I knew why. But there were still so many questions.

I was running out of time to find the answers.

Trudy's words about Calhoun came to mind, and I wondered if his local campaign office was open. And who I might find there.

17

I struck out at the Calhoun campaign office and trudged back to the newsroom, racking my brain for anything about Allison or Grayson I might have missed. I wondered for a second if I wanted the truth, or if I wanted the story I'd been chasing. Which could turn out to be two different things, if Trudy and Kyle were right.

I pulled out the notes from my conversation with Lakshmi and flipped open my computer. At least I'd managed to pull something out on the call girl thing. Bob would have to love an exclusive with one of the girls. Parker hadn't been in his office when I passed, so Shelby was probably still dragging him all over the campus, which meant she didn't have anything.

An arm falling from a dumpster at Richmond American University Thursday morning led Richmond police to a call girl ring operating out of the campus. A former member of the group spoke to the Richmond Telegraph *on condition of anonymity, weaving a tale of powerful men and large stacks of cash.*

"Some of the guys are real bigshots. But either they were old and bald and wanted a young, pretty girl on their arm for some function, or they had wives who weren't into the same things they were in the bedroom," the source said. "I made five thousand [dollars] a night. I kept three, and gave two to [the victim]."

The source identified the victim as a leader in the prostitution operation, but said she was unsure who else might have been involved.

I finished with some scattered information about Allison and her murder, withholding her involvement with Grayson until I knew if anyone else had it yet. I smiled as I sent it to Bob. The smile faded when I clicked into my browser to check Charlie's coverage.

"Son of a bitch."

I had a call girl as an anonymous source and a link to the sorority house.

Charlie had the madam. On camera. Being led out of an ivy-covered building in handcuffs, Aaron standing at the foot of the steps to ward off the gaggle of reporters.

I watched the footage with a building wave of nausea.

The goddamned dean was running the whole thing, huge white letters across the bottom of my screen screamed, right under "Channel Four exclusive investigation." Charlie had officially kicked my ass. The camera panned to the left and I groaned out loud.

Shelby was talking to a uniformed RAU security officer, scribbling as fast as she could and grinning like a Kardashian in front of a paparazzi.

Why the hell hadn't I heard they were making an arrest?

I fumbled for my scanner. No static. I fiddled with the switch and shook it.

Dead battery.

"Dammit!" It was louder than I intended, and Melanie popped her head over the wall between our cubes.

"You miss a fire sale at Saks or something, doll?" she asked.

"I wish," I said. "I missed the story of the...well, of the day. Maybe the month. But really, when you're only as good as what you have today, what the hell does it matter?"

I dropped my head onto my desk with a dull thunk. I hate losing. And I'm not good at it.

"Oh, shit. Is that the dean of the college of fine arts?" Melanie asked from behind me. I had forgotten she was an RAU alum.

"Yup."

"Running a call girl ring? Daaaamn." She drug out the word and wolf-whistled for good measure. "That's one sexy story. No pun intended."

"Yup."

I got up and turned toward Bob's office, figuring it better to throw myself on the sword than to wait for him to come hunting for me.

"What have you got to say for yourself?" he asked, not turning his eyes from the monitor— which I knew without looking was streaming Charlie's feed—when I tapped on the open door.

"I screwed up." I dropped into my chair. "I could say my scanner died and I was busy trying to get the exclusive interview I just sent you, but you don't care, and it doesn't really matter. Charlie beat me. And it's making me sick to my stomach how badly she beat me."

"She's got you whipped today," he said, leaning on one hand and massaging his temples. "Andrews called me ten minutes ago. Shelby's leading page one with your story going as a companion piece. And she's on the courthouse for a trial period effective Monday. I'm sorry, kid."

I closed my eyes.

"This thing with Grayson—"

Bob's head snapped up. "I told you to back off. Nichelle, I couldn't love you more if I'd raised you, and you know it. But I swear to God, if you tell me you blew this story and made me look like a fool in front of the wunderkind upstairs chasing politics after I told you to drop it, I'll put you on leave. I might even fire you."

"I wasn't chasing Grayson today," I said. "I was interviewing the hooker. I tried to give Grayson to Trudy after I talked to you about it last week, but she doesn't want it. She said she didn't believe it and wouldn't take it 'til after the election. But there's something there, Bob."

"You have enough to do keeping the part of your job you have left," he said. "You don't need to try to do someone else's, too. Trudy knows D.C. better that most of the guys who work up there. Let it go. Pull something out on this and I'll put you on it with her after the election, if you want."

But...

The word didn't make it out of my mouth. Bob had never been so mad at me. More than that, he was disappointed. And that sucked.

"Yes, sir."

I went back to my desk, checking my watch.

I wasn't due to meet Parker for two hours, but I wanted to be in the newsroom for Shelby to gloat over when they got back about as much as I wanted to trade my Louboutins for Birkenstocks.

I stuffed my laptop and charger into my bag and told Melanie goodnight.

"We all have shit days," she said, laying a sympathetic hand on my arm. "You'll get her tomorrow. It will be okay."

I nodded, thinking about Shelby covering the courthouse and wanting to kick something.

"I have to get out of here," I choked out.

"Wine. Sleep. Kick ass," she called after me.

Halfway to the garage, I had a flash of the bracelet on Allison's wrist.

Lucinda Eckersly said her son's whore liked diamonds. But the girl who'd found the body said the bracelet on Allison's wrist was fake. It didn't make sense, unless she'd sold the real one, maybe? What if Grayson was still possessive? Or Eckersly was offering to take Allison away from the mess she'd gotten herself into? Bob's purple face followed close on the heels of that.

But Eckersly wasn't Grayson. I desperately needed a way to redeem myself. Answers about the dead girl would do it. Maybe I could find them in the huge white house.

* * *

I squealed to a stop in front of the Eckersly home, ignoring my sore ankle as I sprinted up the steps.

I yanked the doorbell pull and after about a minute, I reached for the cord again, but Doreen swung the door inward before I could pull it.

"Miss Clarke! How nice of you to call again." She beamed, the picture of old southern hospitality. In this part of the world, people weren't expected to call for an appointment or schedule a meeting. Dropping by was not only acceptable, but welcome. "Miss Lucinda doesn't get much company nowadays, and she liked you."

"I'm glad." I smiled. "She's a firecracker. I liked her, too. Is she up for visitors this evening?"

"She's in the great room watching TV. Did you hear about the poor little girl they found in the dumpster this morning? Such a tragedy."

"Indeed." I stepped through the door.

"I'll just tell Miss Lucinda you're here," Doreen said, scuttling off into the reaches of the enormous house.

I browsed the art and artifacts decking the walls, my eyes coming to rest on a gun rack over the doors that led to the dining room. There were three long-barrel rifles in it. They all looked old, and two of them had ornate carvings on the stocks. Like the one William Eckersly held in the photo in the study.

"Nichelle!" The raspy, wispy voice came from behind me, and I turned with a smile, filing the gun in the back of my mind and grinning wider when I saw that she didn't have a lit cigarette. Maybe I could talk to her for a bit and not risk getting blown up.

"Mrs. Eckersly." I reached down and squeezed her outstretched hand. "How are you?"

She gave me a shrewd once over.

"I think you know how I am, or you wouldn't be here, sugar."

I nodded. "I suspected as much."

"Come on in." She took a drag off her oxygen mask and wheeled herself into the front parlor. She stopped her chair opposite a sofa that would comfortably seat seven and gestured for me to sit down.

"Your son knew Allison?" I asked, reaching into my bag for a notebook and pen.

"Was that her name?" Lucinda chuckled. "Fits her. Perky little thing. That's Billy's whore. Wouldn't say I was sorry, either, but I'm a Christian woman and she was somebody's little girl. Sad situation. Billy tore out of here when the news first came on this morning, and I haven't heard from him since."

I pictured the man from the photos I'd seen on my last visit, wondering about the marks on Allison's neck for a moment. Eckersly was a big guy, and a farmer. Which meant he probably had strong hands. That comment about the men liking to think the girls were "theirs" could go both ways. What if Eckersly found out Allison was seeing Grayson?

"Do you know if Billy knew that Allison saw other men?" I asked.

"I don't know why she'd need to. Billy spent fifteen thousand dollars last month on her 'fees' and dinners and gifts. What twenty-two-year-old girl needs more than that?"

"So he didn't think she had other clients?"

She snorted softly. "He didn't think he was her client. Damned fool thinks he was in love with her. Told me the other night he wasn't paying her to screw him, he was helping put her through school. 'The William Eckersly scholarship program,' he said."

"That's a hell of an application process," I muttered.

"You can say that again," she answered.

"I'm sorry," I said. "I didn't mean for you to hear that."

"Never apologize to anyone for telling the truth, child," she said. "If there's one thing I've learned in near-eighty years walking this Earth, it's that."

"You are very direct," I stopped writing and smiled at her.

"It's a privilege of old age. I get to say what I think and not give a damn whether anybody likes it or not."

"Mrs. Eckersly, did your son kill Allison?"

She cackled. "There you go, sugar. Just honesty. No, I don't believe he did. Thought she was the love of his life. I'm pretty sure the reason he bought her that big diamond bracelet was that he was eyeballing the wedding rings."

"Do you know where he was between midnight and six this morning?"

"I'm sure he was in bed."

"But you don't know that for a fact? You didn't see him come in?" I tried to keep the excitement out of my voice. It would undoubtedly be weeks before the police would be able to get a list of clients out of the madam, because she'd have top-notch attorneys who would keep her from giving them anything incriminating, so they'd have to get warrants and find it. Which meant they wouldn't be looking at Eckersly for a good while. Maybe there was a way to get back on Andrews' good side sitting right in front of me. Sex was a powerful motive for murder. What if he'd found out she was sleeping with other men and just gone apeshit and throttled her? Strangling was almost always a crime of passion.

"I didn't see him come in, but he often stays in the fields or in the city until after I go to bed." Lucinda looked wary.

"Would Doreen have heard him come in?"

"Possibly." Lucinda didn't snap, but I could see the wheels turning. She was pissed at her son, but family is family, especially in the country. Power of attorney be damned, she didn't want him charged with murder.

"You're not going to tell me anything else, are you?" I closed my notebook.

She stared at the fireplace, focusing on the Eckersly family crest above the mantle. "Jesus. Do you really think my boy could have killed that girl?"

"I don't know, Mrs. Eckersly."

"Could you tell Doreen I need my pills?" She gripped the arm of the wheelchair, her voice wispier than usual.

Shit.

"Doreen!" I jumped to my feet and strode quickly to the door, ignoring the twinge in my ankle. "Mrs. Eckersly needs her medicine!"

Doreen bustled in with a silver tray holding a highball glass full of water and a saucer full of pills.

"Miss Lucinda," she fretted as she handed over the pills one at a time and held the water glass steadily against Mrs. Eckersly's lips. "You know better than to get yourself so worked up." She cut a glance at me. "I think you'd better go."

"Is she going to be all right?"

Doreen laid a protective hand on Lucinda's shoulder as Lucinda groped for her oxygen again.

"She needs to rest. I take good care of Mrs. Eckersly, Miss." She nodded to the door and fixed me with a positively shiver-worthy glare.

18

I was almost to the bar where I was supposed to meet Parker and Mel—early but craving a very large glass of Moscato—when my phone rang.

I fished it out of my bag with one hand, keeping my eyes on the increasingly heavy traffic in front of me as parking garages throughout the city began to empty.

"Clarke," I said, pressing it to my shoulder with one cheek.

"What is it your gut is telling you, again?" Kyle's words were clipped.

"What? Why? I thought you had your man."

"I thought I did, too, but the goddamn tire tracks don't match any vehicle Billings owns," he said. "So either you're right and he didn't do it, or I need to figure a way around this before the judge gets wind of this report. I'm searching rental car records for five states and pulling everything else I can think of, but so far I haven't found a damned thing. I've been at it for hours and everything's blurring together. The defense attorneys have the report and are requesting a meeting with the judge tomorrow morning. Can you come up here and talk me through this?"

So much for my glass of wine. "I'll be there in twenty minutes."

I stopped at a light and sent Parker a text.

"Change of plans. Rain check?"

I was to the next light when my cell phone binged his reply.

"No wound-licking. Shelby got lucky. Practically tripped over the cops leading the dean out."

"Changes nothing," I tapped back. "But thanks."

I pulled the car easily into a street space in front of the federal building a few minutes later. Most of the worker bees had gone home for the evening. Inside, I handed my I.D. to the guard at the desk and waited for Kyle to come escort me inside.

"Thanks." He flashed a tight grin as he opened the door for me.

"Don't mention it. It's not every day I get invited into the middle of a federal investigation, Mr. Special Agent. How much of this do I get on the record?"

"Can I answer that after I figure out what the hell's going on here?" He led me down a long, sterile hallway to a conference room and flipped on the lights, waving me toward a table stacked with file folders and boxes of records that looked like months—or years—worth of work.

"Holy shit, Kyle." I whistled. "What is Billings into?"

"Are we on the record?" He flattened his palms on the table and leaned toward me, his eyes probing.

I held his gaze for a long second.

Something worth promising him we weren't was in those folders. I could find a way to confirm what he gave me later.

"Not if you don't want to be."

"He's up to his ass in dirty money and shady deals." Kyle flipped open a folder and pushed it across the table. "He's even got connections in the goddamned Mafia. But he's a slippery sonofabitch. I've never been able to get anything to stick."

I inhaled sharply at his mention of the Mafia, flipping through eight-by-ten glossies of Billings in various places and with various people, scanning the images for Joey and hating that I felt a little sick at the idea. But it would explain how he knew what was going on.

"So you had him on the gun and you thought you'd gotten your big break," I said, thinking about the guns I'd seen in Eckersly's foyer. Kyle had said the one that killed Amesworth was rare, so I wasn't sure how likely it was that there was another one in the Richmond area, but it was worth bringing up. "That's why you went so hard at it with the prosecutor."

"If he gets off, he'll disappear," Kyle said. "Or insulate himself so well I'll never get at him again, and all this work will have been for nothing. So what have you got?"

I tapped my index finger on the black laminate table, still staring at the last photo. Billings was sitting at an outdoor cafe table with a man in a dark suit, and a young woman in large sunglasses whose face was partially hidden behind her hair. No Joey. Thank God. I wasn't supposed to care, but I did anyway.

I shook my head slowly as I raised my eyes to Kyle's. I knew that look. It was the same one that had gotten me to give up my virginity in a secluded spot along the banks of Lake Ray Hubbard.

Kyle was begging.

"I want an exclusive on the whole thing," I said. "Not just whatever we get on the murder, but all of this," I waved a hand at the records on the table. "The ATF talks to no one until the *Telegraph* runs the story. Print, not just online."

"I don't have any control over what the media relations people do," he said, but I could see his thought pattern clearly. He was figuring a way around it the same way he'd figured a way around my bra that long-ago July evening.

"You'll find a way." I flashed a grin and arched one eyebrow.

"I suppose I'll have to." He grinned back.

"All right," I leaned back in the chair. "I don't think Billings is your boy. Not on the murder."

"So you said. But why?"

"Well, for one, he's on house arrest. Was he at RAU in the wee hours this morning?"

"No, he was at home all night. I pull the reports every morning. Why?"

"Then he didn't kill Allison."

"Who?"

"Do you own a TV? The call girl at RAU. It's been all over since early this morning." I grimaced.

"All over the TV? But not the newspaper?" He tilted his head to one side.

"It's been a shit day."

He leaned his elbows on the table and dropped his eyelids halfway, smiling a slow smile that used to make my pulse flutter. I didn't want to admit it still did. "I could help with that."

"Slow down, Captain Hormones," I said, clearing my throat and dropping my eyes back to the photos. "I want my job back."

"You lost your job?" His mouth dropped open. "What the hell happened to you today?"

"Not all of it. Just half." I shook my head and tapped the pictures, pushing them back to the middle of the table. "I really don't want to talk about it. Who are these people?"

"New York Mafia, mostly," he said. "I told you, there's a contraband cigarette trafficking ring running the east coast that steals enough in tax money every year to run a medium-sized country. Well, Billings provides their product at a good rate for a cut of the action."

"How can he do that and still keep his job?"

"They have about thirty fronts set up, some of them as cigarette wholesalers," he said. "And they run an above-board operation in three different states. So on paper, Billings isn't doing anything he shouldn't. But some of the trucks are overweight." He dug through a box and produced a file folder full of weigh station reports. "Only the ones going from the Raymond Garfield factory to certain wholesalers. And only in South Carolina and New York, where the state taxes are some of the highest in the country."

"So there are more cartons in there than they're reporting," I said, flipping through the logs and comparing the weights. "How many cigarettes are there in three hundred pounds?"

"About a hundred and thirty-five thousand." Kyle said.

"And this isn't enough for a warrant?" I asked.

"Not with the kind of defense lawyers Billings can afford," Kyle sighed. "I know he's doing it, but they'll say the trucks were carrying...I don't know. Bananas. Luggage. Without an inspection of the contents, I can't prove they're not. And without knowing which trucks are carrying too much, I can't get a warrant to check them. I petitioned for one to cover the whole Raymond Garfield fleet for a month about a year ago, and the judge said there weren't grounds. Trucks turn up overweight every once in a while. These guys are good."

"And the Mafia is running this contraband tobacco thing?"

"There's a shit ton of money in it, and it takes massive organization," he said. "No one else could handle one this big. I've busted little one-off operations where people fake the tax stamps or just buy packs here, where the taxes are low, and resell them out of alleys in New York, where they're high. People buy a sixty-dollar carton of Marlboros in an alley for fifty dollars, and the thief still has fifteen in profit per carton because the taxes are so high there. But these guys...They wouldn't have this operation up and running if Billings wasn't supplying their product. There's no other way they could do this volume without it looking suspicious."

I nodded, flipping through the labels on the folders in the box, which were mostly numeric codes I didn't understand.

"And if you get him, you might get them," I said.

"Bingo. Organized crime is a tough nut to crack. They have a lot of practice covering their asses. But if Billings turns on them to save his own ass—" Kyle smiled slightly. "Well. That's the kind of bust that could make a guy's career."

"And the kind of story that could shut Les Simpson up once and for all," I muttered, pulling a folder free from the box.

Kyle leaned forward. "So, what do you say, Nicey?"

"Do I get my exclusive?" I asked.

"I will do everything in my power," he said. "You have my word."

"Show me what's what," I said, waving my hands over the table. "I don't get your numbering system. Where's your file on the murder?"

He pushed a fat folder toward me and flipped it open. A smiling, work I.D. photo of the deceased lay over a glossy of the gnawed-on remains.

"Jesus," I whispered, turning to the forensics report.

"So someone killed him and dumped him almost right away?" I said. "Blunt force head trauma and gunshot wound. Which was the cause of death?"

"The shot."

I nodded.

"Did you get the DNA back on the samples they took?"

"Still waiting. The lab is backed up."

I looked at the report again.

"But the hair was blond. Billings isn't blond."

"No, but the victim was. And the hair doesn't always come from the killer."

I rolled my eyes upward to look at him from under my lashes. "Especially when the investigating officers don't want it to?" I asked, but my brain was considering Grayson and his silver-at-the-temples chestnut coif. Blond hair didn't come from the senator, either.

What if we were both wrong?

If the murders were connected, then it had to be someone who knew Allison, too.

A photo I'd seen in Lucinda Eckersly's parlor flashed through my brain.

Eckersly was hunting, with that old rifle. And he had blond hair peeking out from under his flannel hunting cap.

"Kyle, tell me about the gun," I said, picturing the carvings on the stock of the old rifle hanging over the dining room doorway in the Eckersly's foyer.

He shoved a printout of a picture across the table and I caught a sharp breath. I wished I had a picture of Eckersly's gun to make sure I was right about this one being almost identical.

"Did Billings say where he got this gun?"

"He bought it at an auction."

"And you're sure the bullet came from that gun?"

"No."

My head snapped up.

"I thought you said you had him on the gun."

"I'm sure the bullet came from that kind of gun," he said. "He won't produce the weapon, so I can't be certain if it came from his gun. Convenient time for a priceless rifle to go missing."

"What if it didn't come from his gun?" I tapped my pen on the table, my puzzle starting to fall into place. "Bill Eckersly was a client of the dead call girl. He's also involved somehow with Senator Grayson, and maybe Billings, too. I saw a funny looking old fashioned gun in the foyer at his house today. One with a carved stock like this one. And you know something, because you wouldn't have been there when he drove his truck into the jewelry store the other day if you didn't. What do you make of him?"

"He's supplying Billings with tobacco off the books," he said. "He doesn't strike me as the murdering type. Also, what would he have against a lawyer who's half his age and lives forty miles from him?"

I bit my lip. He was right. I had no motive on Amesworth I could pin to Eckersly, which was why I hadn't seriously suspected him before. But the gun matched the one in Kyle's printout. I was more sure of it the longer I stared at it.

"His mother was worried about him losing the farm," I said. "Maybe he wanted more of the money?"

"Then why kill the lobbyist?" Kyle said. "That guy didn't have any control over who gets what percentage of anything."

The jewelry store clerk's comment about the wad of cash he flashed around the store danced through my head. That didn't fit, either. Especially not with the fake bracelet Allison had been wearing.

Allison.

"The girl?" I asked. "Eckersly's mother said he was in love with her, and she was a prostitute. If it's not money, it's usually sex when someone gets killed."

"So you think Eckersly killed Amesworth over the call girl, and then killed her last night because...?"

"She didn't love him? She was going to tell?"

Wait.

I reached for the forensics report.

"There was slight remodeling on the head wound," I said.

"Yeah. He was hit before he was killed," Kyle said.

"Like, hours before he was killed," I sat up straighter, warming to the scenario in my head. "What if the attorney wanted a little pretty college girl company, so he calls up the dean at his alma mater and they send over Allison—"

"And the lawyer is into something she doesn't want to do?" Kyle grinned.

"Exactly." I nodded. "So she cracks him over the head and panics, calls her best client for help—"

"And Eckersly shows up, says he'll take care of it."

"He loads the body in his truck and takes off, but then he shoots the guy and dumps him instead of taking him home. Allison flips her shit, and says she's going to tell someone."

"So now she's dead, too." Kyle closed the folder. "How did she die?"

"Strangled. Eckersly is a big man."

Kyle stared at the wall behind me, and I could see him putting it together in his head.

"You saw the rifle in his house earlier today?" he asked finally.

"And he has blond hair. What kind of tires are you looking for?"

"Big ones."

"The kind that go on a double-dually pickup, maybe?" I pictured the red monstrosity buried in the side of the jewelry shop.

"Yep." Kyle shook his head. "It wasn't Billings, was it?"

"Nope. Is that truck still impounded somewhere?"

He flipped open his laptop and punched a few keys.

"The Richmond PD has it," he said. "Looks like I'm going to check out tire treads."

"Looks like I have a story to write," I stood. "Call me when you have the warrant?"

"You got it, Lois." He opened the door and pulled me into a tight hug as I tried to slip past him. "Thanks for your help. We always did make a pretty good team." He loosened his hold, but didn't let go.

My breath caught as his eyelids lowered again. My eyes fell shut and I leaned toward him.

Stop. Bad idea, kissing a cop. And bad for him, kissing a reporter in a building that didn't have a dust bunny the security cameras couldn't see.

I ducked under Kyle's arm and stepped into the hall.

"We have work to do," I said from a couple of paces away.

Kyle nodded, his smile not quite reaching his eyes.

"I'll call you when we pick him up."

19

I stayed in the tub until the water turned chilly and my fingers were pruned, then drank nearly half a bottle of pinot noir, but still couldn't sit down for more than five minutes. I finally dug out a duster and started attacking my house room by room, thinking about Senator Grayson. And Allison, the dead call girl/campaign volunteer. And Billings, Lakshmi, and Lucinda.

Darcy gave up following me around after an hour and retreated to her bed in the corner of the living room while I dusted the bookshelves, muttering to myself.

"Grayson is dirty, too." I thought about the stamps that were hidden in my closet. Part of one of them had likely been on the murder victim. How did he get that if it was Eckersly?

And what if Kyle let Billings go and never caught up with him again? I'd seen photographic evidence that Billings was a creep. Somehow, making a fortune stealing tax money from schools and social programs while peddling a product that killed people didn't seem any better to me than shooting someone.

"Jeez, Darcy!" I threw the duster into the corner, whirling on my still-sore ankle and putting my hands on my hips. "What the hell is going on here?"

Darcy raised her head, considered me for a few seconds, sniffed the air for signs of food, then plopped her chin back onto her front paws and sighed.

"Me, too, girl." I said, checking my cell phone for a text or missed call from Kyle.

Nothing.

"I'm missing something," I mumbled, retrieving the duster and returning it to the kitchen cabinet.

But the story Kyle and I had come up with made sense. Maybe I was just operating on adrenaline overload.

"Maybe," I said, eyeing my reflection sternly as I reached for my toothbrush and a tube of Colgate, "you just want the senator to be in this so you weren't chasing the wrong guy the whole time."

Then why did he have the stamps?

I didn't have an answer for that, so I pushed it aside. I shut off the bathroom light and returned to the sofa, where I picked up a puzzle piece and started filling in the bottom corner of my meadow, laying my phone on the cushion next to me where I'd be sure to hear it.

I'd finished the bottom half of the jigsaw by the time Kyle's text came at one-thirty.

"Tires match. Picked him up at a motor lodge outside Ashland with a stripper and a nearly-empty fifth of Jack. Guilty?"

"Maybe." I typed back. "Call me when you're free."

* * *

Agents from the Richmond office of the Bureau of Alcohol, Tobacco, Firearms, and Explosives arrested a local farmer early Friday in connection with the murder of Daniel Amesworth, 29, a west end attorney whose remains were found near the city limits last week. William Eckersly, 37, whose family owns the largest tobacco farm in Powhatan county, is also a suspect in the death of RAU student Allison Brantley, whose body was found on the campus Thursday.

"I'm limited by agency policy," ATF Special Agent Kyle Miller said early Friday. "But I can confirm that Mr. Eckersly is a person of interest in two open murder investigations."

· · ·

I had the story ready for Bob when he arrived at seven, and his eyebrows raised higher by degrees as he read through it. By the time he turned the chair to face me, they were almost on top of his head.

"I haven't heard a word about this," he said. "Where the hell did you get it?"

"I'm just that good, I guess," I said. "Consider it a peace offering. I'm sorry I pissed you off yesterday."

"This is quite an amends," he said. "How long do we have before Charlie gets wind of it?"

"He promised me an exclusive until we'd printed it."

Bob shook his head. "Not sure I want to know what you had to do for that."

"Not what you're thinking," I said. "I'm me, not Shelby. Even if I have been acting a little like her lately. I don't want Trudy's job, Bob. Today, I don't even want the *Post*. I just want my beat back the way it was."

"I'm not sure I can promise you that," he said. "This is good, but Les is pretty determined. "

I nodded. "I'm prepared to impress Andrews on a daily basis for as long as it takes."

"Something tells me you'll win him over eventually." Bob grinned. "This will help. I'm going to have Ryan put it on the web now. Twenty-four hours is a long time for something like this to stay quiet in a town like Powhatan. The ATF talking is the least of my worries."

I stood. Bob's voice stopped me in the doorway. "Hey, kid? Nice work."

* * *

I had to be at the courthouse for the dean's arraignment at eleven. I checked the docket for the prosecutor's name at ten-fifteen and grinned when I saw it. DonnaJo. It'd been a while since I'd seen my friend in action, and she was a good lawyer who had a flair for firing off intensely quotable snippets in her arguments. She was also a former beauty queen who usually won points with the jury for her blonde good looks and southern belle charm. Tough break for the dean. I reached for the phone.

"I can't tell you shit until I get into the courtroom, honey," DonnaJo said in place of a hello when she answered.

"Aw, come on, DonnaJo," I said. "I'll buy you a glass of wine after work."

"Not today, doll," she said. "Boss's orders. There are reporters camped out in every corner of this building, and Corry threatened to put me on parking detail if I breathed a word to anyone. Everybody from the Mayor to Ted Grayson has been in his office since yesterday afternoon, and I think he's worried about his own ass. Folks are afraid this mess is going to be the end of the university, and the school is important to the city."

Yeah, and the local politicians are in the dean's little black book.

"Plus, that big murder case he took on himself is about to walk, because the ATF picked someone else up last night," she said. "Come to the hearing; I've got some good stuff."

"I'll see you in a bit."

I typed a couple of things into my notes before I turned my computer off and headed for the elevators. The doors had just started to close when a small hand with a perfect scarlet manicure shot around the edge of the frame.

"Going somewhere, Nichelle?" Shelby stepped into the elevator, her big eyes bigger than usual and a smirk firmly in place on her lips. She pushed the basement button.

"I have a hearing to cover this morning." I smiled and swallowed the "you backstabbing bitch" part of that comment. "It's not Monday yet."

"You should say goodbye to your friends down there." She grinned as the doors closed, but it was the kind of grin I'd expect from a cartoon cat with yellow feathers poking through its teeth as the little old lady searches for her pet canary.

"Don't get too comfortable, Shelby," I said, stepping out of the elevator. "I'm not going anywhere for long."

"We'll see, Nichelle. Enjoy your last day at the courthouse."

The doors closed and I turned and strode to my car. Shelby could gloat all she wanted. I wasn't much for giving up.

I sped toward the courthouse and managed to wedge my car between two of the TV trucks out front by blocking one's door, turning sideways and flattening myself against the car to get out. I hurried through security and into courtroom number six, where DonnaJo was opening her briefcase at the prosecution table. I chose a seat caddy-cornered from her so I could see her face, and watched the gallery fill with reporters and curious lawyers. By the time the judge came in, it was standing room only.

The dean sat, still in the clothes she'd worn to work the day before, her mascara running and her head down to shield her face from the cameras, silent for the duration of the hearing except when she was ordered to stand and offer a plea.

"Not guilty." It was barely above a whisper.

DonnaJo produced bank statements and a witness list that even made the judge raise an eyebrow at the defendant. I held my breath waiting for Grayson's name, but didn't hear it. Two city councilmen and a couple of high-profile state officials, though. And more names would come.

The judge banged his gavel after an hour, holding the dean over for the grand jury with no bond. Wow. A no-bond was rare, even in murder cases. This lady was in deep shit.

On my way out, I saw Kyle standing outside the front door shouting into his iPhone. I paused, looking toward the TV reporters who were scrambling to get the dean's hearing ready for the noon broadcasts, which were already half over. I turned back to Kyle, wondering what he was mad about.

"On what planet does it take six days to get a fucking rush ballistics analysis?" He spat. "I dropped that weapon off at six a.m. I don't give two shits if you're doing work for the President himself, I want my report by tomorrow morning."

He clicked off the call and shook his head, then looked up at me.

"Ever feel like you're surrounded by lazy assholes?"

"I've been there. You found Eckersly's rifle?"

"Right where you said it was. His mother is a spitfire, isn't she? She squawked about it being a family heirloom and threatened to sue if we so much as breathed on the damned thing. It's a beauty," he said. "But seriously. All the hell I'm asking them to do is fire it into a bucket of sand and compare the casing with the one they pulled out of Amesworth. How long does that fucking take? If I could do it myself, I would. But the difference in the striations from two such similar guns might be pretty subtle, and I could miss it. I don't want to make another mistake."

"I do know that feeling," I said. "And well. Speaking of, I'd better get back to work."

"Want to grab a drink later?" he asked.

"I've been up for essentially twenty-seven hours right now," I said. "But I'll call you tomorrow, if you want."

I wasn't sure I would, but seeing the way his blue eyes lit when I offered, I wasn't sure I wouldn't, either.

"See you. Thanks for talking me through it last night."

"Thanks for giving me the exclusive. I'm off my editor's shit list. Now I just have to impress the publisher."

"I have utter faith in you." He grinned.

"Have fun with your interrogation."

"Always." He winked and disappeared into the courthouse.

20

Charlie had Eckersly's arrest at noon and six, but Kyle didn't talk to her, which had to be frustrating the hell out of her. The ATF's public information people were every bit as forthcoming as the FBI's—which is to say they weren't forthcoming at all. But the dean's hearing and the aftermath of the bust at the university was the big story of the day, and by the time I finished my piece on the hearing, got it to Bob, and made the corrections he wanted, nearly everyone else had gone home.

I was exhausted, and had pushed through the afternoon with a lot of help from the coffeemaker. But there were a couple of police reports I wanted to read before I went home.

I went back to the break room in search of more caffeine, reading a printout of a new burglary report as I waited for a fresh pot to brew. I filled my mug and reached for the upper cabinet to get my syrup bottle, momentarily forgetting it wasn't there. People suck sometimes. I made a mental note to fill an empty one with soap and leave it for the bandit at some point.

I added three packets of Splenda to my cup and grabbed the robbery report, which looked much more in line with the cat burglar than Grayson's house had. Turning to go back to my desk, I wondered what the chances were that Aaron was still at work.

I tried his office and his cell and left messages in both places, setting the printout on top of my inbox and turning to my laptop. Eckersly had the right tires on his pickup, and he might have motive. Billings, a tobacco executive, was running contraband cigarettes he was making from tobacco he was getting from Eckersly. And the two of them were bribing Senator Grayson, who was into call girls and kink.

Something still didn't fit. Grayson was the wacky-jigsawed odd piece of this puzzle, but I couldn't put my finger on why.

"Did Grayson want out?" I wondered aloud.

I typed his name into my Google bar.

Same stories, same homepages, and social accounts I'd seen before.

I clicked to the images. There was a new shot from a campaign rally two days before. Grayson's son had grown up since the last campaign, though he was mostly hidden behind the woman holding the senator's hand. But she wasn't the same woman from the family photo I'd seen before. That woman was a brunette who needed to lose about sixty pounds and looked uncomfortable in her own skin. This woman was a petite blonde with a winning smile.

I clicked to the image source and scrolled to the caption. Senator Ted Grayson, his wife, Katharine, and son, Jack, at a campaign rally in Williamsburg.

I typed Katherine Grayson into the search bar and clicked the images.

The very first one was a side by side, part of a story in *Washington Monthly* about Mrs. Grayson's transformation. According to the article, she'd grown up very poor, gone to Princeton on a scholarship, married well, but gained weight with her pregnancy and lost her self-esteem for a number of years. Then she lost sixty-five pounds, colored her hair, and adopted a new life philosophy of envisioning everything she wanted, all thanks to a yoga retreat in the Blue Ridge Mountains.

"Would she murder someone to get her vision?" I wondered aloud, staring at her perfect, Estee Lauder rose smile.

"Sex. And money." I closed my eyes for a second, then stared at the photos for another long minute. Katherine Grayson had a very nice life. And her husband's extracurricular activities could erase it. Her status and income depended on his. Damn damn damn.

I snatched up the phone and called Kyle.

Voicemail.

I clicked open an email and typed out a message.

"Bad news. I think we got it wrong again. Have those hairs from Amesworth's jacket checked for bleach. Call me when you get this."

I stared at the photos for another minute, a familiar nagging in the back of my brain telling me I knew her from somewhere.

"She's a senator's wife," I said aloud, stifling a yawn as I closed my laptop and shoved it into my bag. "It's not like her picture hasn't ever been in the news."

I turned Grayson, his wife, and Allison over and around in my mind on the short drive home. There was something there, but I was too tired to see it. Maybe a good night's sleep would shake whatever it was loose.

I unlocked the kitchen door and stepped into the house.

Something exploded on the far side of the room, flashing orange in the dark. A millisecond later, my shoulder caught fire. I staggered backward, the small of my back hitting the sharp edge of the tile countertop. I didn't really feel it, though. I couldn't concentrate on anything but my shoulder, which felt warm and sticky when I grabbed it. I slid down the front of the cabinet to sit on the floor, the coppery tang of blood in my nostrils making me nauseous.

I was pretty sure I'd just been shot.

* * *

Joey's warning floated through my head, followed closely by all the articles I'd read about the Mafia and every warning I'd blown off in the past couple of weeks. Was I about to become a Mafia statistic? Or was Mrs. Grayson still trigger happy?

Footfalls on the tile floor brought my attacker closer, and my whole body flinched when someone kicked my foot. Between the darkness and the blinding pain, I couldn't see.

"Who—who are you?" I stammered.

"I'm nobody." Male. Young. He stepped into the light spilling through the open kitchen door. "But my father is somebody. And he's going to stay that way."

"Jack." My mouth fell open. He was even wearing the same t-shirt he'd been wearing at the body dump site. Which was where I'd seen Katherine Grayson's blonde bob. She just hadn't been smiling that night. "Jack Grayson. Oh, kid, what have you done?"

"What I had to," he said. "My parents can't go down for this."

The pain in my shoulder and sheer exhaustion were taking their toll, because he wasn't making any sense. The parents couldn't go to jail, but the kid was going to kill me. What is this, *Clue*? "I'm not following you. Did everybody do it?"

"Technically, my mom killed that asshole Amesworth," Jack leaned a hip against the table, keeping the gun trained on me.

"How do you technically kill someone?"

"She begged him to stop bringing my dad money. She was terrified Calhoun's staff would get wind of it, and it would cost my dad the election. Amesworth laughed and told her he didn't have any say so over who Billings was bribing or for how long, and then told her if she was better in the sack her husband wouldn't need money for whores. She hauled off and slapped him. He got rough with her. I was coming in from a late class, and I heard the whole thing. I grabbed the closest heavy thing and swung as hard as I could. What else could I do?"

He was getting chatty in his defensiveness. Okay, tell me all about it, kid. "You fractured his skull," I said.

"It made a weird noise," he said. "He fell on my mom. And he bled. A lot. I pulled him onto the floor, and I lost it. I thought he was dead. He didn't look like he was breathing. I wasn't trying to kill him. My mom said I'd saved her and maybe saved our family, but we couldn't just claim it was self-defense. It would be a complete scandal for my dad's campaign. We did what we had to and rolled him up in a shower curtain and threw him in the back of that hillbilly pickup that my dad borrowed for his hunting trip. We drove to the woods. But when we pulled him out of the truck, he started moaning and moving. There was a rifle in the gun rack, and my mom grabbed it and shot him in the head. She said no one would ever believe us and he'd ruin our whole lives."

"But you couldn't stay away," I said.

"I had nightmares. I went back out there to make sure he was still buried, and something had dug him up. Tina was with me. She flipped out. I had to call the cops and report it."

The pain in my shoulder had dulled to a throb, but the wet warmth on my blouse was spreading, and I was getting lightheaded. Think, Nichelle.

What was in the cabinet behind me?

"So you haven't done anything, really," I said, reaching my good hand behind me and trying to open the cabinet. My weight was keeping it shut, and I couldn't move without him noticing. "You didn't kill him, and the cops don't have any idea you had anything to do with it. So why don't you go home, before you do something that really will ruin your life. I'll get some stitches and go to bed, and everyone's happy."

He stared for a second, then threw back his head and laughed. It was loud and hollow, telling me I was running out of stalling time. I scooted forward a few inches and flipped the cabinet open as discreetly as possible with the dark as my cover.

"Lady, I'm at William and Mary on scholarship. I'm eighteen and I'm a junior in college. I'm not stupid. How many college kids can hack into the ATF's email system? I got the message you sent your agent friend earlier. He will not. And my mother isn't going to prison because my father can't keep his dick in his pants."

Shit. That meant Kyle was probably drinking beer with his team, celebrating Eckersly's arrest while I was here with Captain Sociopath. No one was coming to save me. I felt around in the cabinet, trying not to move my arm enough for him to notice. My fingers closed around the handle of a heavy iron skillet. I'd have to get close enough to whack him with it before he could shoot me. How? I squeezed the handle so hard the iron bit into my palm and leveled a stare at Jack.

"If Kyle doesn't know, then your secret is safe, right? I'm not telling anyone."

"You're a reporter. It's your job to tell people shit that's none of their business."

"Not when I'd like to avoid getting shot again."

He chuckled.

"You're nice. I looked you up—pictures of your dog, shoes, and fluffy-bunny quotes was all I found. You were nice to us that night in the woods, too. I was really hoping you wouldn't figure this out. Your agent friend is way off the mark. I've been watching his emails for weeks." I remembered Kyle saying something about a bug in the ATF computer system. And Grayson's kid on a computer scholarship. Nice time to catch up, Nichelle.

"Jack, you don't want to do this," I said. "You had nightmares about Amesworth, right? And you didn't kill him. How do you know that won't happen again?"

"The whore isn't haunting me."

I grimaced. "Oh, kid."

"It wasn't as hard as I was afraid it would be," he said. "I just waited for her to come out of the building and got behind her with a guitar string and pulled. She didn't even fight, really. A couple of scratches, a kick, and that was it."

"Why?"

"This was all her fault."

Nice logic there, smart guy.

"How?"

"She was the reason my dad needed the money, wasn't she? Then she emailed him last week. Said she figured out where he was getting the money to pay her and she'd go to Calhoun's campaign with the whole story if he didn't make her a local campaign manager. But if he does that, everyone thinks he's screwing the pretty young intern, anyway, right? No way to win."

"Okay." I tried to force my brain to find the words that would keep me alive. "So she's dead. Who else knows? If Billings was going to talk, he'd have done it already, right? He's been on house arrest and charged with murder for a week. He has other friends that he really doesn't want to piss off by cutting deals with the ATF. Prison could be the least of that guy's worries."

He straightened up.

"You're a fast talker, Miss Clarke, but I'm afraid I don't believe you." He leveled the gun. "I even tried to scare you off. You should have taken the hint."

"Darcy!" I panicked.

I heard muffled yapping and claws on wood.

"She's in the bathroom," Jack said. "You don't think I'd actually hurt a dog, do you? I'm not a monster."

"Jack?" I tugged the pan to the edge of the shelf, done talking to the sociopath.

"Yeah?" He cocked his head to one side.

"Look out."

He turned to look over his shoulder reflexively, and the cookie sheets inside the cabinet crashed when I wrenched the skillet free. Darcy's scratching popped the broken door unlatched and she raced in, barking. Jack stumbled toward me, waving the gun the other way and firing a shot at the refrigerator.

"Darcy!"

She kept barking. I whipped the pan around to my front, used my injured arm to steady it, and swung with my good one.

The reverberation when the skillet connected with his knees sent a shockwave into my bleeding shoulder that made me scream, but he screamed louder, tumbling sideways onto the floor. The gun skittered across the linoleum into the dark.

"You bitch!" Jack howled.

"You should have taken me up on that offer, Jack." I tried to get to my feet and failed, my sore ankle giving at the worst possible time and causing me to lose my balance. He scrambled for the gun, and I willed myself to stand, fighting wooziness when I managed to pull it off.

My foot protested the two steps toward him as his fingers closed around the gun. Shit.

I raised the pan and brought it down on his hip, and he yelped and froze for an instant, but didn't let go of the gun. I lifted one foot and stomped my pump down on his empty hand with all the force I could muster, leaning all my weight on that leg. There was no doubt I was doing further damage to my sprain, but I knew from the crunch under my heel I wasn't the only one feeling it.

He screamed again, finally letting go of the gun. I dove for it, snatching it up by the barrel and flipping it around. I didn't have the first damned clue how to shoot it, but I figured I had decent odds of hitting something at that range.

"Don't move." My voice shook.

I wasn't sure if he replied, because my heart pounding in my ears was the only thing I could hear for a good thirty seconds. When it faded, he was still howling.

"My hand! You broke my fucking hand!"

The indignation would have been funny, if I'd had the capacity to laugh.

"Maybe you shouldn't have tried to kill me."

I backed carefully toward the door, my only thought that I needed to get to the car and get the hell out of there, when I heard footfalls on the steps. I held my breath.

"Nichelle?" The door flew into the wall and light flooded the room. "What the hell is going on in here?"

"Thank God." I handed Joey the gun and sagged into a chair. "Joey, meet Jack Grayson. He shot me."

"She hit me with a fucking frying pan and then crushed my hand," Jack howled.

"Shut up, kid. And be still." Joey shoved the gun into the back of his waistband and knelt in front of me, probing my shoulder with his fingers. "Always too late to save the day." He brushed my hair out of my face and smiled.

"Can you take me to St. Vincent's?" I asked. "I don't feel so good."

"You have a plan for dealing with the kid?"

"Kyle. My phone's over there somewhere." I waved a hand toward the door and collapsed across the tabletop.

21

I opened my eyes to find Joey pressing a dish towel over my wound and Kyle barking orders at a handful of agents who were cordoning off my kitchen as a crime scene. Jack was gone.

"Can I get medical attention now?" I asked when Kyle stopped and put a hand over mine, shaking his head.

"Of all the calls to miss," he said. " I'm so sorry. I wouldn't have seen this coming in a million years."

"S'ok. I was calling to tell you to go arrest that little psychopath's mother, but then I emailed you, and he intercepted the email. You might want to get your tech guys on that. He said he's been reading your emails for weeks. He was here when I got home." I laid my head back on the table and Joey's hands tightened on my shoulder.

"I need to get her to a doctor." Joey said. "What the hell is taking that ambulance so long?"

"What was your role in all of this?" Kyle asked. "I still don't think I caught your name."

"I didn't offer it," Joey said. "All I did was stop in to see a friend and walk in on the tail end of the attack. She had disarmed him already. I can't tell you anything."

The two of them eyed each other warily.

"Bleeding. Hospital." I smiled wanly, trying to get their attention off each other.

"I could've walked there by now," Joey said, scooping me into his arms.

"I'll be by in a while." Kyle glared as Joey turned for the door. I didn't have the energy to care. I laid my head on Joey's shoulder and mumbled an apology for getting blood on his suit.

"Not like it's never happened before." His lips grazed my ear as he whispered, walking down the steps and settling me into the passenger seat of his Lincoln. "Though I'd rather not wear any more of your blood, if you don't mind."

I smiled and leaned back against the seat. "I'd like that."

Joey laughed when I pulled out my cell phone and started typing. I shushed him, firing off an email to Bob with a short, hit-the-highlights story on Jack Grayson. My shoulder throbbed, but damned if I was going to lose this headline to Charlie—or worse, Shelby—while I was getting stitched up. I called Bob to give him a heads-up since it was so late, and he roared "what?" so loud my ear rang when I told him I'd been shot. Assuring him I was fine, I rushed him off the phone when Joey pulled into the ER lot at St. Vincent's. I didn't like upsetting Bob, but I needed him to get the story up before Charlie caught wind of it.

A pair of stout nurses who clearly thought Joey shot me banished him to the waiting room and gave me the domestic violence inquisition, but after repeated assurance that he'd had nothing to do with it, they let him come in while a doctor tended to my shoulder.

The shortest nurse continued to give Joey the stink eye, even with me hiding my face in his shoulder and him stroking my hair as the doctor stitched up the wounds—which were on both sides, since the bullet went clean through.

"She should've been a nun." Joey laughed as the woman shot him another glare on her way to get a second unit of blood for me. "I feel like I'm back in Sister Mary Paul's classroom in ninth grade. She didn't like me so much, either."

"How could anyone dislike you?" I blurted, thinking I shouldn't say that out loud, but unable to fight off the haze from the pain medication enough to censor it.

"Plenty of people dislike me." He cradled my jaw in one hand, running a thumb lightly along my cheekbone. "I'm glad you're not one of them. But can you do me a favor? The next time I tell you to stay the hell out of something, will you listen?"

"Very possibly," I slurred sleepily. "I didn't believe you. And I never suspected Jack. Did you know it was him?"

"No. I was pretty sure it was his father, just like you." He dropped his hand to my lap and grabbed the one of mine that didn't have an IV in it. "Grayson's been talking to a few of my associates about their interest in keeping the taxes on cigarettes as high as they can go. He figured out Billings was double-dipping. He's been taking money from us for product under the table, and then doing the company's dirty work paying off politicians. Grayson decided he could eat his cake and have it, too. Vote his conscience on the tax hikes, but still have the money coming in for his girl.

"It was just coming in from my side instead of big tobacco. I thought he had it out with the lobbyist and shot him. But I knew poking around him would lead you back to some," he paused, "associates of mine. I worried about you pissing them off. Then I saw your story this morning and thought the farmer did it. But for a kid to be able to murder two people—almost three—in cold blood? Damn."

"I'm glad it wasn't you," I said, squeezing his hand.

"I would love it if you'd stop thinking I killed every dead guy who turns up in your day."

"I'm getting there."

My cell phone binged, but it sounded impossibly far away. I didn't have the energy to look around for it.

"That's my cue." Joey flipped the phone into my lap and crossed to the door. "Your federal agent friend is in the parking lot. Wants to know what room we're in."

"Hurry back," I said.

He turned from the doorway and smiled. "I don't think you're getting rid of me this time."

Kyle shoved the door open and strode to the side of the bed less than three minutes later, grasping my free hand and knitting his eyebrows together as he hovered.

"Goddammit, I feel like a first-class moron. Some supercop I turned out to be. I am so, so sorry, Nicey. I was so far from thinking it was that kid, I'd have suspected Lex Luthor first."

"The mother. I found pictures of her online tonight and recognized her, but I didn't place her at the body recovery until after I got home. Jack cracked Amesworth over the head because mom's begging him to leave her hubby alone turned ugly. They thought he was dead, but then they got him out to the woods and he woke up. She shot him with the rifle Grayson borrowed from Eckersly. So they both did it?"

"There's more, apparently–Billings and Eckersly had cooked up their own cigarette trafficking operation when the higher tax rates passed here."

"I see," I said, fighting to keep my eyes open.

He perched on the edge of my cot, eyeing the units of blood hanging from the IV stand. "They didn't need Grayson on their payroll anymore. So he stole a set of Virginia tax stamps from Amesworth's office and tried to blackmail Billings. Threatened to rat him out to the mob for bigfooting their territory while he's still selling them product. Billings and Eckersly were buying the stamps through a front at that jewelry store, paying real money for fake diamonds and taking the stamps with the receipts. Billings sent his boy Eckersly to talk the senator down because the two of them are tight. Eckersly is a big contributor to political campaigns. When that didn't work, Billings sent Eckersly to steal the stamps."

"Damn," I said. "Covering politics is not as much fun as I thought."

"You okay?" He laid a hand on my arm.

"I'm so tired," I sighed. "Sleep deprivation, adrenaline, blood loss. I want to sleep until next week."

"There's about a dozen reporters on your lawn driving your dog batshit, and a couple of your friends from the PD are in the waiting room."

"Aw, hell. Seriously?"

"Sorry. I issued an all call to your house when your friend called me. Where'd he go, by the way?"

"Coffee. He'll be back. I think."

"Who is that guy, Nichelle? There's something about him I don't like."

"Besides the fact that there's something about him I do?" I needed to deflect that question for as long as I could. "You promised me an exclusive. No talking to the TV guys," I slurred, my eyelids dropping shut. .

As I drifted off, I felt Kyle's lips against my forehead and heard his voice from the other end of a tunnel. "I don't want to talk to anyone but you."

* * *

Kyle had a crew clean up the blood in my kitchen before Joey took me home the next evening. He walked me inside and checked the whole house to make me feel safe before he left me with a brief kiss and a promise to call the next day.

"So I get to talk to you on the phone now?" I asked, leaning against the doorframe and smiling. "I'm moving up in the world."

"I still say I'm more charming in person," he said.

I locked the door behind him and fed Darcy before I climbed into bed with my laptop. It took more than an hour to piece together everything I knew about Grayson for Sunday's front page, and by the time I finished typing and emailed the file to Bob, my shoulder was burning again. I took a Vicodin and managed to find a comfortable position with the help of several strategically-placed pillows, dozing the evening away.

Convincing my mom to stay in Texas was no easy feat, but her bridezilla client's wedding was in less than a week, and I begged her not to throw the account away because of me, tossing in a tiny fib about Kyle taking care of me to make her feel better. Kyle did call on Sunday. So did Joey. I snuggled back into my pillows after each conversation wondering what I was going to do about the two of them.

* * *

Whether it was the blood transfusions or the narcotic-induced full weekend of sleep, I felt like a new woman by Monday morning. My arm was in a sling, and would stay that way for three weeks. Instead of skipping the gym altogether, I settled for walking on the treadmill, watching a recap of Charlie's weekend coverage of the Ted Grayson scandal on the flatscreens that lined the wall. He'd resigned when my story about Jack went live, bribery and solicitation charges notwithstanding. I already knew that, but she had a tidbit on a possible challenger for Calhoun in the swiftly-coming election that I hadn't seen.

"Knock yourself out, Trudy," I said. "I can't wait to read it."

I walked into Bob's office at five 'til eight, sporting a pair of sapphire Louboutins that almost matched the color of my hospital-issue sling.

"Miss Clarke." Rick Andrews, our publisher, was in my usual chair. He rose when I walked in, putting a hand out and smiling. "Welcome back."

"You have no idea how glad I am to be here, sir," I said, shaking his hand with my uninjured one.

"We're very glad to have you. Your piece yesterday was outstanding, and the fallout from all this is just beginning, so I'm told." He smiled stiffly, and I thought about what Bob had said about Grayson being his friend. But not that good a friend, apparently.

"I'm on top of it," I said.

"So you've shown. I came down this morning to congratulate you, and extend the gratitude of this newspaper. But I also owe you an apology. Bob tells me you were working on this investigation last week, and I had no idea. The courthouse is yours again, if you want it back."

"I would love that." I smiled.

"Good." He stepped aside, and I lowered myself gently into my chair. Andrews and Bob exchanged nods.

"I'll leave you to running your newsroom, Bob," Andrews said from the doorway.

"I appreciate that, Rick."

Bob swiveled his chair toward me and I flashed a grin.

"Not bad in terms of making up for getting my ass kicked, huh?"

He narrowed his eyes at the sling.

"Are you ever going to learn?"

"I hope so." I moved my shoulder gingerly. "This is way less glamorous than it looks on TV."

"But you're still rocking the shoes," Parker said, shaking his head and sitting down across from me. "I'm going to appoint myself your full time bodyguard. Mel says someone has to do it."

"That could work," I said. "Will you drive me around, too?"

He rolled his eyes and looked at Bob. "Can you give her something less dangerous to cover? Like, I don't know, a war?"

Bob laughed. "Her escapades are always good for sales," he said. "Besides, this one got the other half of her beat away from Shelby."

"She's going to be pissed." I smiled at the thought.

"She threatened to quit," Bob said. "Les talked her out of it."

"Damn." I shook my head.

"Hey, before I forget; I left your coffee syrup on your desk, Clarke," Parker said. "Sorry it took me a couple of days to get it back to you. I had to go to three different stores to find the sugar-free one. It really is good, though. And better for me than sugar and half-and-half. Thanks."

Parker. I smiled, not even able to muster a little of the annoyance I'd felt as the syrup disappeared by degrees. "We'll take turns buying?"

"Works for me, Lois," he said.

Everyone filed in for the staff meeting, which Trudy finished off with a call for applause.

"I'm a big girl, and I can admit when I'm wrong. It's rare," she said, grinning at me, "but it happens. Nichelle, honey, you have my congratulations and thanks, and best wishes for a speedy recovery. I also owe you an apology. I should have listened to you last week. I thought I knew my people better than anyone else could. I won't make that mistake again. So, you know, anytime you feel like tipping me to the story of the year, bring it on. I promise to listen."

"Thanks, Trudy." I returned the smile. "No hard feelings?"

"Are you kidding? I'm going to be up for a Pulitzer by the time I get through with Grayson. I owe you a bottle of wine. Or a pair of new shoes."

"Size nine." I chirped. Everyone laughed.

Back at my desk, I scanned through police reports. Nothing except another robbery. This one looked to be the work of the cat burglar, too—which sounded nice and safe.

I opened my email, finger on the delete key for the usual Monday morning blitzkrieg of "Miracle Weight Loss!" and "Penis Enlargement Now!" spam.

At the top of my inbox, sent less than five minutes ago from a washintonpost.com address, was a subject line: brava. My heart in my throat, I clicked it open. It was from the politics editor.

"Nicely done. I'll have an eye out for your byline."

"Holy headlines, Lois." I sat back in the chair and smiled.

SMALL TOWN SPIN: Nichelle Clarke #3

Crime reporter Nichelle Clarke ventures out to a tiny Chesapeake Bay island community, helping a friend search for answers in the wake of unthinkable tragedy. But in small towns like this, some rocks are never meant to be overturned...

T.J. had the world in the palm of his hand. He was handsome. Popular in school. Smart. A stellar athlete. The son of superstar pro quarterback Tony Okerson, he seemed destined to follow in his father's footsteps to a career of gridiron glory.

That bright, shining dream ends when T.J.'s lifeless body is found on a rocky shoreline near his family's Chesapeake Bay home.

Due to his father's past fame, the tragedy ignites a media frenzy in the normally serene island community. Through a mutual friend, the grieving parents turn to reporter Nichelle Clarke for help. Nichelle agrees to write the story herself and attempt to quell the national media circus.

But as Nichelle begins to explore the facts surrounding the death, she discovers some shocking details. Something doesn't fit. And while the local sheriff wants to stamp the case a drug overdose and move on, Nichelle becomes convinced that foul play may have been involved.

To the townsfolk, Nichelle is an outsider, putting her nose where it doesn't belong. But in her experience, that's exactly where the most damning secrets are kept. And the further she follows the evidence trail, the more Nichelle realizes that this sleepy coastal village is anything but innocent...

ACKNOWLEDGMENTS

There might only be one name on the cover, but it takes a lot of effort from many people to create a novel. I am indebted to everyone who helped with this one.

My friend Jody Hynds Klann has my eternal gratitude for making sure the science (if not always the time frames) in my forensics are correct.

Another general thanks to the city of Richmond. I love living here, I love writing about this place, and I am honored and humbled by the support I've gotten from the media and the business and cultural communities here. Major gratitude to Fountain Bookstore, The Library of Virginia, and Barnes and Noble for hosting events and helping me meet readers. Book people are wonderful people.

Massive thanks to wonderful book people for the success of *Front Page Fatality:* Laura Levine and Harley Jane Kozak, I am such a fan of your work, and the blurbs you sent still make me grin. Dru Ann Love, Jessica DeLuna, Lynn Farris, Bella McGuire, and all the other bloggers who loved Nichelle and shared that online, thank you for helping get the word out.

Andrew Watts and the team at Severn River Publishing: thank you for making the process fun, for giving Nichelle's stories new life and new vision, and for keeping me in the loop. It's a joy to work with you.

Kate, Courtney, Julz, Kristin, Meredith, Debra, Jo, Allison, Stephanie, Michelle, Caryn, Linda, Sherry, Jen, Kim, Jenny, Debbie, Susan, Angela, Lisa, Kym, Rebecca, Anne, Ezster, and Corby: I can't imagine life without you girls! Thanks so much for your cheerleading, support, and rooftop-shouting.

Jay Roecker, I am privileged to call you my friend, and thank you for your unending support.

Last, but never ever least, a big thank you to my littles for understanding when mommy needs time to write. The most awesome thing about this is watching you guys be as proud of me as I always am of you.

As always, any mistakes are mine alone.

ABOUT THE AUTHOR

LynDee Walker is the national bestselling author of two crime fiction series featuring strong heroines and "twisty, absorbing" mysteries. Her first Nichelle Clarke crime thriller, FRONT PAGE FATALITY, was nominated for the Agatha Award for best first novel and is an Amazon Charts Bestseller. In 2018, she introduced readers to Texas Ranger Faith McClellan in FEAR NO TRUTH. Reviews have praised her work as "well-crafted, compelling, and fast-paced," and "an edge-of-your-seat ride" with "a spider web of twists and turns that will keep you reading until the end."

Before she started writing fiction, LynDee was an award-winning journalist who covered everything from ribbon cuttings to high level police corruption, and worked closely with the various law enforcement agencies that she reported on. Her work has appeared in newspapers and magazines across the U.S.

Aside from books, LynDee loves her family, her readers, travel, and coffee. She lives in Richmond, Virginia, where she is working on her next novel when she's not juggling laundry and children's sports schedules.

Sign up for LynDee Walker's reader list at
severnriverbooks.com/authors/lyndee-walker
lyndee@severnriverbooks.com